CRADLE
OF THE
DEEP

CRADLE
OF THE
DEEP

A CRIME NOVEL

DIETRICH
KALTEIS

Published by ECW Press
665 Gerrard Street East
Toronto, Ontario, Canada M4M 1Y2
416-694-3348 / info@ecwpress.com

Cover design: Michel Vrana
Author photo credit: Andrea Kalteis

LIBRARY AND ARCHIVES CANADA CATALOGUING IN PUBLICATION

Title: Cradle of the deep : a crime novel / Dietrich Kalteis.

Names: Kalteis, Dietrich, 1954– author.

Identifiers: Canadiana (print) 20200263854
Canadiana (ebook) 20200263889

ISBN 978-1-77041-526-3 (softcover)
ISBN 978-1-77305-580-0 (PDF)
ISBN 978-1-77305-579-4 (ePUB)

Classification: LCC PS8621.A474 C73 2020
DDC C813/.6—dc23

The publication of *Cradle of the Deep* has been generously supported by the Canada Council for the Arts which last year invested $153 million to bring the arts to Canadians throughout the country and is funded in part by the Government of Canada. *Nous remercions le Conseil des arts du Canada de son soutien. L'an dernier, le Conseil a investi 153 millions de dollars pour mettre de l'art dans la vie des Canadiennes et des Canadiens de tout le pays. Ce livre est financé en partie par le gouvernement du Canada.* We acknowledge the support of the Ontario Arts Council (OAC), an agency of the Government of Ontario, which last year funded 1,737 individual artists and 1,095 organizations in 223 communities across Ontario for a total of $52.1 million. We also acknowledge the contribution of the Government of Ontario through the Ontario Book Publishing Tax Credit, and through Ontario Creates for the marketing of this book.

 Canada Council for the Arts   Conseil des Arts du Canada

PRINTED AND BOUND IN CANADA   PRINTING: MARQUIS   5   4   3   2   1

MIX
Paper from
responsible sources
FSC® C103567

For Charlie
The embodiment of loving kindness —
and a true friend

. . . *one*

Six months in and Bobbi Ricci couldn't take any more, couldn't lie there listening to whatever was hibernating down Lonzo's throat. The gasping and grunting thing with its wet sucking breath. Snoring like a Lawn-Boy. Skin around the old man's neck loose and wrinkled, hair sticking from his ears like a crop. Sounded like he had some growing down his throat, too, the man gagging on it. I look at you, I feel old, Bobbi was thinking.

She gave him the grooming kit for his birthday, came in a nice case of full-grain leather. What do you get a crook turning sixty? Lonzo ripped off the gift wrap and let it fall, popped its latch, looked at the velvet inside, the little scissors and the tweezers, the eyebrow brush, saying, "So, what am I supposed to do with this?"

"Same thing you do with your car key, stick it in your ear and wiggle it around, call it grooming. Was thinking it would help you look nice, that's all," Bobbi said, couldn't believe this guy.

"You saying I don't look nice?" Graying hair combed in a swirl to hide the pink dome, bluish veins like a road map above his ankles, ass like a deflated tire. The crime boss flapping open his leopard housecoat, standing in his boxers, checking himself sideways in the dressing mirror, back of his walk-in closet, his in-breath taking off the extra inches, the man patting what he called his tummy — a crime boss with a tummy. Saying, "Not bad, a man my age, uh?"

Called him a regular Spencer Tracy, then Bobbi ended it by saying, "You don't want it, I'll take it back, get you something else."

"Yeah, if you don't mind." Handing it back, then seeing she was pouting, Lonzo saying, "You don't want to take it back, then don't say you do. Like you don't know your mind." Waving his hand around, he stepped on the gift wrap, mumbling something in Italian and walking from the room, Bobbi standing there holding the leather case. Thinking about jabbing him with the nail file.

Enough light slanted through the bedroom window now, shadow lines across his sleeping face. Lonzo splayed in his king bed with his head twisted to the side. Sucking air through his mouth, his jowl flat against his pillow. Guessing if the moon was full, she'd see the drool collecting at the corner of his mouth. That milky pool he got when he'd been eating pasta with the cream sauce, his favorite dish. That familiar sniff of garlic and Old Spice. Bobbi thinking, God, close your mouth.

Tomasino Alonzo Palmieri, everybody calling him Lonzo, long-time underboss to Joey Bananas, big into laundry and cheese back east, even bigger into guns and drugs, sent from Brooklyn to Montreal, kicking a foot up the backside of the supremacist bikers running the port, pushing them out, taking over the container terminals. Lonzo getting it done, then getting sent to take care of the fledgling western interests. Organized crime spreading like syphilis, Lonzo on the West Coast gaining a toehold on the docks of Vancouver, infiltrating the workforce, squeezing out bikers like pimples, taking over the guns and drugs coming from China.

Lonzo held out his hand and twenty guys jumped, ready to kiss the ring. Recruited the Clark Parkers to do the down-and-dirty, the arson and strong-arm stuff. Lonzo keeping Lee Trane on the payroll, doing the wet work. Getting it done with no questions, and no links back to the organization.

Calling himself a businessman, Lonzo liked to joke he was clean compared to the mayor, a fat fuck wanting to bulldoze Chinatown, make way for a goddamned freeway, all the time lining his own pockets. A story Bobbi heard a dozen times over, getting hard to look interested.

Had to admit it, the money and the tough-guy routine got her attention at first — Bobbi Ricci liked the danger about the man, didn't matter he had about eighteen years on her, a body turning into an old catcher's mitt. Snapped his fingers and got what he wanted. Had a goon like a shadow called Aldo, kept an eye out for the boss, lived above Lonzo's three-car garage, made sure the old man got older. Opened doors for him and rode shotgun in the limo. Hung out in the outer office when Lonzo conducted business at the vending machine company, or when he went inspecting his chain of laundromats, a half-dozen places scattered from Whalley to Deep Cove, calling them Lonzomats, his right-hand man Carmen Roth working magic laundering the lettuce.

For a while Bobbi got a kick riding around in back of the limo, Lonzo taking her to the finest places in the city to eat, always getting a table. Five months and she saw him as a bore, the man telling the same stories, spouting facts about Coke machines and laundry. Those suspenders on his ankle socks getting to her, the sprigs of Don King hair under his armpits, sprouting from his ears, too.

The best thing about climbing in his bed: the sex was quick and once a week, tops, with the lights off.

Her left arm started tingling now, Lonzo's head weighing on it. Flexing her fingers, she tried to ease her arm out, but didn't chance it. Hard to believe this was the guy who caught her with Carmen "the Accountant" Roth at that Eastside bistro, a few months back, a block from the original Lonzomat, the two of them just having lunch, talking about dry cleaning. Back then she saw Lonzo more as a mad dog than a bore, coming in that bistro, throwing his fist with the big ring, standing over Carmen as he flopped under the table, wine glasses and candle tipping. Leaning down, Lonzo saying, "What'd I tell you about going with the *bambolinas*, uh?" Pointing a finger at her, losing the anger, saying, "How about we dance?" Saying her name the Italian way, Roberta Ricci, made it sound like music.

"*Bambolina*, you said, that what I am?" Bobbi said, sliding from her seat, acting hurt, avoiding the spilled Dolcetto. "Okay if I help him up, or you gonna see it like flirting?" She tugged Carmen by the arm, got him sitting in his chair, saying sorry and thanking him for lunch.

Holding the door for her, Lonzo saying, "Nice Italian girl, what it means. And so you know, it don't look good, a nice Italian girl eating with the *ebreo*, one who writes with his pencils."

Not sure what that meant, Bobbi saying, "What makes you think I'm so nice?" Glancing back, seeing the waiter handing Carmen a napkin, asking if there'd be anything else.

"Nice, but not too nice." Joking, Lonzo led her out the front door, past a kid struggling on the ground with the sandwich board, Bobbi wondering what happened to the kid, Lonzo saying never mind that, leading her over to his Caddy by the curb.

Thinking about it now, Bobbi remembered the way Lonzo did it, just walked in and took what he wanted. Didn't need Aldo, his personal goon, to do it for him. It wasn't the force, just the attitude, the man in charge. It turned her on. Now he was just an old guy about twenty years out of time, nothing 1973 about him, and suffering from short-man syndrome. Bobbi pretty sure most men had it, no matter what their height. It just turned out Lonzo had it in spades.

Glancing at the clock, she decided it was time to make her move. Her arm tingling more, pinned under his snoring head. Bobbi was getting out, not sticking around, waiting for him to fall victim to the hazards of his line of work, like getting shot, or opening his car door and *bam!* — chunks of Lonzo raining across his lawn, clogging the pool filter. She could see it happening, and if she hung around, it could be her getting in the Caddy, going to do a little shopping on Robson, maybe catching one in a crossfire. Since coming from Montreal, Lonzo had gained plenty of enemies.

The plan came to her a few days back while Bobbi was putting on her face in the bathroom down the hall. She caught his reflection in the mirror, Lonzo in the master bedroom, with the door open, crouching at his walk-in closet, taking out all his shoes. Thinking he was acting odd, she switched off the light and tucked behind the door and watched through the crack. Lonzo taking out the closet's bottom shelf, lifting a Gucci case from under the false floor, working the combination and popping its luggage lock. Looking around to make sure he was alone, he grabbed a bundle of bills, slipped it inside his jacket, put the shelf and shoes back. Bobbi eased the bathroom door shut and went back to drawing on her lipstick, facing the mirror when he walked down the hall, opened the door, called her his doll and clapped her fanny, fingers grabbing like he was checking a melon, saying, "*A dopo*, baby." Heard him go down the stairs, off on what he called business, riding in back of the Cadillac, his driver Denny behind the wheel, his goon Aldo riding up front.

Pressing her lips together, looking at herself in the mirror, Bobbi went into his room, moved the Ferragamos and Gucci shoes, took out the shelf and stared down at the twin cases hidden there. Trying different lock combinations — using the digits for his birthday, her birthday, his phone, his address, the date he arrived from the old country — coming up with nothing. Imagined one was stuffed with Yankee hundreds, the other with Canadian, the Trudeau government allowing the dollar to float, going for parity. Betting Lonzo covered his ass either way, depending which way he had to run. When the time came, he'd grab the twins and he'd be out the back door. Bobbi knowing he'd leave her behind.

She set the shoes back: loafers, Oxfords and brogues, same order she found them. Bobbi thinking how to run off with the twins herself and live to spend the cash.

Couldn't get it out of her mind. Hardly slept in her room down the hall that night. Next morning, she took the Corsair Lonzo kept for the cook, driving over the Lion's Gate bridge to Commercial, looking for this dealer she used to cop from, a guy with Sonny Bono hair busking on the side, calling himself Boppin' Beppe. Just up the street from the deli where Lonzo's cook got the scallopini and capocollo the boss liked, olives coming from the hillsides of Puglia. Said he could taste the old country in every bite.

A blue-sequined jacket on the back of the chair he was sitting on, Beppe leaned back outside Vito's Cafe, an acoustic guitar across his lap, hawking eight-tracks of his greatest hits, *Best of Boppin' Beppe*, a dozen tapes lined up in the open guitar case.

Beppe eyed her getting out and walking up.

"Hey, Bep, you remember me?"

"Be a hard one to forget." Looking her over. "Guessing you want a fix-up, huh?"

"Not into it anymore, and not for me I'm asking, it's for a friend." Bobbi thinking this guy's jacket was like a warning light to any law enforcement within a square block, all those sequins.

"Sure I got what you need."

"Another guy who knows what I need, huh?" Bobbi gave a tired smile and bent for an eight-track cartridge from the guitar case, the homespun label with Beppe on the cover, wearing cool shades, Bobbi reading the notes and titles on the back, thinking, Yeah, somebody else's greatest hits. Betting Beppe had never been inside a recording studio in his life. Saying, "You any good?"

"Well, music's a matter of taste, but, hell yeah, I'm good, maybe not at catching a break, but far as the music goes, how about you judge for yourself?" Glancing up the street, saying, "But guess you're after what makes the world spin faster, for this friend, you say."

"Yeah." Still reading the back, she said, "Dion DiMucci, that the guy from the Belmonts? Love that one 'Runaround Sue.'"

"Yeah, sure, can't go wrong with the Belmonts . . . named after the street where they lived."

"That right?"

"Good back in the day, then Dion went on his own, doing some blues before forming the Wanderers. But nothing hit like the early Belmonts. Got two tracks on there, his early stuff, 'Tag Along' and 'Movin' Man.' Be a couple more on my next one. Feels good paying the man some tribute. Now you want me to guess, or you gonna spell it out, what you come for?" Smiling the gold tooth he traded for the enamel original.

"Well, I'm looking for something with some kick."

"We talking like black tar, something like that?"

"The kind of kick can knock out a horse."

"Can get you Black Beauties, Stardust, China White. You just name your pleasure."

"Pleasure's not mine, like I said, it's for a friend, well, not exactly a friend. And, not exactly a pleasure, something that puts him in, or, more out . . . you know, the kind of situation that gives me the upper hand, if you follow?"

"So, this not-exactly friend wants it with some kick, like over the moon."

"Way over."

"Well, got some purple haze around, send your friend tripping. Or some blow just come in, hardly stepped on. Get him into orbit."

"Don't worry about tripping or orbits. Just think knocking out a horse."

"Hmm, okay, like that." Beppe nodding, trying to follow along. "And this not-so-friend, not supposed to know about it, huh?"

"Never sees it coming."

"Uh-huh, okay, I get the picture."

"That a problem?"

"Not for me, but for your not-so-friend —"

"So, you can help me out?" She tapped the eight-track against her hand.

"Thinking some Mickey Finn'd do the job, or you want, can get my hands on some ketamine, does the same kind of job." Beppe pulled his lips into a smile, showing the gold tooth.

"Long as it knocks out a horse."

"Then let's go with the Mickey, tried and true."

She reached in her bag, started to pull out a ten.

"Whoa, whoa, not like that, come on, girl. Just be cool and have it ready, and that ten spot's gonna need a twin, along with a fiver for the tape, a pleasure in its own right." Beppe leaned the guitar gently against the bricks, took the jacket from the chair and wrapped it over his shoulders, saying, "Way we do it, you grease my palm on the down-low when I come back, you dig?"

She said she did and sat in the chair, feigning interest in the song titles on the back of the cartridge. Eyes wandering across to Franco's Spaghetti House, a decent early-morning crowd coming for coffee, a food market next to it, sign advertising "Frutta e Verdura." A billiard hall on the corner, a TV facing out to the street, some soccer match playing, an empty chair out front. Reached in her bag and counted off the bills, she had the cash ready.

"'Dream Lover,' you do it like the original?" she said, getting up and giving up the chair when he came strolling back, the sequined jacket over his shoulders like a cape. The man all rock star.

"Just like Bobby Darin, who else?" Careful draping the jacket over the back of the chair, lining up the shoulders, Beppe sat, saying a lot of artists had covered it, even Dion himself, but to his mind nobody did it like Bobby Darin. Then told her he was aching to cut a new album.

Bobbi smiled, thinking he looked more like he was going into rehab, feeling sad for him, the man living on rock and roll dreams.

Reaching in his jacket for a pen, he took the eight-track from her and scrawled his name on the label, handing it back, something like folded paper stuck up between the pinch roller and tape guide. The guy doing it like a magic trick. Taking the bills from her palm like he was giving her a handshake.

"You drop that in your not-so-friend's drink, coffee, whatever, and get set for a quiet night."

Bobbi slipped the tape in her bag, asking if he knew "Dock of the Bay."

"My man, Otis."

Told him it was the kind of sound suited his voice. "Just give it your own spin. Maybe something for the new one. But, hey, what do I know?" Smiling, guessing everybody was a music producer these days, then moving, not giving a backward glance, she stepped into the street, opening the door and getting in the Corsair.

Back at the house, she stashed the folded paper in her tampon box, the drawer next to her bed in the guest room, where she stayed when Lonzo wasn't in a romantic mood, which was most of the time. The man liked sleeping on his own, with the eyeshades on. Sparing her from the snoring, Bobbi staying in the next room, thinking who could sleep in the same room with this guy.

Taking Beppe's tape, she went in the living room, pushed it in the Zenith and pressed play. Not a bad recording, and surprise, the guy could sing, not in Dion DiMucci's league, but not bad, either. Surprised some label hadn't snatched Beppe off the street, getting him to sign and cut a record deal. Guessing it was true what she'd heard about Canadian talent having a bitch of a time catching a break and getting any kind of airplay. Boppin' Beppe selling his homemade tapes and dope down in Little Italy, across from a place selling cold cuts, meantime Anne Murray was selling millions singing about snowbirds.

When Lonzo came home that day, she was dancing around the living room in her socks, jeans and a T-shirt, going from the tighten-up to the flick, had the coffee table pushed over to the window, the girl working up a sweat, Boppin' Beppe serving up some righteous Jackie Wilson.

Snapping his fingers but not to the music, he told her to turn down that *merda*. Looking at the tab indents in his shag rug where the coffee table belonged.

"Hey, this guy's Italian." She caught her breath, collecting herself, saying, "Think you ought to give him a chance."

"Italian, huh? Guy's a mangia-cake, singing like he's in a jungle. You want Italian, real Italian . . ." He stepped around the sofa, flipped open the console's door, pointing to his 78s and LPs. "Then you put on some Nico Fidenco, Riccardo del Turco or Sergio Bruni, the voice of Napoli. Guys who really sing, not this *canadese* doing that doo-wop shit." Telling her he didn't want to hear it again, percolating into his walls.

·

The man had been truly offended. Practically had to beg him to take her out that night. Promised to knock his socks off for being a good sport. Thinking of those old-man garters he wore. Finally, talked him into getting Aldo to drive them into the city, catching a set of Nat Adderley at Oil Can Harry's.

Sitting in back of the Calais Coupe, Lonzo turned to her, hand starting on her knee, moving up her leg, saying, "Now, you got me going from mangia-cakes to moolies. Putting up with more jungle music. How about if somebody sees me, a place like this?"

"Gonna think you're cool." Bobbi parted her legs, let his fingers walk along her thigh, forcing a smile like it was cute.

Two drinks into the first set before Lonzo went to the men's. Bobbi dumped the powder from the folded tissue into his Wallbanger. Swirled it around his glass till it dissolved.

Polishing off the drink, he leaned close, saying in her ear, "This fucking song's about food?"

"Just called 'Cantaloupe Island,' nothing to do with food." Looking in his eyes for a sign the dope was starting to work. Hoping Beppe got it right.

Looking for a waiter to fetch him another Wallbanger, saying this eight-ball with the horn sounded worse than the Fudge, the last band she dragged him to see, that time when he fired his driver, made Denny Barrenko get out in the middle of the street, like the traffic was his fault. Now he was back to telling her she owed him, wanted his socks blown off.

"Yeah, it'll be big, alright," Bobbi promised. "One you're never gonna forget."

Lonzo smiled, saying now she was talking.

Leaving right after the set, Lonzo told Aldo to drive them home, complaining he felt like shit, wobbly on his feet, blaming the music. Bobbi reaching from the back, telling Aldo to put on the eight-track, the big man slipping Boppin' Beppe into the player. "This Diamond Ring" filling the Cadillac.

Lonzo too zonked to notice, bobbed his head a few times, eyes glazing over by the time they crossed the Lion's Gate. Aldo having to help the boss out of the car, getting him in the door and up the stairs, the boss's knees weak, his legs going out from under him, eyes rolling like a pinball. The man mumbling gibberish.

Concerned about the boss, Aldo thinking he should call Lonzo's doctor, Bobbi saying he just had one too many. Flopping him on the bed, tugging off his shoes and loosening his belt, she listened for Aldo to trod down the stairs, hearing him going out the door, crunching gravel underfoot, and going to the coach house over the garage.

Lying in his bed, Lonzo set a weak hand on her ass, blubbering something about knocking his socks off.

"Sure, baby. Get ready, here it comes." Pulled his socks and dumb garters off, then his pants, tossed them on the floor. Lonzo was out cold as she took her time getting out of her dress, standing over him in her bra and panties, that slobber starting at the corners of his mouth. Turning out the lamp, she sat on the bed and waited, making sure the Mickey took. Looking past the tipped blinds, waiting for the light in the coach house to go out.

She laid back against the pillows, and Lonzo flopped an arm across her stomach, Bobbi unstrapping his Rolex, tugging and wiggling the diamond ring from his finger.

The light went off in the coach house, Bobbi waiting till she was sure, going barefoot past the bank of windows rising to the ceiling, the panorama of the city lost behind a bank of clouds, top of the British Properties. Great view when it wasn't raining. The lit pool shimmering, raindrops forming little circles on the surface. A shimmering reflection on the cabana. This place Lonzo loved bragging about, six bedrooms, a manicured acre of lawn, the tennis court out behind the pool, the three-car garage with the coach house on top.

Slipping on his robe, she went and sat on the toilet, doing that deep breathing that never did any good and played it through one more time. Deciding on the bell-bottoms, going from the tunic top with the paisley to the cashmere turtleneck, picking the patent Oxfords over the platforms with the disco heels. Tiptoeing around the bed, she took the Beretta and his car keys from his nightstand. She'd go to his closet, move the shoes and shelves, take the twins and grab her clothes from the guest room, then get the hell out of there. Pray there was enough cash in the twins to put an ocean between her and Lonzo, thinking Paris was a good start.

Careful not to bump the furniture. Sounded like the beast down Lonzo's throat got snagged between an inhale and exhale, his mouth hanging open like a carp. Then there was something else, a scraping sound, made her stop mid-step.

The floorboards creaked out in the hall. Her heart jumped, she nearly cried out. Had to be Aldo coming to check on the old man. Or worse, somebody coming to kill him, his shitty disposition catching up with him.

Bobbi's breath caught, her hand gripped the Beretta at the door. Telling herself she could do it, empty the clip if she had to. Replaying what Lonzo explained about the cross-bolt safety mounted on the frame, under the hammer, how you aim for the middle, both hands on the grip.

The knob gave a slight rattle. Wishing she'd locked it after they got him in the bed. *You can't be too careful.* His words going around her head. Stepping easy to the backside of the door, her finger light on the trigger.

The knob turned some more.

For one wild second, she wanted to jump at the bed, shake Lonzo awake and press the gun in his hand, point his arm at the door, but the old man was out cold, useless and snoring.

The door eased open, faint light from the skylight coming in. Bobbi's heart was jumping more, her hands trembling. She raised the barrel just above the knob, and she counted to three.

. . . two

Denny Barrenko picked up three rules for breaking into places. First, be smooth going in, but keep an edge, and don't overthink it. Two, no drugs, no booze. Okay, a toke or two so you go in smooth. Three, forget what you missed the first time, and never go back. Greed spelled prison. Three rules, simple as that.

Handed down from Wilson Landa, an American brother with a wild tangle of hair, ducking conscription, the guy hailing from Bozeman, sharing the three-room flat on Hastings. Five draft resisters in three rooms living in view of Woodward's, letters painted on the clay bricks, the place selling hardware, oil skins and linoleum, groceries and boys' pants. Denny and Wilson liked spending afternoons when it wasn't raining out on the fire escape, passing joints, talking shit about music and guys they knew getting drafted and sent to 'Nam. The U.S. starting to pull out combat troops, the boys going home. Wilson and Denny wondering when they'd get to go home, the odds of Nixon giving some amnesty.

Wasn't easy finding work this side of the border, Wilson pushing broom before going into the business for himself, robbing from the rich, breaking into places from Kits to West Point Grey.

"Sticking your neck out, brother." Denny thinking what it would mean getting busted this side of the border, Mounties rumored to be a fierce bunch, always getting their man. Locking him up, then deporting his ass.

"Doing what we're doing beats going with the river rats up the Mekong. You wanna talk about sticking it out." Twisting up another one, Wilson had lit it and shared his views on the Tet Offensive, sure Nixon wasn't done fucking around, not wanting to go down as the first commander-in-chief to lose a war. Passing Denny the joint, saying, "Why Tricky Dick blitz-bombed Hanoi the way he did, his way of saying Merry fucking Christmas."

Then Wilson got on about his three rules, how he came up with them after tripping a motion sensor, running out the back of some place, jumping through a hedge. "Assholes get shit like motion sensors, ought to have a sign on the lawn, give some fair warning, you know. Like 'Beware of Dog.'" Wilson saying how he waited for the family to drive off after their Cheerios, Daddy in a suit and tie, pulling out in a nice Lincoln, mother packing the uniformed kids in back of the station wagon. Picking the back-door lock, Wilson slipped in and got as far as the drink caddy in the front room, was helping himself to the Sauza when the alarm horn went off. "Scared the livin' shit out of me, man."

The two of them sat buzzed, laughing about it.

"So, why do you do it?"

"You kidding. Made a grand last week alone, hawking a watch, a handful of necklaces and shit, two-fifty in cash. Got this pawn shop, guy buys what I bring in and doesn't ask questions. Know what I'm saying?"

Generally, he got a kick out of Wilson's stories, Denny

toking and sharing a couple tales of his own, told him about his job chauffeuring for this old dude Lonzo who owned this vending machine outfit and a string of laundromats called Lonzomats. Always had a goon riding shotgun, a three-hundred-pounder with a gun under the jacket. Driving the old guy around in the back of a Cadillac Calais, a tuxedo-black coupe with the chrome and whitewalls. Denny wearing a cap and a nice navy jacket. Denny sure the guy was into more than pop machines and pressing shirts.

"You just drive the guy around, huh?"

"Run the odd package, fetch some take-out, airport pick-ups, drop off a party doll the morning after, stuff like that."

"Gopher on wheels, huh?" Wilson smiling, saying it wasn't a bad gig.

Shrugging, Denny said it kept him in SpaghettiOs and reefer. It wasn't bad, but it wasn't much compared to Wilson clearing a G-note a week, just for breaking in a couple places, abiding by his three rules.

He hadn't thought much about Wilson's rules again until he got canned, being told to take off the cap and jacket, giving them back. Wrongful dismissal if there ever was. The old man Lonzo shit-canning him, told him to get out of the Caddy, middle of a city street. That was six months ago, Denny still pissed about it.

Now he was rhyming them off, Wilson's three rules, driving the shitbox Bug, the one he borrowed from the flatmates, keeping three cars behind the Caddy Calais, the very one he used to drive. Aldo the goon driving, Lonzo and his latest party doll, Bobbi Ricci, riding in back. Crossing the Lion's Gate from the north, rolling through the park and along West Georgia, the Caddy turning at Bidwell. Denny thinking Aldo should have gone straight, turning on Alberni, hitting heavy traffic all the way over to Thurlow. Denny, keeping them in sight, stopped halfway up the block as the Caddy pulled out front of Oil Can Harry's, Aldo getting out and going around and holding the door for Lonzo and Bobbi. The sign out front claimed Nat Adderley and his horn were playing tonight. Denny driving by, glancing over. Lonzo saying something to Aldo, then slipping the guy at the door a tip, putting his fat fingers on Bobbi Ricci's ass, escorting her into the club. The old son of a bitch.

"Jive Samba" rolled around his head as Denny drove back, would have loved catching a set or two, Nat being one of the unsung heroes of jazz. But Denny kept his focus on breaking into the old man's house, get himself the compensation he was due, make up for the wrongful dismissal. Humming some of that Adderley and thinking about dark-haired Bobbi Ricci, recalling her brown eyes in the rearview, the way she looked back at him — like he mattered — riding in back with the old man.

Now he drove the Bug back through the Causeway and crossed the Lion's Gate, the forty horses complaining all the way up the slant of Chartwell Drive, chugging and coughing exhaust notes up to the top of the Properties. Parked it by Vinson Creek, yanked up the parking brake, then Denny walked, making it look natural, like Lonzo was expecting him to drop by for cocktails. A yew hedge blocked the view from the street, Denny keeping his eyes and ears sharp, ready to run if he saw the Caddy coming back. Picking the *Province* off the driveway, he strolled to the house and around the side, an eye up at the coach house over the triple garage, Denny reaching the glass cutter in his pocket. No alarm company stickers on Lonzo's windows, no surveillance cameras under the eaves. The lights were all off.

Recalling that time Lonzo shot off his mouth from the back seat, Denny driving the old man and Bobbi Ricci to this Italian supper club on Commercial, only place Lonzo said you could get a decent chop, Tuscan-style, the way he liked it. Bobbi sat next to the man in her fur, a couple of inches taller in her heels, a couple decades younger with the nice hourglass curves, that pouty mouth and the bored look in her eyes. Denny used to say the odd thing to Aldo the goon in the passenger seat, taking up space and happy to pass the time.

That last time Denny did the driving, Bobbi Ricci said she didn't remember Lonzo locking up. Lonzo saying what *stronzo*'d break into his place, any two-bit crook knowing who he was, and what he'd do to anybody who tried. Being armed to the teeth was the only security a man needed. Lonzo gritting his teeth, leaning across the seat, asking Aldo, "You see these teeth, right?"

Aldo turning his neck, nodding and agreeing the boss could take care of himself.

The old man saying, "Then what do I need you for?" Still gritting his teeth, adding a growl for effect.

Aldo giving a sideways, bored look at Denny, his eyes saying, "You believe this shit?"

Bobbi saying, "It's good you got Aldo, don't kid yourself . . ."

"Who's kidding? Man lives over my garage, eats my food, watches my TV. Me, I'm inside, armed to the teeth." Showing them again.

"Jeez, Lonz, come on, take it easy," she said. "Aldo loves you, guy'd jump in front of a bullet for you."

"Just saying I can take care of myself." Lonzo reaching across, putting a pudgy hand on the big man's shoulder, patting it, saying, "You're my number one, Aldo, you know that, uh? Five days a week, the two days I give you off."

"How about a dog, could get one for the days I ain't around, watch over you and the place," Aldo said, like he cared.

"On account you worry for me, uh?" Lonzo not waiting on an answer, looking at the back of Denny's head, saying, "How about you, Denny, you wanna work seven days, drive me anyplace I say? Like I can't do it myself."

"Do whatever you say." Denny glanced sideways at Aldo, then stole a look at the rear-view, his eyes meeting Bobbi's.

"I think a dog's a great idea," Bobbi piped in. "One of them German ones, bigger teeth than yours."

Lonzo saying, "Yeah, you think so?" Sounding pissed.

Denny saying, "She's looking out for you, too."

"How about you fuckin' drive, what I pay you for." Lonzo thumped his big ring against the back of the driver's seat. "Guy telling me what's what."

"Was me that said it, Lonz," Bobbi said. "Was thinking a Doberman, Rottweiler, something like that. You know, for when you're not around."

"Fuck Doberman, I go that way, I get a Corso, Italian dog eats them kraut ones for lunch. I ever want something shitting on my lawn, yeah, I'll go Italian."

"Suit yourself," she said, shrugging. "Still, a good idea."

"When I need *protezione*, I got me." Lonzo bared his teeth again, banged his fist with the ring against the back of Aldo's seat, glaring at Denny in the rear-view, growling, showing the mad dog some more. "Am I right?"

"You got it, boss," the big man said, not turning his head, the spit landing on back of his neck.

"One thing, don't got to clean up after a gun." Patting his jacket, where Lonzo kept his Beretta, still glaring at the back of Denny.

Bobbi play-slapped his arm, saying, "All this macho, God, crack a window." Rolling her eyes at Denny in the rear-view.

Denny liked the way she did it, maybe he smiled then. Remembering it now. Something just between them, maybe Lonzo caught the passing look.

A week later Lonzo canned him, Denny driving them into the city, the Caddy caught in late-afternoon traffic, en route to the Coliseum, catch the Vanilla Fudge concert, Bobbi's idea.

Lonzo bitching about it all the way across the bridge and through Stanley Park, "Be a good sport, and where's it get me? Some band named after food. The fuck am I doing?"

Denny was wondering how Bobbi talked the old man into it, going to a rock concert.

"'Cause you're a good sport, Lonz, a real one-of-a-kind guy." She patted the liver spots, back of his hand, saying, "Good to try new things, Lonz, get a bigger view of the world." Eyes meeting Denny's again. "Why we're catching the Fudge?" Telling him about the way they did "You Keep Me Hanging On," how it had soul. Sure he'd get it.

"Sounds like bullshit, you ask me. I want soul I put on the Sergio Bruni or Pino Donaggio, guys like that."

Denny making the mistake of saying, "Who?"

"How about eyes on the fuckin' road? Think you got enough problems."

"They got this other one they do," Bobbi said, patting the hand again. "'Shotgun.'"

Denny drove on, thinking Bobbi was alright. No idea why she went with a guy like Lonzo. Same reason he and Aldo were in the front, doing it for the money.

"The fuck you doing now?" Lonzo punched at the back of his seat, saying, "Get in the fucking other lane."

Catching that mix of garlic and aftershave, Denny negotiated the traffic backed up past Denman. Turning to say, "Looks like everybody's in town, Friday night."

"On account you don't pay attention," Lonzo said. "Told you, take the Iron Worker's."

"When'd you say that?" Denny glanced at Aldo. Aldo not meeting his look.

Lonzo shook his head, told him to turn on Pender and cut to the water.

Against his better judgement, Denny squeezed over a lane to make the turn. Ten minutes before they got to Burrard.

Lonzo punched the back of his seat again. "Get down to Waterfront, by the spur lines."

"Looks like it's clearing ahead," Denny said. "East Hastings's a better bet."

"Water-fucking-front. I got to spell it for you?"

Spray on the back of his neck, turning the wheel, Denny doing like he was told.

"Ought to make you cop for the tickets, take it outta your pay, making us miss the opening act. What's it, Led Balloon?"

"Zeppelin," Bobbi said, taking the hand with the ring, putting it on her thigh. "And how about you just take it — *Owww!*"

Denny looked at the rear-view, swerved, looking over his shoulder, Lonzo catching her wrist and squeezing it. He started to turn in the seat, Aldo waving a finger at him. And he swung the Caddy onto Waterfront, the traffic getting worse, getting wedged behind a tour bus, blue exhaust coming in the vents.

"Fuck you doing now, getting us gassed?" Letting go of her wrist, Lonzo punched at the back of Denny's seat again, his eyebrows bunching together.

Denny kept his cool, wiped a hand across the back of his neck, looking for a way around the traffic.

"Not a big deal, we miss the opening act." Bobbi told

Lonzo he wouldn't like it anyway, the singer with his long hair and shirt open, the band playing real loud.

Steering around the bus, Denny turned at Main and got onto Powell, like driving in a parking lot, cars jammed and horns honking.

Making conversation, Bobbi told Lonzo the Fudge remade a classic, "'Für Elise.' You know it?" Patting his arm, saying he was gonna love it.

"Mean if we ever get there."

"And 'Season of the Witch.' You know it? Better than the way Donovan did it."

"Don who?"

Aldo nodded, agreeing that the Fudge did it better.

Bobbi held Lonzo's hand, stopped him from punching the seats.

Denny made his last lane change to a protest of honking horns. The lights were out at Victoria, emergency lights flashing up ahead.

"The way you drive, gonna call you Nancy fuckin' Sinatra. Man's got no instincts for this kind of work."

"Come on, Lonz," Bobbi said. "Traffic's not his fault."

"I get caught in a real-life situation, one where I need a guy knows something, Nancy ain't the guy. Ain't no Mario Andretti."

"That's why you got Aldo."

"Yeah, but how about it's his two nights off? Nancy here can't cut it."

"Yeah, but you got the mad-dog growl." Denny not sure why he said it, just getting sick of this guy.

"The fuck'd you say?"

Feeling more spit land on his neck, Denny said, "Gonna be there in five minutes, okay?"

"Get the fuck out, I'm gonna get us there in two."

Denny turned to look at him.

"You fuckin' heard me, Nancy." Leaning in and showing the mad-dog teeth, Lonzo shoved open his door, tore free of Bobbi and was out of the car.

"Come on, Lonz, supposed to be showing me a good time." Bobbi tried to catch his hand.

Lonzo storming around the front, past the hood ornament. "It's layoff time, you bozo Nancy." He reached inside his jacket, standing there, saying, "Open the yap again, you gonna get early retirement. *Capisce*?" Waiting for Denny to get out.

Looking over at Aldo, back at Bobbi, he shrugged, then Denny got out, left the door hanging, stepping between bumpers. Not looking back, the crazy man still yelling after him.

When he finally got on the right bus, it dawned on him, he was out of work, out of luck and out of country. Going back to the flat with Wilson and the other guys who'd torched their draft notices. Back to getting the morning paper and scouring the classifieds, living on SpaghettiOs and Sanka. Funny, the only thing he was thinking about was the way Bobbi Ricci looked at him in the rear-view. Like she'd miss him.

Found himself doing the odd three-hour stint in the dish pit at an Indian joint, the place hot as hell with the two tandoor ovens, his clothes soaked with sweat. Friday mornings, he delivered the community newspaper, getting up at four. Six months since Lonzo had kicked him out of the car on the way to see Vanilla Fudge.

•

Rain was light and cold, Denny arriving at the Strathcona address. A one-time factory near Venables and Clark, the windows almost all knocked out and boarded, the place that used to make sensible shoes. Some city official calling this part of town gentrifying, fine shops and apartments going in, a car dealer with a Lincoln in the showroom window, a Ma and Pa place with its windows soaped, a White Lunch taking its place, ladies strolling with dogs that fit in a purse. Walking past weather-beaten down-and-outs on the sidewalk, pretending they weren't there. Denny tugged up the hood of his denim. Feeling like he hit a new low.

The heads in the line ahead of him bowed against the drizzle, twenty or so hopefuls applying for the same job, some A-list entertainer needing a personal assistant, a Hollywood crew coming to town to film a movie. The job posting didn't say who the star was, just that the successful applicant needed no experience, only a valid driver's license and a good attitude. Denny guessing he fit the bill.

The rain let up a bit by the time the door opened, the next applicant going in and the door shutting again, the line inching forward. The rain and wind gaining strength once more. The two young women under a black umbrella in front of him didn't notice Denny was getting wet. The two of them talking about this film called *Five Easy Pieces*, starring Jack Nicholson and Karen Black. Both women getting gooey and dreamy about Jack.

A couple of fat drops snuck down the back of his neck, Denny seeing the guy out front of the bistro across the street, wearing a rain slicker and what he believed they called a sou'wester hat, walking back and forth, rain splashing off the sandwich board he wore. Denny thinking, what kind of job was that, walking the block, wearing that rig, rain or shine, letting the world know soup, salad and an entree was under five bucks.

The Caddy pulling up out front of the place pulled him from his thoughts, flicking its four-ways. Denny recognized the tuxedo-black ride, the stacked headlights on, the very one he drove when he was wearing the cap and jacket. Squinting through the rain, he saw Aldo sitting shotgun, the new driver getting out, guessing he was wearing the same cap and jacket, going around the rear and opening the back door. Lonzo stepping out, the guy who shit-canned him in front of Bobbi Ricci, left him in the middle of the street. Denny going all these months with no real work, just another resister on the wrong side of things, with no prospects in sight.

Lonzo did the two-step with the kid carrying the sandwich board, trying to go left, then right, then shoving him out of his way, knocking him down. Mad Dog Lonzo, likely showed the kid his blunt teeth, doing that fucking growl. The women under the umbrella missed it, still tossing celebrity names around, Paul Newman, Marlon Brando and Dino. Their voices getting giggly and rising up an octave.

"Asshole," Denny said. His eyes followed Lonzo walking past the kid with the now-busted sandwich board.

Both women turned, giving Denny lemon-sucking looks.

"You not see that?" Denny pointed across the street, Lonzo pulling open the bistro's door, going in, the sandwich-board guy lost from view behind the far side of the Caddy.

Both women clicking their teeth and turning their backs, their umbrella blocking him out. Talking in hushed tones. Denny shrugged into his jacket, feeling the rain seeping through the denim.

•

The way he did it, Lonzo had the new guy pull up out front, flick on the four-ways, told him to leave the Caddy running, told Aldo to sit tight, he had this. Then he walked into the bistro, the place going for a Euro look. Some guy with long hair, wearing a rain slicker and a sandwich board blocking his way. Lonzo stepped right, the guy stepped the same way. Lonzo tried left, the guy doing it, too, misstepping and smiling like it was funny. Taking it the wrong way, Lonzo gave him a shove, fucking hippie kid. Awkward with the sign, the hippie went down and turned turtle. Not giving him another look, Lonzo went into the place. The waiter stepped aside, forced a smile and asked if he'd like a table by the window.

"I look like I'd eat here?" Walking like he knew the way, Lonzo weaved past the tables, up to the couple at the corner booth, nice romantic spot with checked linens, a toast caddy, little jam pot on the tablecloth, both of them having coffee. Cracking his knuckles to get their attention, he smiled and waved a finger at Carmen Roth, his business associate. Flashed the big ring at the guy who did the laundry, pushing his pencils and making the dirty money clean. Then smiled at Bobbi Ricci, said she was looking nice today and asked if she wanted to dance.

"You hearing music, Lonz? 'Cause if you do . . ." Carmen Roth smiled back and looped a finger at his temple, thought Lonzo was joking, grinning at Bobbi. Stuck his fork in his scrambled eggs, tipped it in a puddle of Tabasco, aiming for his mouth when the fist caught him.

Lonzo grabbed a fistful of shirt, kept Carmen from sliding from the chair. Flicking scrambled egg from the hand with the ring.

Carmen reeled and spit bits of egg, trying to come up for air. Cocking his fist, Lonzo promised another rocket, the ring gleaming. Asking, "How about it, Carm, you hear the music now?"

Jumping from her chair, Bobbi said, "Goddamn it, Lonz, we're having breakfast here. Wanted me to learn about the business, right?"

Coughing egg and blinking, Carmen waved a hand in surrender, trying to say he was just showing her the ropes.

"Only rope she sees is mine, *capisce*?" Letting go, Lonzo pulled it together and smiled, picked up Carmen's napkin, wiping his hands, then held out the one with the ring, asking her, "Now, how about that dance?"

"Gonna hit me if I say no?"

"I'm a lover, not a fighter, you know that, babe." Patting Carmen on the shoulder, saying if he wanted to talk business, do it at the office.

Snatching her bag off the back of her chair, Bobbi said sorry and thanked Carmen for breakfast, let Lonzo lead her past the tables, all eyes on them. The waiter keeping his distance, snapping his fingers for the busboy to go clean up Carmen Roth.

Stepping past the front desk, Lonzo took a little mint, pressed a fin in the waiter's hand, saying, "See my friend gets some Tums." Holding open the door for Bobbi. "Serves him right, eating in a place like this."

"I ask where we're going?" Bobbi let him take her arm, lead her to the car, Aldo nodding to her from the front, the new driver getting out, going around the back, getting the door.

"Little place I know." Lonzo stepped around the hippie kid with the sandwich board, the kid still trying to get his feet under him.

Lonzo getting in behind her, saying, "Feel like a little Italian?"

"You mean like Zanotti's? Won't be open yet."

"Talking about my place."

"Said you wanted to dance." Bobbi getting in, sliding across.

"Yeah, after."

The guy with the sandwich board got his feet under him, the board cracked, bent and ruined. Lonzo got back out and went back over and pressed a couple bucks in his hand and told him, "Get a real job, kid. This is embarrassing, uh."

. . . three

Denny watched the Mad Dog coming out with Bobbi Ricci, the new driver opening the back door, getting them inside. The car pulled from the curb, wipers swishing, front tire splashing the guy with the sandwich board.

The job line shuffled like a chain gang, rain finding a way past the sole of his sneaker. Remembered the way Bobbi looked at him in the rear-view that time, something passing between them. His shoe squished as he stepped. If it wasn't for the need to eat, Denny would have walked from the line. Five more minutes and the door opened again, the recruiter sticking out her candy-floss fro, looking surprised it was raining, saying sorry, but that was it for today. "We'll see the final applicants tomorrow at nine. Word to the wise, be a smidge early." Twisting her mouth into what passed for apology, she shut the door. The star remained a mystery.

"Smidge this," Denny said, doing a crotch grab, the two women turning, narrowing their eyes, taking their umbrella and walking off.

Back at the flat, he tugged off the wet socks and shirt, slinging them on the radiator, telling Wilson about seeing the son of a bitch who fired him, watching Wilson roll a joint. Denny could only take a couple tokes before the asthma had him coughing. Got a nice buzz, the weed Wilson copped from this guy who delivered it from up in Whistler. Then he stood under the shower, the hot water staving off pneumonia, Denny thinking how to get even with a guy like Lonzo. Remembering the way Bobbi Ricci had looked at him.

Friendlier skies the next morning. Denny grabbed a paper from the box, helped himself to a grapefruit at the Asian market, stood along a wall on East Hastings, peeling the fruit, eyeing the classifieds.

Caught the crosstown back to Strathcona, gave the driver a line about forgetting his change, ended up standing third in line with no sign of the two women with the umbrella. A do-gooder with a stoop coming by with a bible under his arm, passing out take-out coffee from a tray, Grab-n-Go printed on the styrofoam. Saying, "You up with Jesus, brother?"

"Every chance I get," Denny told him, taking a cup, asking about cream and sugar.

The coffee still warm when the recruiter with the 'fro opened the door, calling him in.

"Take a seat." The chick with the 'fro and love beads hanging around her neck, a peace ring on her finger, said her name was Candice but he could call her Candy. "From California, huh, cool." Flattening his folded résumé, stained along its edges, she asked what he thought about what was going on.

"Sounds like a movie star looking for help."

"The war, you know, what's going on?" Candy looking at the paper. "See you're from the States."

"Oh, that, yeah well, mostly what I hear on the news, same as you, I guess." Denny shrugged. "Nixon shutting things down, the way it sounds. Pulling the troops out."

Leaning in, her 'fro looked like it might tip, Candice saying, "So, that happens, where's that put you. I mean, can we count on you to stick around, if you don't mind me getting personal? Totally cool if you're, you know, on the dodge, I mean."

"Candy, right? Well, war's not my thing, the reason I'm here. No shame not serving my uncle, the way I see it."

"Totally cool, man."

"But I like it here, Canada's a nice place. Might just stick around," Denny said.

"That how you ended up here, dodging? I mean, if you . . ."

"No, it's fine." Saying he was 4-F, explaining he couldn't serve on account of his asthma. Didn't tell her about the demonstration at Berkeley, one that turned into a riot. Somehow ended with him getting his picture in the *Examiner*, looked like he was throwing something. The gestapo coming around his apartment block, looking for him. Denny figuring it was a good time to split.

"Cool. Okay." Candy looked at her list of questions, saying, "You got experience in the biz. I mean, being from California, you've probably seen them around, huh, the stars?"

"Where I come from's mostly musicians. Movie stars, we keep them mostly in L.A. But sure, I seen some around. Guy from the show about Eddy's father. Guess I know how to act around them."

Candy moved her finger down the page, the driving job on his résumé, asking about it.

"Old gent I was driving sat in back while I did the chauffeuring. Doctors' appointments, lawn bowling, picking stuff up, that kind of thing. Got to know the city real well, but

I'm looking for something more, you know, something with a challenge."

"Sure, I get that." She scribbled a note on her pad, explained the job was on-call, seven days a week.

"More hours the better."

"Cool." Asked if he was on any kind of medication, marked down no when he told her just the inhaler, told him the job could involve travel.

"You mean like across Canada?"

"Could be down to L.A. That a problem?"

"Naw, be like going home." Denny smiled, thinking it would be more like getting arrested on sight.

"Candidate we're seeking's got to be discreet, you know, no loose lips, talking about it. Privacy's a big deal."

"Well, I'm no snitch, Candy." Denny put on the smile, thought it was working.

Turning the résumé over, she asked about college.

Denny gave her the line about the school of hard knocks, guessing these days you needed a degree to fetch shit for entertainers.

Last question, she asked about temperament, how he handled somebody else's.

Not sure he understood the question.

"Anybody ever throw anything at you, and if so, how did you resolve it?"

"Resolve it?"

"Yeah, you know, make it right, smooth it over."

"These A-listers kinda cranky, huh?" Denny smiled, trying to picture somebody like Walter Brennan throwing something at him, a guy he could bench-press.

"Mostly you make pick-ups, stuff like that," Candy said, hand touching her 'fro again.

"Long as it ain't the stuff they throw at me." Smiling at his own joke.

Putting down her clipboard, she thanked him for coming, offered a hand, felt damp like she just licked it.

"Got a good feeling, just got to run it by the higher-ups." Said she'd be in touch, pressing the peace ring into his palm, her look saying she'd give him the job in a second. All he had to do was reach out and take it.

Going out the door, Denny passed the two women from yesterday, minus the umbrella. They stepped wide around him. The same guy with the sandwich board paced out front of the bistro across the street, advertising a breakfast special Denny couldn't afford. Denny guessing there was a lineup for that job, too.

•

On the bus back to the flat, thoughts of payback crept in. Replaying the scene from the day before in his mind, Lonzo walking into that bistro and coming out with Bobbi Ricci, pulling her along none too gently. Remembering Lonzo bragging about having more getaway cash stashed in his place than guys like Denny and Aldo made in a lifetime, then laughing about it.

Denny saying, "How about somebody breaks in?"

Lonzo gave the mad-dog look, baring the teeth. "Some *ladro* tries taking what's mine . . . *Grrr*."

Money stashed in the house, there for the taking. Denny believed it, replaying Wilson's three rules, thinking how he'd do it. Sketching the rooms in his mind from the couple times he stood in the foyer, waiting for the man, thinking where a guy like that would stash it.

Drove the Bug to the top of the Properties and staked

out the place, watched the Caddy come and go, relearned the man's routines, the time of day Aldo went with him to the Lonzomats, when they came back, when Aldo had his two nights off. Making notes and making sure Lonzo hadn't had second thoughts about a dog. Parking up the street every morning for a week, watching the place, Denny driving home with the rush-hour crowd, expecting Candy to call about the job, feeling he aced that interview. He'd rob this son of a bitch, have some easy money, take the new job, cater to some spoiled A-lister. Do it until Nixon granted amnesty, then he'd go home, use Lonzo's cash to set himself up in business. Maybe buy his own limo, drive rich folks around. Maybe get to know one or two, where they lived, their patterns. If he ran short on cash, he could break into their places when they went out, observing the three rules.

Remembering a piece he read in the *Sun* about a burglar doing a B&E over in Deep Cove, getting cornered by one of those German breeds not interested in waiting for the cops. The crook locked himself in an upstairs john, the dog snarling and bashing against the door. Calling for help out the window, the guy calling the cops on himself. Two uniforms talking to reporters while canine control got the dog muzzled and under control, the cops charging the guy with a pillowcase stuffed with goodies. Never going to live that one down in any house of corrections. But Denny knew the only dog he had to worry about was the Mad Dog himself, worse than any guard dog.

•

Keeping an eye on the Cadillac over the Lion's Gate, Denny kept the Bug chugging a few cars back. Could make out the vanity plate: Lo1. Wondering what he needed a plate like that for, the only Cadillac the man owned.

Pulling up out front of Oil Can Harry's, he watched Lonzo and Bobbi get out. Aldo and the driver drove off for their supper break. Denny knowing this was it, his one shot. Circling the block, he headed back to the North Shore.

Lights were coming on by the time he drove to the top of the Properties. The Bug grouching up that winding Chartwell Drive, shuddering and sputtering past the fancy houses, a trail of exhaust coming out the tailpipe. Rich folks with their valuables and secrets, places worth a hundred grand or more, cars that cost five Gs in the driveways — LeBarons, Continentals, Rivieras, New Yorkers, 98s, Eldorados, most driveways with more than one.

Denny seeing this as a bold move, not a stupid mistake.

. . . *four*

The steel wheel of Wilson's glass cutter doing the job, Denny with a picture of Toller Cranston on ice, then cranking the latch and crawling through the basement window, barely squeezing his shoulders through. Landed in the set tub with a thunk, got his feet on the floor. Stood still, listening for any sounds. The pen light leading him past racks of wine bottles, a stationary bike and dumbbells on a rack. Denny checking his Timex, shining the narrow light around, looking for where Lonzo might have stashed the cash.

Going up the steps, he flapped open the cupboards and cabinets in the kitchen, felt around, went in the living room, checked around the fireplace, looked behind a couple of paintings, the drapes, feeling around and under the dining furniture. Nothing. Forty-five minutes gone before he started up the stairs, froze halfway up when he heard a thump.

Then came voices, a key scraping in a lock before he pushed himself the rest of the way up, ducking into the first room, left the door open and quiet as he could, he got inside the closet, easing the door almost shut, smelling mothballs. Straining to hear the voices and thumping from downstairs.

Had to be Lonzo and Bobbi coming back early. Footsteps thumping to the top of the stairs, he heard Aldo and Bobbi talking, Lonzo babbling something, then giggling at his own words.

After a while, the place went quiet, then somewhere a door closed, Denny finally daring to step from the closet, careful not to knock any hangers. Putting his head out, peeking past the door, the quiet making him want to rush down the stairs and out of there. Run to the Bug, sputter away — the worst idea of his life.

Telling himself to keep it cool, sucking some deep air, he finally moved through the dark, light stepping along the hall, fingers touching the wall like feelers, guiding him along. He stopped at every room door and listened. Not daring to flick on the penlight, he went in the next room, its door half-open, feeling along the walls, under the bed, behind the furniture, careful not to knock into anything. No secret stash.

The next bedroom's door hung wide open, woman's clothing in the closet, the space smelling nice, guessing this was Bobbi Ricci's room. Taking the time to put his nose against something flimsy, a dress or blouse on the rack, he couldn't tell. Guessing by the quiet in the place, she had gone home tonight, this room kept for her when she stayed over, either she couldn't stomach it, or it was true what he'd heard, Lonzo didn't sleep with his women. At the end of the hall, Denny stopped and put an ear to the double doors of the master bedroom.

Sounded like a phlegmy musical, a chorus of wheezes and snorts coming through the wood. Knowing if he didn't check the room now, he'd never have the balls to come back. Putting his hand on the knob, he turned it slow, pushing himself to do it. Inching it open. The light from the window showed Lonzo splayed across the king bed — alone — the boss's mouth open wide enough to drop in a softball.

Edging in, he bent low and slid his fingers along the edge of the bed, crept to the nightstand, close to the snoring mouth, feeling around for the pistol, the old man bragging about it, the most important thing a man needed by his bed. Easing the drawer of the nightstand, he felt inside — something like a used tissue sticking to his fingers. Denny shaking it off, then going low over to the dresser. He was reaching and thought he was touching Lonzo's wallet on top, that's when something cold pressed against his ear. Denny freezing.

·

Bobbi inched the Beretta from his ear, recognition as he turned his head. She sighed, wagging the barrel meant she wanted him in the john. Taking Lonzo's wallet from him, she tucked it in the pocket of the bathrobe, kept the barrel on him. Easing the bathroom door almost closed behind her, wagging for Denny to back up to the toilet.

"The hell you doing, Denny?" Whispering it.

Denny replaying the look that passed between them in Lonzo's rear-view, him pretending not to eavesdrop on their conversations in the back seat. Giving a lift of a shoulder, saying, "The man owes me." His eyes going to the pistol, guessing if he had to get shot, he'd want her doing it. She wagged it again, told him to sit on the throne.

"So, you shoot me, you gonna wake him."

"Yeah, haven't decided. But, maybe there's a way ..." Bobbi thinking fast, taking a few moments before coming up with, "You give me a hand, and maybe you come out of this, get to walk away."

"A hand doing what?" Fearing she was planning to off the old man.

Slowly pulling back the bathroom door, she waved the barrel for him to follow, then tiptoed through the bedroom to the double closet. She eased open the slider, whispering for him to move the shoes and lift out the bottom shelf. Putting a forefinger to her lips. Standing aside, cinching the bathrobe and waiting.

Nobody needing to tell him to be quiet. Bending for the shoes, he lined them on the broadloom, lifted out the shelf easy without a sound, reached in and pulled out the twins, two Gucci cases. Knowing what they held. Trying to guess by their weight how much was in each one.

Whispering to him, "What you came for, right, come-uppance?" Waving the pistol again, making him put them down, put back the shelf and shoes like he found them, then he took both cases and followed her through the bedroom to the door. Lonzo lying there, out cold with his mouth in a big wide O, snoring like it was opera.

In the hall, Bobbi leaned close to him, saying, "Stay." Pointing the pistol, letting him know she'd do it, she left him at the top of the stairs, and she disappeared into the room he guessed was hers, the one that smelled nice.

He stood there weighing his odds, rushing down the stairs and getting out of there with the twins, Lonzo's get-away cash, what he came for. Not sure why he didn't.

Then she was back, a cashmere turtleneck and bell-bottoms over an arm, a pair of Oxfords in her hand, the Beretta in the other. Nodding for him to go down ahead of her. At the bottom, she said, "Wait."

She dropped the bathrobe, not too dark to make out the black bra and panties. Bobbi getting into the turtleneck and bell-bottoms, looking at him, saying, "You mind?"

Saying he was sorry, Denny turned away.

Getting into her clothes, she stepped into the shoes, then led him along the hall and through the kitchen, grabbing the eight-track cartridge that said *Boppin' Beppe* on it from beside the knife block, going out the side door, telling him not to let it slam. Denny carrying the bags, catching the door with his shoulder. Again, feeling like the hired help.

Flicking on the fluorescent light in the garage, he watched as she used the auxiliary key and popped the Caddy's trunk, told him to lay the twins by the spare. Then tossed him the keys and said, "You drive."

Back to playing chauffeur. Raising the garage door, knowing Aldo was right above and would hear it, he got in and backed down the driveway and was rolling along Chartwell, passing the Bug by the creek. Halfway down the hill he pulled the knob and put on the headlights, thinking he'd call and let Wilson know where to pick up the Bug, get it out of there before it got impounded. The lights of the city glimmered down the hill past the dark mass of Stanley Park. Denny checking the rear-view, nobody following them.

"You gonna keep pointing that?" he said, nodding at the pistol in her lap, the barrel looking at him.

She said nothing and didn't move the gun away.

"How you stand it, that racket, the guy snoring like that?"

"Shit I dropped in his cocktail, must've kicked up his sinuses." She said it staring straight ahead.

"You drugged him?" Denny looked at her, kind of surprised.

"Just watch the road. No way I wanted him waking up, middle of me walking out."

"With his getaway cash."

"Guess he owed me, too."

"Never pictured it, the two of you like a couple."

"This you going all Dear Abby now?"

"None of my business, just saying ..."

"Saying you never snore?"

"Not like that. God, nobody does it like that."

"Yeah, well, guess we'll see."

Not sure what she meant, Denny steered down the hill. Flashing lights and a barrier as he turned onto Taylor Way. His heart back in his throat, thinking it was the cops. Turned out to be a work crew in safety vests, one guy setting out the orange cones, three others dealing with a burst water main. A flagger waving them along a single lane along the wide boulevard, past the cones, tires sloshing water at the underside.

He took the ramp to the right, onto the No. 1, going west, then north.

"Why not that way?" Bobbi pointing to the ramp under the bridge, the road going south.

"Just a hunch." A long time since he sat behind the wheel, this fine car with the Delco stereo, speakers front and back, power everything: antenna, doors and windows, six-way seats, the sunroof and front-seat heater.

"Watch the speed, don't need no attention." The Beretta in her lap, still pointing his way.

Switching on the cruise control, he adjusted the steering the way he used to set it, slid the seat to where he liked it, Denny rolling across the top of town, the dark of the inlet, the city lights beyond it to the south. Neither of them saying much till they passed Caulfield.

"So, Bobbi, that short for something?"

She looked at him. "We making polite conversation now, huh?"

"Just asking, see what you prefer. Bobbi with an I, maybe two Bs. Guessing it's Italian, like Roberta. Going by the dark eyes and hair."

"How about just girl with a gun."

Horseshoe Bay was coming up on the left, the No. 1 sweeping north, Bobbi saying, "So, why tonight?"

He told about seeing Lonzo pull up outside the Eastside bistro, knocking down the guy with the sandwich board, coming out with her on his arm, Denny standing across the street in a job line.

"Somebody else looking for a driver?"

"Assistant to an A-lister, movie star."

"So, I'm guessing you didn't get it."

"Thought the recruiter, this chick with a 'fro, would call, but haven't heard a word."

"You never know ..."

"Anyway, seeing him got me thinking about it, thinking he owed me."

"So, you broke in looking for payback. Guy wronged you and had it coming, the way he kicked you out, middle of the street. Humiliated you. Told you about his hidden money, bragging what a big man he was, and got your wheels turning."

"Yeah, he couldn't help but brag about it. But it was when you told him to get a dog. The way he was growling, showing his teeth, saying who had the stones to rob him. Like he was daring me to do it."

"Yeah, I remember. But you know, Denny, you ask me, the man owes you shit. You make your bed, you lie in it."

"Maybe so, and hey, you got the gun, otherwise I might say at least it was my own bed I was lying in."

"Got a point. Still you sucked up plenty, talking across the back seat. You and Aldo, guys like you ..." She was shaking her head.

"How you mean, guys like me?"

"Wrong thinkers."

"What's so wrong, we got two bags of the man's cash in the trunk." Denny nicked his head to the back. "One each, right?"

"There you go, more wrong thinking." Bobbi waving the pistol, then reaching in her bag, taking the *Boppin' Beppe* eight-track and pushing it in the player. "Runaround Sue" coming on.

"This that Engelbert guy?"

"Boppin' Beppe. Guy you never heard of. One who gave me the stuff knocked out Lonzo. Paid five bucks for it."

"Come with the tape?"

"Five bucks was for the tape."

"The guy can sing, give him that." Denny tapped his fingers on top of the wheel, along to the music, looking from her, to the Beretta, then back out the windshield. "So, we are splitting it, right?"

"Thinking about it."

Denny frowned. "The man kicked me out, middle of the street. Six months of living on SpagettiOs. Got to be worth something."

"Try faking Os, six months of that. Take the noodles and sauce anytime." She looked at the blur of Horseshoe Bay going past on the left, hardly any lights on. Saying, "Told Beppe he ought to try some Otis, the man's got the voice for it."

"Yeah, see what you mean, and maybe ought to change his name."

"You don't like Beppe?"

"It's not helping."

"That guy Dorsey called himself Engelbert, guy does alright. Brian Wilson called his outfit the Pendletons, Creedence was the Golliwogs," she said.

"Really into it, the music, huh?"

"I like what I like, guess it gets me dancing or feeling mellow."

"So, we're in this, getting along, talking music. How about you put that away?" Eyes on the Beretta. "Go a long way, getting me mellow."

"I like you edgy."

"Feel like if I say electric Dylan beats folk Dylan, maybe I get shot."

"Used to be Zimmerman, now Dylan's just Dylan. You don't like him, may as well say you don't like music, electric or folk, either way. Never understand the fan that time at Newport, trying to take an axe to Dylan's power cables." She tucked the pistol in her handbag, looked at a sign whizzing by. "B.Ceeing is believing." Then looked back at him. "From the way you talk, you're from the States, right?"

"Walnut Creek, near San Francisco."

"Place of love-ins, sit-downs. Free love, everybody turning on."

"Some of that going on, mostly back when the Dead were the Warlocks. More dope than love, you ask me. A place where oral sex is a felony."

"No shit."

"The week I split some free-love folk tipped the fuzz and stopped some gay parade. You heard of Harvey Milk?"

She shook her head.

"People down there are uneasy about lots going on, protesting the war, anti-nukes, Nixon, you name it. Got nothing like that up here."

"Burned my bra one time," she said.

He looked at her. "No kidding?"

"Drove down to this demonstration, called it the spirit of equality."

"Set the thing on fire, huh?" He smiled, tried to picture it.

"The thing?" She frowned, telling him she drove to Atlantic City, a bunch of girls building an oversized Miss

America out of papier mâché. Painted the bathing suit red, white and blue. Made a freedom trash can from foil. "All us girls tossing in our curlers, girdles, bras, fake eyelashes, anything that binds and cinches. A symbol, you know. Ripped up a *Playboy* for kindling and lit the can on fire. All of us girls dancing topless and singing 'We Shall Overcome' 'round the fire."

Denny smiled, liked that they were talking, less threatened by the pistol in her lap.

"You try squeezing in a girdle sometime, strap on a bra and shoes that pinch. All designed by a man."

"Yeah, guess I get that."

"Anyway, it was fun till this ex-miss wannabe showed up, with her puffed hair, fake boobs and heels. A 'Vote for Nixon' pin on her D-cup. Had a bunch of others with her. Started calling us bull dykes, this ex-miss poking an acrylic fingernail at me. All it took, and it got me boiling."

"You set her straight, huh?"

"Knocked her on her ass." Bobbi made a balled fist.

Denny grinned at the small hand, but getting a new appreciation.

Beppe's tape got caught in the guides, and Bobbi tapped the heel of her hand at the deck, pressed eject, the AM coming on, the newscaster finishing an update on the rain of bombs on Cambodia, calling it a series of tactical air raids. She carefully un-looped the tape from the pins, smoothed it between her fingers, hoping it was alright. Using a finger, she wound it back up.

Denny saying, "Not what we need, dropping more bombs on the innocent."

"Really a draft dodger, huh?"

"More partial to conscientious objector. But yeah, I'm against the violence going on."

Whistling past the Welcome to Squamish sign, Bobbi told him to hang a right at the light, wanted him to pull into town, look for a place serving coffee, hoping it would keep her sharp.

Getting in the exit lane, he considered she could be planning something, like leaving him flat, to go in search of a Greyhound stop. Taking the Caddy and the bags of stash, keeping it all for herself.

Angle parking, the street empty except for a lone Skylark, a puke-teal color. A grocery with its covered racks next to a dark TD Bank, a cleaners and an all-night trucker joint called Tazza's on the corner, its lights on, a couple of long-hauls out in the vacant lot around the side.

"Make mine black." She pointed to the payphone out front of the grocery. "Gonna make a call."

"You know somebody up here?"

"Guy I know's got a chalet, up someplace called Alta Lake."

"This guy know Lonzo?"

"Carmen Roth, the guy from the bistro, the one Lonzo decked."

Denny nodded, looking worried. "Not sure that's a good idea."

"You hear me ask you?"

"Betting your life on it — mine, too."

Bobbi smiled, holding out her hand. "Let me have the keys."

Hesitated before handing them over, then he got out, felt the bite of night air and went for coffee, thinking if she was still there when he got back, he'd check the twins for bugs.

Walking in the all-night joint, he nodded to a gray-bearded man in an apron and white cap, the guy looking up from the daily news spread on the counter. A pair of truckers at the far end, chowing down. Stepping up, Denny ordered two with shoes, the guy in the apron giving him a tired look, groaning as he straightened, leaving his paper, getting a couple of styro cups, filling them from a pot on a warmer, popping on lids and charging him half a buck, pointing to the creamers and sugar packets on the side counter. Looking out past the reversed lettering on the glass, Denny could see Bobbi at the phone box, a light on over her head, the receiver in her hand.

•

Talking to directory assistance, Bobbi made the call collect, checking the coin return for her dime, noticed her hand was shaking. Screwing up her nerve as she waited through the ringing, and hearing the click at the other end.

The groggy voice saying, "Who the fuck's this?"

Twisting on a smile, she said, "I wake you, Lonz?" Her voice not as strong as she wanted.

A sharp intake of breath on the line, Bobbi having second thoughts about making the call at all, wondering if he could tap it, find out where she was. "How you doing, baby, you feeling okay?" she asked.

"I'm talking to a ghost."

"I want to explain . . ." And she told him about dropping a little something in his drink at the club.

"Where you at?"

No answer.

"And who's with you? No way you got the brains for this."

"He had nothing to do with it —" Stopping herself, wanting him to know there was another guy, and wanting to show she did have the brains. Then screwing up her courage, like the time she punched that woman for calling her a bull dyke. What she said was, "You know you snore, baby?"

"The fuck you say?"

"You're one raspy old pudge." Bobbi not holding back. "Got a neck like a turkey, cat whiskers coming from your ears. Two of us walk down the street, I'm looking across your head, like the surface of the moon, liver spots for craters. And in bed, my God, nothing mad-dog about you. You flop off me, and I want to get you a warm milk. You ask me, you got what was coming to you." Bobbi's free hand was a fist, her fingernails digging into her palm, the other hand choking the receiver. Not sure where it was all coming from. Tears felt hot rolling down both cheeks when she ripped at the receiver, yanking at the cord. Frustrated when it didn't rip free. Bobbi taking the receiver and slamming it down. Looking around from the phone booth. Saw Denny was back in the car. Nobody else around. Her heart was pounding, tears going hot to cold in the night air. Leaning against the side glass, she wiped at them, watched her frosty exhale, looked like she was smoking.

•

A styro in each hand, creamers, sugar packets and stir sticks balanced on top, the *Squamish Times* wedged under his arm. Passing the Skylark, thinking of switching rides, Denny set the cups on the roof and tugged open the door. Getting behind the wheel, he set a styro on the dash, looking at Bobbi at the phone box, hoping this guy Carmen came through with the chalet, let them hide out a day or so. Denny fixed his coffee, thinking of a cozy fire, nice and warm, just the two of them counting out the cash, helping themselves to Carmen's liquor.

If that didn't work out, he knew this guy in Whistler, another hour north. Rubin Stevens grew some righteous weed — a friendly type of guy, the kind you could look up and drop in on — the guy who made the run to Vancouver every couple of weeks, dropping off a quarter-pound of homegrown to Wilson and his flat-mates, each of them chipping in seventy-five bucks. Kept Denny's head on right, with a good buzz, but needing to suck on his Medihaler, dealing with his asthma. Betting if he hadn't dodged his uncle after getting on the news, the asthma would have kept him from conscription, his uncle putting him down as 4-F, like he told that job recruiter.

Pulling down the armrest, he balanced his cup, peeled off the lid and dumped in sugar and a couple of creamers. Stirring the stick, he took a sip, surprised the coffee wasn't bad.

Turning on the dome light, he flipped through the local rag, not sure why he took it, the counter man folding it and offering it to him. A mix of headlines and local news. Nothing about the U.S. troop withdrawal. Turning the page, he scanned one about town council debating improvements to the 99, the article dubbing it the killer highway. Denny thinking especially if Lonzo caught up with them.

Bobbi stood by the phone, her back to him, Denny flipping the page, an ad telling him to watch for $1.49 day at the local grocer this Wednesday. A cartoon that wasn't funny. Skimmed a local story about a beekeeper visited by aliens. A photo of the guy smiling, pointing to where the yellow lights beamed in the sky. Next story about loggers going back to work after a shutdown. Nothing on the war at all, Denny wondering if Canadians knew one was even going on. Folding the paper, sticking it between the console and seat.

Coming back and getting in, Bobbi took the cup off the dash.

"You get him?"

"No answer."

"Saw you talking."

"Oh, that was Lonzo." Said it just like that. She smiled at him and snapped the lid and took a sip, saying, "It's not bad."

Denny just looked at her.

"Just seeing if he was okay, an old man with all that shit in his bloodstream, can't be good, right?"

"You asked him if he's okay?"

"The way he was yelling, could tell he was."

"You're something, you know it?"

"Tried to show him I cared, nothing personal . . . was hoping to ask about the combination."

"The locked cases?"

"Since we were talking."

"Jesus."

"But he starts with the growling and freaking out. Practically spitting in the phone, about what he's gonna do . . . yadda yadda."

"Us?"

"Just figured it's a shame to cut up good luggage. The way I feel, I mean, you got any idea what Guccis go for?"

"You said 'us.'"

"What?"

"Tell me exactly."

"Told him about dropping a little something in his drink at Oil Can's, time he went to the can, middle of the set."

"You said my name, didn't you?"

She shrugged, sipped her coffee. "What's he gonna do?"

"I don't know, start by tracing the number." Denny looked up, a guy walking to the Skylark, getting in. "Find out where we're at."

"Man's still so doped, lucky he can stand."

"But he's got people do his shit for him."

She shrugged. "Even if he finds the phone box. So what? Not like we're gonna hang around and wait for him."

"We got to dump this car, check the bags for bugs." Denny thinking it through, had to keep driving north. Lonzo would have people coming from the south, looking for them. Reaching his Medihaler, he thumbed the button on top and dragged on it.

"You're getting paranoid." Bobbi flipped on the dome light, sipped more coffee, feeling better, settling down, getting lipstick on the styro's edge. Taking the paper, she flapped it open and scanned it. "Got a rock festival coming. A place like this, you believe it?"

Denny held out his hand for the keys.

"Place called Paradise Valley. Got some big names signed." She kept reading, putting her hand in her bag, feeling for the keys. "The Guess Who, Flying Burritos, Joni Mitchell." Dangling the keys off her finger.

"Gonna be a million miles from here." The Skylark pulled out, driving off. Denny starting the car, backing out and finding the ramp to the 99. Saying, "Wanted me to think I was coming back with the coffee and you'd be gone, right?"

"You caught that, huh?" Bobbi smiling, folding the paper, sticking it under the seat.

"Always playing."

"Could've left you at the house, bleeding on the rug, with the old boy snoring on the bed."

Denny switched off the dome light and was back on the 99, feeling better as the Caddy found the limit, passing the Brackendale turnoff, passing a Ford Hauler and a Dodge D. Denny watching his speed.

Sitting quiet awhile, Bobbi looked at him, saying, "We got to give up the Caddy, I'm thinking nothing less than mid-size." Popped off her Oxfords, folded her legs up on the seat, rubbed one foot, smiling as she said, "You know the little Mercedes?"

"Yeah, you got a color in mind?" Denny glanced at the Beretta back in her lap, thinking he ought to grab it. Back to going ten over the posted speed, saying, "Can't believe you did that, told him about us, you and me."

"Just slipped out," she lied.

"You like stirring it up, huh?"

"A little." She crinkled her nose, tried looking cute.

Checking the fuel gauge, the needle at a quarter tank. Should be enough to make it to Whistler, the pines flashing past in the headlights beam. Glancing back at the Beretta. "You ever shoot one?"

Lifting it, looking at it, the barrel still pointing his way. "Looks easy enough."

. . . five

North of Garibaldi, Daisy Lake glinted through the pines to the east. Bobbi sat curled with her legs on the seat, bell-bottoms over her bare feet. Fishing a file from her bag, she ran it across the tips of her nails, saying, "Done with that old life, tired of the way things been going."

"Yeah, well, you got enough to retire on if you want."

"And I earned every penny. See, that's my point, I earned it. What I'm wondering, what'd you do?"

He didn't have anything to say to her. A few miles on, he rolled into Whistler without asking her, following the sign to Creekside. Plastic over the windows of some place called Tokum Corners.

"The hell you doing now?" Bobbi looked around, passing a cabin, like the one the Clampetts lived in. Then an A frame with a sign out front: sales office. Lots for sale. A Canadian flag wagging off a pole, a map showing available lots and proposed ski trails.

"Know a guy here, since your man Carmen didn't pan out," Denny said. "Maybe give us a place to get cleaned up, let me check the cases for bugs, find something to eat."

"Hey!" Bobbi was holding the Beretta, pissed off, feeling

she was losing control, this driver not taking her serious. "You wanna do anything, like keep breathing, how about you run it by me. How'd that be?"

"Know what I think, think you got control issues. But let me ask you one: You even know how to drive?"

Bobbi not sure what to do about it, Denny pulling into a muddy parking spot, tilting the telescopic wheel, sliding the bench seat back, making legroom, kicking off his sneakers. "I'm gonna crash, and you can't drive. So, why not put that away, catch some winks yourself. Gonna feel better in the morning." And that was it. He tipped his head against the cold window, closing his eyes.

Bobbi stuck the barrel into his ribs.

He didn't open his eyes, just said, "You keep doing that, I'm gonna take it from you." And he rolled his hip, getting the best fit between the wheel and the seat.

Bobbi looked at him turning away from her, the man going to sleep. Clicking her door lock, she kept the pistol on him, thinking it through. Then dropping it in her bag, she wished him a stiff neck by dawn, then put her own head against the cold glass and was asleep in seconds.

·

She was screaming herself awake, Bobbi jumping with her hand to her throat, hitting her head on the headliner. One hand on the dash, the other on the door handle.

Denny caught her in his arms, saying it was alright.

And she let him hold her, put her body against him, catching her breath, letting the real take hold, saying to him, "Saw Lonzo, at the window, breathing on the glass, Jesus, tapping that damn ring." Looking out the side window, thinking of those fucking teeth.

"Just a dream." He kept holding her, looking about, nobody out there.

Bobbi got her breathing to slow, her heart stopped pounding in her chest. Sweat on her skin made her tremble. She eased away from him.

Denny leaned back against his door and repositioned his legs, not much room between the seat and the wheel, six feet tall and uncomfortable as hell. He said something about the scent she wore, told her he smelled it back at Lonzo's place.

Guessing he was trying to make her feel easy, she said, "Got to be the Prell."

"The what?"

"Shampoo. All it is."

"Yeah well, it's nice."

"Thanks, I guess." Bobbi looking at this guy she'd been holding a gun on. Smiling in the dark.

"You want, I can turn on the heat," he said.

"Yeah, I wouldn't mind." Thinking she was sounding vulnerable, even with the pistol in her lap.

Turning the key to accessory, the instrument panel lights coming on. Just ahead of six in the morning, Denny telling her it would get light in an hour or so, the clock's red hand sweeping off the seconds. Letting the engine run about ten minutes before shutting it off, he fell to sleep again, and she did, too, stirring when a food delivery van drove past.

. . . *six*

"Kind of broad does a thing like that, dopes a man when he's not looking, steals him blind and takes his Cadillac? She wants to be my ex? I'll give her an X. Carve it across her eyes." Lonzo grinding his teeth for Lee Trane.

"Yeah, I get it," Lee Trane said, trying not to look bored. Told him Bobbi Ricci's phone call had come from a phone box in Squamish. Had it traced when Lonzo first called him, somebody he knew at Bell, saying, "I'll find them, count on that."

"Fuckin' right you will. My goddamn head's thick as soup," Lonzo said, his hand rubbing across his forehead. In spite of the Mickey, he'd had the presence to leave the bed-side phone off the hook after she called, stumbling down-stairs, dialing Lee from the kitchen phone, waking him and telling him he had a job for him, saying, "Starting now, that's when." Wanted Bobbi to face him, on her knees like a sacri-fice. And Denny the driver, wanted him in little bits. Lonzo spitting into the phone's mouthpiece.

Before coming over, Lee told him to call it in to law enforcement, report the Caddy stolen. Then said he'd be right over.

"Don't need the damn cops," Lonzo said.

"They find the car, they gonna give us an idea which way they went." Lee standing in the hall now, looking at the old man, saying, "And Lonz, you did good not hanging up the other line till my guy made the trace."

"You got me mixed up with a moron?"

"Just saying . . ." Fuck, try paying this guy a compliment.

Lonzo went on saying how he nearly ripped the phone cord from the wall when she called, wanted to throw the damn thing out the window, hear it splash in the pool. He went and poured three fingers of Chivas, not offering Lee one, looked up at the painting on the wall, the nude by Mariani, kept talking about what he was going to do to Bobbi Ricci. He downed the drink, saying he'd been betrayed, getting robbed like that. "And that draft-dodging fuck likely . . ." Then he crossed himself, the photo of his mother on the mantle. Mama, see what they done to your boy.

"*Pagheranno, Mamma.*" Pouring another three fingers, saying, "And where the fuck was Aldo the whole time?" Turning and seeing Lee Trane had gone.

•

The red-haired cop scratched under his cap, standing at the door, scribbling out the stolen vehicle report, knowing this guy Tomasino Alonzo Palmieri was a known dirtbag, but guessing he had the kind of clout that could make his career on the force one of misery.

"So, how you gonna get it back? A Cadillac, worth more than a Johnny Law like you makes in a year." Betting this kid was Irish, that fucking red hair under the cap and freckles on his face like dirt.

"Doing all we can, Mr. Palmieri," mispronouncing the name. "Every man from the chief on down takes this sort of thing serious." The cop nodded. "Put out an APB, get a detective on it, doing whatever it takes."

The other cop looked at his partner, then away past Lonzo's hedge.

"You screwing with me, you boy scouts?" Lonzo looked at the name on the shield.

"Just doing the job, sir."

"How about next time I see Donaldson at the club, I mention your name, tell him what a gem this Walsh is he's got working for him?"

"Like I said, sir, we're doing all we can."

"Neighborhood like this, a man gets his car jacked while he's sleeping in his bed. All the while you're out there doing what you can."

The cops turned down the walk, Lonzo slapped the door shut, ripped off a slipper and tomahawked it across the room, took out a lamp. Reached the bottle of Chivas off the booze trolley, started for the stairs.

The ringing phone stopped him.

•

Had it traced to the pay box in Squamish an hour after he left the old man's place.

"Yeah? So, find her and bring her back."

"How about the driver?" Lee said.

"Him, you do what you want; fact, use your imagination. Think little pieces."

"Got it."

"And Lee?"

"Yeah?"

"Take a couple of boys. Want this done pronto."

"That's why you send me, alone."

"Did I say let's debate?"

"Look, you're the boss, I get that, but this is my thing, huh?"

"Fine." Lonzo sighed. "Just bring her back, goddamn it." Hanging up, thinking he'd put a couple more boys on it anyway.

•

Lee looking at the phone in his hand, saying, "Ain't love grand." Making another call, his contact at 312 Main, a sergeant named Buckley. Needed to locate the Cadillac, asked Buckley to put the word out. Explained the old man's girlfriend might be driving it. Buckley sounding like he was getting a kick out of it.

Lee packed an overnight bag, extra pants and shirt, some toiletries. The .38 snub nose with the two-inch barrel under the Jockeys and socks. Reliable and good up-close, easy to tuck under a jacket. A box of hollow point rounds. His cop-issue cuffs. Laying the twelve-gauge in the hidden compartment, the trunk of the T-Bird.

Buckley called back within the hour, read from a report: Lonzo's license plates were found on a Cutlass belonging to the sales manager at Whistler Chalets, the guy phoning it in. "Sounds to me your boy Lonzo's having trouble with the ladies, alright."

"You're a funny guy, Buck. Next time I see him, I'll tell him how you laughed it up." Hanging up, Lee took his stuff and got in his car and drove north, thinking about Bobbi Ricci. Not bad-looking, and not dumb either, taking Lonzo for his money. Letting Lonzo's one-time chauffeur do the driving, picturing her riding in back with the Guccis, taking off with the man's half-million. Only talked to her a couple times, usually with Lonzo there — the kind of woman he wouldn't mind getting with himself. Be a shame to drag her back to face the son of a bitch, a pretty good idea what the old man would do to her.

. . . seven

Looking at the morning gray, Denny listened to the rhythm of her breathing as she slept. Stealing a look at her, the line of her neck and her dark hair sweeping down, face gentle like a child's, and no sign of the pistol.

With the color of morning coming, he got out to stretch, his breath huffing out, the slope of Whistler to his right. The air cold and thin up here, going in and out of his lungs as he took in that slope, snow halfway up. Thinking about it, the frosting in the pine tops making everything look new. Taken from his thoughts when the food van pulled out on the wheel ruts he came in on, hearing muck slap up at its underbelly.

The flag angling off the A-frame flapped. Getting back in, he switched on the ignition and turned up the heater again. Cupping his hands, he blew into them. Bobbi sleeping through it.

Thinking it through, he figured their best chance was to head to Lillooet and swing around on the 12, go past Hell's Gate and end up in Hope. Lonzo would have people looking. Likely he had a trace on the line. Bobbi calling the old man from the Squamish phone box, asking if he was okay, her way of rubbing it in. Denny sure she let him know he was in on it. A damn stupid move.

Could reach for the Beretta now, tell her to get out, take the cases and split for the east and disappear. Looking at her sleeping, her head against the passenger window. Yeah, Denny could do it, reach over and have it all. And he kept watching her, trying to catch that scent of Prell again.

Just past seven before she stirred. Denny watching her most of the time.

Yawning and balling her fingers, not enough room to stretch, she combed fingers through her hair. Saying, "Want to tell me again why we're here?"

"Told you, this guy I know, hoping he helps us out." Didn't say more, he got out, looking at the A-frame of logs and boards with the map out front, the flag hanging now. Up the hill he saw a neon sign out front of a place called the Spuzzum Spoon. Lights coming from inside told him it was opening for breakfast. Asked Bobbi if she could eat, and the two of them walked to it along a dirt path.

Paneled in pine with a plywood floor, a sunburst clock making it twenty past the hour. A waitress, her hair long and blonde and tied in a tail, crowned by a colored head-band, a tie-dyed apron over a man's flannel shirt, jeans, rainbow-striped socks tucked into clogs. She welcomed them and told them to sit where they wanted, three tables and a counter with a mix of stools and chairs, nobody else in the place. Said she was Jane, and this was her place.

Going to the round table by the window, Denny scraped back a pioneer chair, sitting with a view of the Caddy and the road coming in. Jane stepped from behind the counter, Denny putting her look down as fresh-scrubbed mountain girl.

Jane saying, "Breakfast sandwich's chopped egg and chive, your choice of coffee or tea. The tea's herbal or chai."

"Coffee sounds good," Bobbi said, crossing her arms, feeling the mountain cold snap through the turtleneck.

Denny scanned the menu above the counter, a cartoon miner with a flop hat and axe telling him to Drink Mountain Dew. "It'll tickle yore innards." Going for coffee, too, with the breakfast sandwich, white being his bread choice, said sure to the sweet pickle, asking Jane, "Spuzzum, that's over by Hells Gate, no?" Remembered seeing it on the map out front of the A-frame.

"You got it right, just south of the Nipple." Giving him a playful look, she turned, her ponytail swung as she fetched the coffee, setting down the mugs. "Dogwood Valley's the place I opened the first Spoon."

"Like franchising."

"More like a grease fire, burned the place useless. This lease came up, so here I am, the name's the only thing that got saved." Putting on a smile, she disappeared again, coming back in a few minutes, setting his plate down. Saying to Bobbi, "Sure I can't get you something, hon? Fresh bagels just come in, got the Philli cheese goes with it."

"Too early to eat." Bobbi waited for Jane to go, taking half of Denny's sandwich, nicely toasted and cut on the diagonal, taking a tiny bite.

"Not hungry?"

She shrugged, tipping it so the chopped egg and mayo didn't spill out, taking a bigger bite, licking mayo from the corner of her mouth. "There, happy?"

The door opened, cold air and a good-looking guy coming in, a cigarette tipped from his mouth. Ski vest open, stubbled jaw, denim shirt untucked, pants inside his untied boots, a toque on his head, red pom-pom like garnish. "How you folks doing?" Smiling over as he perched on a swivel seat at the counter, palms drumming on his thighs. Not one of Lonzo's crew. Denny thinking it was a ski bum nursing a night-after. Waiting for Jane, the guy blew a stream of smoke over the counter.

Coming from the back, Jane was happy to see him, coming around the counter, arms held wide, saying, "Hey Chill, how you feeling, my man?" Kissing his cheek.

"You tell me, babe." Hugging her to him, bending back and lifting her feet off the ground.

"Shoulda seen the Rube last night, *ooh-wee*." Looked over at Denny and Bobbi, trying to keep his voice low. "So blasted, the man peed off the porch, passed out in mid-whizz, you believe it?" Tipping his hand, showing how he fell, his voice lower again, but being heard. "Still holding his business when we stood him back up, snow falling off him." Grinning, Chill dragged on his smoke.

"Hope there's no frostbite." Jane glanced over, like she just remembered about Denny and Bobbi.

"Man's unkillable, bent a bit maybe, but be as good as new, just needs a few hours." Chill did a slow spin on the stool for a better look at Bobbi and Denny, mainly Bobbi. Puffing smoke, saying, "You two here looking for a lot, building one of them dream boxes?"

Denny looked out the window, an Olds Cutlass pulling next to the Caddy, a guy with a briefcase getting out, checking out the Cadillac. Wasn't one of Lonzo's guys, in his middle years, the look of a balding accountant in a navy blazer, unlocking the door to the A-frame and going inside. Denny saying to the guy at the counter, "Don't get it, buying a place up here, just to ski down a hill."

"You sure sound like city, no offense." Jane came around, refilling their cups.

"Chalets and lodges and chairlifts. Mud all over the place. Putting in a gondola'll take you right to the top." Chill pointed up the mountain. A final drag, looking around for an ashtray, not finding one, careful not to let the long ash fall. "All the peace and quiet anybody'd want, except for these assholes bulldozing everything." The ash fell, and Chill got up, put a boot on it, went to the door and flicked his butt outside, noted the Cadillac by the sales office. Asking, "Sure you ain't scoping a place, driving a car like that?"

"Guy you mentioned, the Rube, swan-diving while he pees, that Rubin Stevens by any chance?" Denny said.

"Could be, 'less you got a badge, brother."

"I look like that?" Denny grinned.

"Never know these days. How you know him, the Rube?"

"Comes by, this place I stay in the city."

Chill nodded like he was getting the picture. "Uh, one of the draft dodgers, right? Bunch of you in a flat, smoking pot, not working, waiting for Nixon to say, 'Come on home, boys.'"

"We prefer conscientious objectors. But, so, where do I find Rubin?"

"Could try the Roundhouse, or, hold on . . . maybe Toad Hall." Tugging out his pack of Craven As, pinching one out. "Sure you ain't thinking of building, huh?"

Jane telling Chill he was being weird again.

Chill shrugged and lit another smoke. "Guys in hard hats tearing out the trees, plowing up the mountain, slapping up tacky cabins, overcharging, driving up costs. Mucking up a good thing, calling it progress, and you call me weird."

Jane said to Denny. "Chill's not for it, in case you can't tell."

"Driving stakes in the heart of the land, then raping it. Don't give a shit they're messing up the folks already here." Chill blew smoke, checking Bobbi out, not bothered that she was with Denny. "Guys in their shiny shoes and two-buck smiles, send in the dozers, tearing down the places we live, scaring off the wildlife, screwing up all of Soo Valley."

"They forcing you to sell?" Bobbi said, feeling for the guy.

"Can't sell what's not his," Jane said.

Bobbi putting it together, saying, "So, what, you're like a squatter?"

"What I do, I find an empty place, nobody living in it." Chill shrugged, "Clean it up, give it some love. For that you call me a squatter."

"What then, a ski bum?" Bobbi being playful.

Jane laughed, going back around the counter. "How about member of the Underpaid Canadian Ski Team?"

"Well, of that I'm guilty." Denny laughed. "Ski the white months and swim the green ones." Saluting to his temple, the cigarette between his fingers. "Living right over at Toad Hall, least till the hard hats tear it to the ground."

"This the place where Rubin's at?" Denny suppressed a cough, the smoke bothering him.

"You want, can take you right over, help you wake his sorry ass."

"That what you do up here, ski and swim, huh?" Bobbi said, trying to picture it.

"Yeah, and we hike and bike, and paddle and party. Generally speaking, it's a big mess around, a little naked volleyball now and again, over by Green Lake, you know, the bunch of us living free and off the land."

Jane asked the paying customers if they wanted refills.

"Thanks, doll." Chill held out his cup, cigarette down to a butt, pinched between fingers. "Well, was a good run, I guess." He looked at Denny, saying, "Drove all this way in your Cadillac, up here scoring some weed, huh?" Chill tipped up the cup, still eyeing Bobbi, saying, "If that's all you need, can fix you up with some myself. Same good shit as the Rube, same price, too, twenty an ounce. Save you the trouble trying to wake the man."

"Don't mind waking him, but thanks anyway." Denny not liking the way this guy kept eye-fucking Bobbi, doing it like it was cute. "Plus, we never paid more than fifteen a lid."

"Man's giving you the deep discount, huh?" Chill nodded, eyes meeting Denny's. "Help you objectors make your rent, give you some margin, let you sell a little herb on the side while you hunt for honest work, Canadian jobs, waiting on the war to end."

"Uncle wouldn't take me anyway." Denny taking the Medihaler from his pocket, pressing the button and taking a puff.

"The hell's that?" Chill asked, blowing a cloud.

"Little baby that gets me classified as unfit to serve." Denny holding it up.

"Read about guys like you coming up with ways to dodge: pooping their pants, not showering for a month, going in hand in hand like homos." Chill coming and taking it from him, looking at it. "Heard that fighter Cassius say, 'Ain't no Viet Cong ever called me nigger.' Rather sit in jail than go to war." Chill read the print down the side. "'Eighty percent of particles from half to four microns radius.' What's it, like fresh air?"

"Yeah, on account of asthma and smoke don't mix." Denny taking it back, dropping it in his pocket.

"But you're here buying pot."

"Maybe I eat it."

"Mean like brownies?"

"And hash butter, lollipops, gummy bears."

"Gummy bears, huh?"

"Just got to mix in gelatin, some fruit juice. Pour it in a mould and let it set."

"Yeah." Chill saying he'd try it sometime. Adding, "Got no problem with you dodging, man. Don't get me wrong. Wouldn't join Uncle Sam and his baby killers myself. Sooner go make it in my pants or go hand in hand, kiss some guy on the mouth."

"So, can you point us to Toad Hall, or not?" Denny smiling, trying not to show his impatience.

"Do you one better . . ." Chill brought his cup over and drew out a chair and swung it around, sat on it backwards. "Walk you over there myself. No problemo."

"That'd be nice," Bobbi said, taking the plate, offering Chill the rest of Denny's sandwich. Saying she could do with stretching her legs.

"Hey, thanks. This the egg?" Chill bit into it, opening one of the small foiled pads of butter, asking Jane if this place had a knife.

Jane going to get one, coming back, giving Chill the knife and laying the tab in front of Denny.

Spreading butter on the top of the bread, Chill shooed a fly, reached another pat of butter.

Paying the check, Denny got up and left a fifty-cent tip, just wanting to get out of there. Going to the door, telling them he'd follow in his car, stepping in the early sun with the flies buzzing around the stoop, going to the Cadillac, thinking he'd sit behind the wheel till they came out.

A station wagon pulled up in front of the A-frame, parked on the other side of the salesman's Cutlass, a middle-aged couple getting out of the Town and Country, woodgrain down its sides. The salesman stepped to the door, brushing at a lapel. "Welcome to Whistler, folks." Spreading his arms like the muck and mountains behind him were something to behold, shaking their hands and holding the door for them, getting them inside.

Denny checked his wallet, down to his last ten bucks. Needed to get into the Gucci cases, get some of Lonzo's cash. Hearing the salesman's voice from inside, hitting the couple

with buzzwords: "Best ones are going fast" and "solid investment" and "great potential." Watching the salesman lead the
couple out the back door, armed them with brochures and
literature, showing the staked lots. Reminded him of markers
in some unknown soldiers' graveyard.

Once they were out back of the A-frame, Denny took
Bobbi's nail file off the dash, and he went to the rear bumper
and got to work, switching the plates from the Caddy to the
Cutlass. Looking around, making sure nobody saw him do
it. Getting back in, he rolled past the Spuzzum Spoon, his
wheels slipping in the ruts. Seeing Bobbi and Chill walking
up ahead, Chill with his hand on her arm, keeping her from
slipping in the muck.

·

Denny parked the Caddy next to a Microbus, green and
painted with flowers and peace signs. A bumper sticker
reading: "Gas, Ass or Grass. No One Rides for Free."
Another one that read: "Let the Rabbit Eat Trix."

Getting out, not believing what he was seeing, guys and
chicks standing naked on the porch, a fleshy line hanging
out in nature, a dozen of them arm in arm. One guy holding
up a pair of skis, another strapping on a ski helmet, another
guy pulling on a toque standing between two chicks in
nothing but ski boots. Some tanned, some pallid. All happy
and high and singing. Buffalo Springfield blasting from
inside: "Stop, hey, what's that sound?" A naked photogra-
pher setting up his tripod, bare feet in the muck of the yard.

A lantern hung from a beam, next to a big rusting bell,
an old bench seat pulled from the Microbus used like garden
furniture. Toad Hall etched on a wood sign, nailed to the
battered roof.

"No Show!" A wiry guy with hair past his shoulders called out to Denny, throwing out his arms, coming down the steps, tinted ski goggles the only thing he had on, pushing them up on his forehead. Denny calling him Rubin Stevens, the Rube walking to him with a big dumb grin. Putting Denny in a bear hug, forgetting he was naked, practically hoisting the smaller man off the ground. Then holding him at arm's length, saying, "Look at you, brother."

Denny backed a step, glad to see him, the smell of pot and last night's beer coming off him like a fog. "The hell you doin', Rubin. You gonna freeze your ass, man. Likely get busted to boot."

"Busted, shit. Councilman's third one from the end." Rubin turning to the line and pointing. "Guy shriveling next to him's an auxiliary Mountie."

The guy wearing the ski helmet threw them a military salute, a beer bottle in one hand. Looking down at his crotch, then at the woman next to him, blaming the cold for what he called the shrivels.

The blonde on the other side of the guy with the helmet called to Chill to come get naked, say cheese with her.

"How you say no to that?" Tossing off his vest, then the shirt, peeling off his pants and hurrying on tiptoes up the steps, Chill called to Bobbi, "I'll save you a spot."

Bobbi saying it was a bit nippy, thanking him just the same, saying she'd keep an eye on his threads, gathering his pile of clothes that still felt warm, holding them against her.

Pale ass jiggling, Chill hopped up and down on the porch boards, shouting, *"Woo-hoo!"*

"So, what brings you, my man?" Rubin said to Denny, arm around his shoulder. "Was gonna come see you boys next week, got some new shit'll blow your mind."

"Sounds good, Rubin. But, uh, could use a lid now, if you got it, and uh, maybe a place to get cleaned up, maybe crash for a bit." Denny thinking he only had the ten bucks left. Needed to get into the Guccis, grab more cash and check the cases for bugs.

Rubin burped up some of last night, looked like he might be sick, then it passed. Giving Denny a steady look, Denny guessing he was wondering how this draft dodger just pulled up in a Cadillac with a good-looking woman, looking to score and for a place to hide out.

The chick in ski boots called, "Come on, Rube baby, I'm freezing my tits off here." Crossing her arms over her breasts.

"Hop around, Bunny, till I get there," he called back.

The one holding the skis passed them, saying to the guy next to her, "Spot me, huh, Toulouse?" Got down and did a handstand, her legs going wide, dark hair brushing the boards, her bush to the sky.

Juggling the skis, Toulouse steadied her by an ankle, smiling and taking in the spectacle.

The guy behind the camera clapped his hands, calling, "Okay people, come on, let's get real and do this."

Somebody calling him Kiwi, somebody else calling to Rubin.

"Coming, brother." Hustling back up the steps, Rubin stamped muck from his bare feet and squeezed next to Chill, pulling the goggles down over his eyes. One of the blondes doing a handstand, too. Rubin taking hold of an ankle, getting set to say cheese.

Kiwi looked through the viewfinder, counting to three, laughing as he ran up the steps, nearly falling, but getting in the frame. Everybody smiling as the flashbulb popped.

Bunny got back to her feet, putting a hand to her forehead, saying she loved the head rush, looking down at her chest, saying, "Oh man, look what the cold did." Pointing down at Toulouse, saying, "I'm up and you're down, my man."

Toulouse frowned, blaming the cold, covering up with one hand, wondering out loud, trying to remember where he dropped his pants, all the denim lying on the porch looking the same.

The bunch of them went inside, rummaging clothes on the floor, more on the chairs and tables, everybody getting dressed. Folding up the tripod, Kiwi left the camera on the mount, putting it across his shoulder and going inside.

Denny caught Bobbi by the arm, saying, "Sure you want to go in? Can wait in the car if you want?"

"You kidding, this place is a blast." Still holding Chill's clothes, she went up the steps and inside like she belonged.

Thanking her, taking his clothes and pulling up the jeans, Chill sniffed the flannel shirt and put it on, doing up the buttons.

Bunny went to the stereo by the window, a Pioneer turntable spinning, LPs lined on a shelf of bricks and boards, between bookend speakers. Lifted the tone arm, she slipped the vinyl in its sleeve, then putting on *Cahoots*. The needle scratching at side one. "Life Is a Carnival" coming on. Bunny doing the hip shake as the horns kicked in, singing along about walking on water, drowning in sand.

Denny introducing Bobbi to Rubin. The Rube forgetting he was still naked, giving her a hug, too, saying she was more than welcome. Tugging off the goggles and tossing them over by the turntable.

Bunny said hi to Bobbi, passing her a fat joint. Said she was going to squeeze some OJ with Alice. "You want some, hon?"

"Love some." Bobbi followed her to the kitchen, taking a drag, the music filling the place.

Rubin grinned, saying to Denny, "So, you boys run dry, they send you in a Cadillac instead that shitbox Volksie. Things must be looking up, huh?"

"Here 'cause you got the best weed around, but you know that."

Finding an odd-looking joint behind his ear, Rubin stuck it in his mouth, looking around for matches, somebody tossing him a book. "Rasta buddy calls it a spliff, thick on one end. Calls it herb, rolls 'em back home with palm bark, dips it in honey. Those Rastas knowing about getting close to God."

"That right, huh? Know I got the asthma, right?"

"Yeah, sure." Not hearing him, Rubin went on, "Just got to listen to Marley and Toots, and you understand what he's saying."

"You gonna toss on a robe or something any time soon, man?"

"Well, would you look at that." Rubin looked down, forgetting he was in the buff. Struck a match and fired up the spliff.

The song ended, and Levon Helm started singing about the streets of Rome being filled with rubble. The girls dancing in the kitchen with their glasses of orange juice. A party taking shape.

"After a while you forget you got anything on," Rubin said, still making no move to find pants.

"Hey, your place, your rules." Denny coughed, passing back the spliff. "Oh, and hey, if you got a room, man, some-place we can crash out a bit, catch a few Zs, maybe get cleaned up, you know . . ."

"Sure, brother, right up the stairs, any crib with nobody in it, it's all yours."

"Nobody gonna mind?"

"Nobody's gonna notice, man."

Bobbi came back with a glass of juice, Rubin passing her the joint.

Bobbi saying to Rubin, "You're gonna catch a draft."

Going to the dining table, Rubin reached under it and sorted through the remaining clothes, stepping into some overalls. Richard Manuel belting one about who robbed the cradle, who robbed the grave.

•

Bobbi turned through the bead curtain, into the kitchen. Bunny and Alice were still dancing. Some of the guys sitting at the table against the wall. Kiwi clattered around behind them, opening the fridge, finding the fixings for what he called his must-go stew, telling Denny and Bobbi they were welcome to stick around for a bowl. Then went back to arguing with Toulouse and Chill at the table about the best Stones album ever, saying *Sticky Fingers* topped *Let It Bleed*.

Toulouse saying, "No way, man. Stones are nothing like in the days of Brian Jones. Man, how you top 'Paint It Black?'"

Buttoning his shirt, pulling up the overall straps, Rubin came in, going with *Beggars Banquet*, the one with "Parachute Woman." Taking a butter knife from a drawer, blade blackened, heating it on a spare burner, unfolding some foil from his pocket. Taking a wire with wood handles from the drawer, slicing a chunk of hash, did it like a surgeon, saying to Denny, "Moroccan, man, this shit's the real." Dropping a piece on the red-hot blade, putting to his mouth, sucking in the smoke, offering it around.

Talk around tokes went from "Cowgirl in the Sand" to *Dark Side of the Moon*. Kiwi exhaling, swearing nothing beat "White Bird." Denny coughing, trying to think what time it was, remembering they were on the run.

Heating the knife again, Bobbi watched Rubin watch Denny step out to the Cadillac, betting in spite of being high, he was wondering about this draft dodger with asthma, driving up here in a car like that, bringing a woman like herself, asking for a room. The Rube still watching as Denny came back in with the two cases.

"Let me guess, toothbrush and undies, huh?"

"Got to stay fresh, right?" Denny said.

"That what I'm supposed to say, somebody comes looking?"

"You worried about cops, no need," Denny said. "Nothing like that, man."

"Was thinking more like her old man," Rubin said, smiling at Bobbi. "Guessing he owns the car."

"I look married?" Bobbi said it like she was hurt.

"I say married?"

"Okay, maybe there was a guy . . ."

Rubin looked at the Caddy, back to Denny, "Sugar daddy, and she's the sugar, huh?"

"Doubt he comes looking. Nothing to worry about."

"But if somebody does, you were never here, right?"

"Look, we'll split as soon as we, you know, catch a few winks. Oh, and wouldn't mind scoring a lid for the road."

"We talking a cash sale?"

"Yeah, sure. Gonna pay you for the last time to boot, catch up."

•

Janis was wailing "Cry Baby" from downstairs. The two of them up in the first bedroom, top of the stairs. Denny laid one of the cases on the mess of blankets, glancing back through the beaded curtain, looking at the little combination locks. Took Bobbi's nail file and jabbed it at one of them, twisted and pried till the blade snapped off. Looking over with a smile, offering it to her.

Bobbi looked at it, not taking it.

Walking out of the room, Denny went in search something like a screwdriver.

Turning the case her way, Bobbi spun the dial, tried some more combinations: using the street address of the first Lonzomat, Lonzo's birthday, her birthday, trying to recall anniversaries: first time they went out, first time they made out, that day Lonzo punched out Carmen Roth, the man spitting his scrambled eggs.

Coughing again, Denny came back with the blackened hash knife. Bobbi saying, "This ain't Samsonite, man. Any idea what these babies go for?"

"You got a better idea?" Easing her aside, getting on his knees and going to work.

"A hundred bucks each, easy."

"Yeah, take it out of my end." Pushing the blade along the zipper, he gutted the case along the red and green stripes. Peeling back the side like a flap of skin, looking at the stacks of banded hundreds inside, all U.S. bills.

"Holy shit." Bobbi reached in and took a bundle, rifling it in her hand.

Denny cut the other bag along its stripes while Bobbi counted. More U.S. notes. Denny ripping and feeling under the lining for bugs, finding nothing. Both of them sitting on the blankets, staring at the cash.

"Fifty-fifty, right?" Denny glanced at her handbag by her feet, the Beretta in there.

"The bags come out of your end," she said. "And you go cutting up the car seats, looking for your bugs, that's on you, too."

"Going to switch rides, the next town we get to," Denny said, thinking north was Pemberton, then Lillooet.

"I say we go back the way we came."

"Maybe would've, except you phoned Lonzo, and make no mistake, the guy's sending people, count on that. Not driving back the way they're coming."

Bobbi seeing his point, but not liking the idea of heading farther north.

"We'll blow by Lytton, Boston Bar, Hells Gate. Then south to Hope."

"Like going in a circle."

"Maybe find an airfield and hire a pilot, fly us someplace, Vernon or Nelson, get over the Rockies to Calgary."

"I don't do planes, got this thing."

"Fine, okay, we'll drive." Denny went to the bead curtain. "Gonna see if Rubin's got some bungee, heavy tape, something like that." Denny going down the stairs. Bobbi hearing him coughing, knowing they couldn't stay here. No locks on the doors, people coming and going, the place filled with smoke, enough to keep her buzzed.

Bobbi flopped back on the blanket, the wood floor hard under it, her head spinning, trying to think of her next move. Looking at the orange crates lined along the wall under the window. *Wheels of Fire* thumping from downstairs, this place where the party didn't end. Laid back, thinking she'd rest her eyes a few minutes, her eyes heavy, the weed helping her sleep easy.

... *eight*

Duffey Lake Road was a dark stretch, Bobbi unhappy about leaving the party, heading north. Denny trying to explain why. The neon sign for The Last Spike showed a restaurant, store and gas pump. Not another car in the gravel lot to steal, he pulled in, told the attendant coming out to pump in a couple bucks, paid him and followed Bobbi inside, the place divided between store and restaurant, tables and chairs on one side, store aisles on the other.

She asked the teenage waitress, "Food any good?"

"It's the only place around." The girl shrugged.

Taking a can of Pringles and a pack of Razzles from a shelf, Denny joined Bobbi at a table by the window. The waitress came with menus. Denny going for the hot turkey, getting some slices that looked like they'd been frozen, a gray gravy with lumps, broccoli more limp than green and a Jell-O fruit salad, and coffee to follow. Bobbi ordering grilled cheese.

Lifting the top slice of bread from the sandwich when it arrived, saying to him, "Sketchy place like this, you always go with the grilled cheese. Hard to mess up a couple slices of American melting between slices of Wonder." Eating around the crusts, she took his fork, stuck it in his Jell-O, jabbed a wedge of fruit, put in in her mouth, saying, "Jell-O's okay."

"Yeah, what flavour's red?"

"Strawberry, maybe cherry."

A Biscayne pulled in the gravel lot, headlights going off, drawing to the far side of the pump, two guys getting out and looking around, checking out the Caddy parked to the side. Mopping up some gravy with bread, Denny said, "Got your handbag?"

She followed his look out the window, the two guys talking to the kid at the pump, both turning this way. Neither of them looking like locals. The passenger with some size, wide in the shoulders, a ball cap on his head, said something to the driver. The driver walking past the window, not looking in. The passenger staying by the pump a moment, then going around the back of the place, like he was going to the can.

Denny slid from his chair. "Get ready to go?"

"You mind I finish?" Stabbing at his Jell-O again.

"Let you have some of my Pringles. Come on." Catching her arm, he practically lifted her from the chair, dropped a few bucks on the table, Bobbi snagging her handbag off the back of the chair.

"Get in the car, and don't say nothing," he told her.

She started to object, Denny squeezing her arm, giving a slight shove. Pulling the entrance door, he waited like he was letting the big guy go first. The guy smiled and started to step through, eyes on Denny, started to say something.

"Bet you can't eat just one." Denny tossed the Pringles can to him.

The guy looking at the can in his hands.

Denny swung up his foot, kicking him square. The guy's mouth dropped open, a wheeze coming out, the Pringles dropping from his hand. Snapping the keys from the guy's hand, Denny pulled Bobbi to the Caddy, telling her, "Get in." Throwing the big guy's keys across the two-lane, into the dark of the far ditch.

The guy crumpled by the entrance, the waitress coming to him as Denny drove off, the other guy running from around back.

Bobbi looked at him. "It's Lay's." Then looked over the seat, out the back window.

"What?"

"'Bet you can't eat just one.' Pringles is 'Once you pop, you can't stop.'" Couldn't believe what he just did, turning and settling on the seat.

"Good to know." Denny putting his foot on the gas, saying, "That call you made in Squamish, looks like it's catching up." Denny looked at her, Bobbi with the Beretta back in her hand. "Back to that, huh?"

"You just kicked that guy?"

"Lonzo's guy."

"Or two guys getting coffee. How can you know?"

"What I know, we're still breathing."

. . . *nine*

The lights of Lion's Bay showed up the slope. One hand on the wheel, his other on the armrest, Lee Trane looked up at the mesh holding back the sheer rock wall, kept it from sliding across the killer highway, rock slides common on this stretch, shutting down all the lanes. Checking his speedo, he dared the needle to seventy-five. The two-door T-Bird with the leather buckets, vinyl roof, flip-up headlights, tilt-away steering, select-shift auto, the 390 V-8 purring along the highway.

He'd find them, bring her and the money back, take care of the driver. Other way to do it, he could hang onto the stolen cash and just split. What a man could do with that kind of money. Maybe take Bobbi Ricci with him. Lonzo crowing how he already replaced the stolen half-mil. Said it wasn't about the money, just the principle. Lee shaking his head, this crime boss who he once watched interrogate a Montreal biker, wanting to know what happened to one of his crew. The biker not telling him shit. Lonzo reached with his fingers and pulled the guy's eye from its socket, saying, "An eye for an eye." The old man strong on principles.

Blowing past Squamish, the T-Bird was doing eighty now. Three hundred and ninety horses doing it easy. Mid-afternoon by the time he pulled off at the Whistler exit, Lee slowed on the gravel, just paid for a wax and shine. A stupid-looking A-frame with the sloping sides, he pulled in next to the Cutlass, Lonzo's plates still on the back bumper. Getting out, he looked at the staked lots out past the place, reminded him of a cemetery.

"That your car?" Lee asked the tubby guy coming to the door with his used-car smile, balding and pale, looking like he'd spent too much of his time behind a desk.

"Frank Dormand." A fleshy hand shoved forward.

Lee bet it was a toupee, top of Frank's head, the wrong kind of Ford out front.

"Asked if the car's yours." Lee shook the hand, gave a good squeeze.

"Cutlass with the 442, sure is, mister." Frank Dormand waved him into the office, shaking out the hand. "How you like your Bird?" The chrome insignia made it a V8. "A 390, huh?"

Giving a look at the Cutlass, 442 on its nose, wide center stripe running down the hood. Lee saying, "390 and you got the 442. Guess you got more muscle."

"Not about that, is it? No, not at all."

Lee grinned and pushed past Frank, stepping inside and looking around the office, its peaked roof and sloped sides, windows on both sides looking out at the plotted lots. A desk and a display case of the model development in the middle of the room, a couple of wooden filing cabinets on the back wall.

Leaving the door open, Frank went and slid behind his desk. "Only meant we're both V8 men, you and me knowing about horsepower. 390, 442, what's the diff, right? Fifty-two more horse. *Pfft*, practically nothing."

Lee sat opposite, looking at the table with the model on top, paper chalets and village buildings, plastic cars, model trees and people, a mountain of papier mâché. "People buy places up here, huh? Mud roads, thin air, cold all year round."

"Yeah, but the best skiing in the country, a nice getaway spot, yes sir."

"Middle of no place."

"Well, right now prices are low, but just wait till the runs go in. Got a whole village planned." Frank pointed to the model. "A good investment, this place starts going up, like money in the bank."

"Where my money belongs, in the bank."

Frank spared the rest of the pitch, this guy not here about vacation property.

"Thing I want to know, Frank, is about the switched plates."

Frank leaned back, scratching his head, saying, "Well, the officer came by said the plates belonged to a Cadillac reported stolen. Think it was parked right out front this morning." Frank pointed out the spot where it had been. "Was that yours, the Caddy?"

"My car's right there, Frank. One with fifty-two horse less than yours. Caddy belongs to the man I work for. And sure wasn't him that switched them."

"Meant nothing by it, honest. Look, I want to help ..."

"Sure." Lee grinned, leaning in the chair like he had all day.

"I called soon as I noticed. Got no idea where the guy in the Caddy went."

"He?"

"Was a guy hanging around, youngish, kind with long hair. Guessed the car was his."

"Aside from the hair, what else can you tell me?"

"Sure didn't pass for a guy with a Caddy, you know? More like the ski bums we got up here. Didn't take much note, tell the truth. In my line, you get to know who's here to buy, who's just kicking the tires, you know? This guy, didn't figure him for either, buying or kicking. Wasn't here about land."

"What else?"

"Nothing really. Never talked to him, was busy with the Kushmans, couple that was here to buy, sold them Lot 42." Frank glanced out the side window. "But maybe check at Jane's. Could be the guy had breakfast, was that time of day. Her place the only one open then." Frank pointed toward the Spuzzum Spoon.

Lee got up and started for the door, stopped halfway. "What color?"

"Guy was white, no doubt of that."

"Mean the Caddy?"

"Black, metallic maybe, dark anyway."

Stepping on the wooden porch, Lee looked to the mud track leading to the Spuzzum Spoon, then down at his new brogues, over at the T-Bird's whitewalls. Getting in, he backed out, hit the gas and slung muck off the back wheels. Looking back at the Cutlass now slapped with muck. "Fifty-two fuckin' horse."

Was a decent cup of coffee, the waitress Jane talking about Denny and Bobbi, taking them for a couple. Didn't even give fake names.

"Say where they were heading?" Lee picked up his cup, dropping five on the counter, told her to keep it.

Thanking him, Jane told him to try Toad Hall. "Ask for Chill or the Rube. Maybe help you out."

Told her the coffee was real good, and he went out. Flipping a salute at Frank over at the A-frame, the man taking a rag to the muck on the Cutlass, looking at Lee like he didn't understand why he did it.

Parking by the hippie microbus, Lee went up the wide steps and tapped on the screen, the pot smell and *Cosmos' Factory* coming from inside, "Ooby Dooby" playing. Fucking hippies murdering a perfectly good Roy Orbison number. Knocked a couple more times before some blonde chick came to the door, barefoot in cut-off blue jeans, a faded lumberjack shirt, no buttons done up, no bra, the shirt just tied in a loop, showing her belly, a beaded necklace with a peace sign around her neck. Eyes glassy, face with no makeup.

"Looking for a Chill?"

"That right?"

"Gal at the cafe said I'd find him here. Another guy called Rude."

"I'm Bunny, and you're a pig, right?" She smiled, blinking red-rimmed eyes.

"You want to put a hand in, Bunny," he said, flipping open his jacket. "Feel around for a badge." His eyes rolled down her half-open shirt.

"'Cause if you're a pig, you got to say, right, otherwise it's what . . . a set-up?"

"Entrapment, what they call it."

"A square dude checking me out, the kind who calls tits a rack. Now you sound like you study law." She smiled, surprised he didn't flush.

"The law of nature. Far as cops, I see 'em on TV."

She looked at him a moment more, undid the loop in her shirt and pulled it open. Looked at him looking at her breasts. Disappointed that he didn't react. Left the shirt open and told him to wait, and she went looking for Chill.

"What can I do you for, man?" A tall guy coming to the door, looking down at Lee's dress shoes and straight clothes. The T-Bird out front.

"You Chill?"

"Nope." The guy waited, tapping his bare toes.

"Looking for Bobbi and Denny, the couple in the Cadillac." Lee guessing this was the one the waitress called Rube.

"You see a Cadillac, man?"

Lee wanted to clutch this Rube guy by the throat, make his hippie eyes bug out. "I know they were here, asshole."

A second guy came behind the one who wasn't Chill, greasy hair sticking up, stubbled chin. His shirt done up wrong, buttons not lined up.

The one he guessed was Rube said, "Man's looking for a Bobbi and Denny."

"That right?"

"Chick at the Spoon said they came this way," Lee said.

"Lot of people drop in, man," the second guy said. "Drop in, drop out, come and go, you know?"

Taking a breath, Lee looked around, a big rusting bell, a bench seat pulled from a car, tape patched across its vinyl, several pairs of skis leaning against the wall. Could get high from the fumes coming from the place. Saying, "But not many drive up in a Cadillac, huh?"

"Not into the capitalism trip, man, wouldn't know a Cadillac from a ..." the Rube guy said, pointing at the T-Bird. "Whatever it is you're driving, man."

Lee looked from one to the other, wanting to hit the one who wasn't Chill in the mouth, both looking high enough they wouldn't feel it. Bunny came back, looping up her shirt, stood between Rube and Chill, an arm around each one, Lee shook his head, then he turned for the Bird, thinking, You can't kill everybody.

. . . *ten*

"What the fuck's with you, this the only way you know, north?" She looked around in back of the panel van, the hacked-up Guccis sliding around the metal floor, bungee cords wrapped around them. The interior smelled like somebody cleaned fish and forgot to hose it out. A balled suede jacket stuffed behind the driver's seat, Bobbi reached for it, finding an Expos ball cap in the pocket. She shook the jacket, held it up, dark tan, the kind with the fringes along its sleeves, sweat circles inside the satin lining. Dome fasteners. Something like oil had stained one of the pockets. Tossing it down, she turned in her seat, slid the heater knob to full, not sure it was blowing any warm air, saying, "Sure know how to pick 'em. Only option this thing's got's a bad smell."

"How about you make the best of it?"

"Traded the Cadillac for this, and you're telling me, make the best of it?"

"That what you think, I traded it in. You see a car lot, some guy with a bad tie, haggling a deal? A place like Lillooet, what'd you think we'd find, Beemers and Benz?"

"That's because we're going the wrong way."

"We go south, we head right into Lonzo and his teeth. Thanks to you for making that phone call."

"Those guys, man, you don't know they were Lonzo's."

"They had the look and I wasn't taking chances."

Bobbi banged the heel of her hand against the heater knob, still cool air blowing out.

"Fuck, Denny. I got my gun, I say how it is." No seat heater, no comfy leather. Bobbi looking at the dash. "Not even a fucking eight-track."

"Getting kinda tired of that 'Devil or Angel' anyway," Denny said. "Beppe's okay, got a decent falsetto, but the guy's singing stuff from the days of Brylcreem."

"Shoulda shot you at Lonzo's." Bobbi folded her arms, feeling the cold creeping up from the floorboards, this wreck with its cancerous rust coming through the floor, a good stomp and her foot would go right through. She reached in her bag, flipping open the pack of Craven As she took from Chill back at Toad Hall. Putting one between her lips, pressing in the lighter.

"Know I'm on the Medihaler, right?"

At least the lighter worked. She put the tip of her cigarette to the hot coil and lit up. "You got to make do, what you said, right?" Cracking the window, blowing smoke at it, she jabbed the heater knob again, the plastic tip snapping off, Bobbi flicking it to the floor. "A true piece of shit."

The two of them quiet for a while, the miles ticking by, Denny slowing through a construction zone, pylons and rock rubble along both shoulders. Reaching for the suede jacket, Bobbi laid it across her lap and rested her head against the window, hoping for more sleep. Denny driving past Chasm and 70 Mile House, two lanes of the 97, called the Cariboo Highway.

Clicking on the AM to help him stay awake, he caught

Hazel Dickens doing "Walkin' in My Sleep." Tapping fingers on the wheel to some Lightfoot, blowing by Soda Creek, then some place called Horsefly.

"Could do with a bite," she said, not opening her eyes.

"Yeah, next place I see."

"We stop, how about you don't kick some guy's nuts this time." Bobbi folded the jacket and put it against the window, using it like a pillow. Putting on the ball cap, the Expos logo on the brim, Bobbi tugged it low over her face. Couldn't be dirtier than her hair felt.

"Guys at the flat got *Hockey Night* on the box all winter. Watching the Gump keep it out," Denny said.

Tapping her finger on the logo on the brim. "Baseball, not hockey."

"That right, huh?"

Denny thinking she liked making him feel dumb.

The 97 rolled them into Prince George, Denny pulled into a boarded-up Dairy Delight. Unfolding the map he found in the map pocket, he checked their options. Place with an airport east of town. Tried talking to her about flying out of there.

Bobbi saying no way she was getting in some death trap with a single prop. Sticking a finger on the map, saying, "How about we go east, you ever hear of it? Like Jasper, maybe Edmonton."

"This time of year, mountains are nothing but ice and snow. No way we'd make it through."

"Not in this heap. How about a train station, they got one of those?"

"Yeah, but could be Lonzo's got people checking passenger lists, a goon waiting at every stop."

"So, we give fake names."

"You got fake ID to go along with it?"

"So, you're saying we're fucked?" Bobbi wanting to slap him.

"Can go west for a while." Showing her on the map, tapping the dot for Prince Rupert. "Maybe jump a freighter, get us —"

The patrol car caught his eye, swinging onto the main drag a couple blocks behind them, two cops inside. Denny guessing they might wonder why a van was idling outside a boarded-up ice cream joint. The Guccis in plain view behind his seat, held together with bungee cords. Putting on his turn signal, Denny rolled to the exit, took his time and got on the Yellowhead, swinging west. Keeping his eyes on his sideview.

Putting on the stained jacket, Bobbi wrapped her arms around herself. After a while, she folded her legs up on the seat, huddled under the jacket.

Driving the Yellowhead, Denny was thinking he should have gassed up in Prince George, the needle riding close to empty. Betting Lonzo already knew his Caddy had been found in Lillooet, with the wrong plates on it. Maybe he found out about the van, too, knowing what to look for. Saying to Bobbi, "Okay, we're gonna find you something with a heater."

"How about I pick?"

"Okay, you're thinking something sporty, perhaps a little red coupe, two-seater. That sound right?"

"Fuck off."

"What we need's something to keep Lonzo from connecting the dots."

"That guy you kicked in the nuts. Likely a cop report on that, connecting more dots," she said.

The needle touching the red on the gas gauge, Denny passed Decker Lake, patches of snow between the pine shadows along its shoreline. Pulling out Rube's bag of pot, he tossed it to her, saying, "You know how to roll?" Thinking, screw the asthma, if he had to listen to her, he'd do it with a buzz. Handing her the ZigZags, passing a sign: *"Hey Nixon, don't dump your Agent Orange here."*

"Your boy Nixon, at it again." Bobbi crumbled bud onto a paper, licking and twisting it. "Read something how the army's suspected of dumping shit off our coast."

"First off, he's not my boy."

"And why here?"

"Don't dump in your own backyard, use your neighbor's."

"Why they call it that, Asian Orange?" she asked.

"Agent Orange. Think on account the containers it comes in got orange labels."

"That's a reason?" She pushed in the lighter, saying, "Ask me, you did the right thing, not going. No matter how it ends."

"How you mean, how it ends?"

"I mean the war." Giving him a thoughtful look, saying, "You know anybody over there?"

"Brother did a tour, other guys I was in school with, yeah."

She took the joint back. "He send you letters?"

"When he was alive, yeah." Denny taking a hit, eyes on the road.

"Sorry," Bobbi said, looking like she meant it, taking the joint and dragging on it, saying, "What was his name?"

"Dale."

"You two close?"

"Like brothers."

Handing him the joint, she looked out at the pines whipping past her window. Saying, "If you want to talk about it . . ."

He was quiet a while, then said, "Operation Apache Snow, some place called Hamburger Hill. A pal of ours, guy called Aaron, lived up the street, served with him till he stepped on a toe popper and lost a leg, earned him a medal and got shipped home."

"Yeah, what good's that?"

"Only good part's he didn't die in some jungle, an ocean from home. For anything else good, you got to ask Tricky Dick himself. All I know, Dale isn't coming back." Denny handed back the joint, waved it off, didn't want any more. Rubin's pot quick to get him one toke over the line.

She asked if he was sure he didn't mind talking about it.

"What's it going to change?"

He talked more about the brothers growing up, then she asked about the protests. Denny telling how he stood with a mass of students on the Berkeley steps, protested Nixon being sworn in. Another time a bunch of them set fire to their draft cards, this coming after Dale was gone. Denny doing it in front of the news photographers, making the early edition.

"They wouldn't have sent you anyway, on account of your asthma, right?"

"Guess I was protesting for Dale."

"I get that." She put a hand on his arm. "That how you got on the news?"

"Got on the news a couple times." He smiled. "Blocked this induction center, messing with the recruiters, not letting the boys in. A bunch of us got caught on camera, cops coming around with their clubs in hand, giving us a warning, then right away started swinging. So, I ducked away from that scene. Other time I was at this anti-war parade when it turned ugly."

"You holding up signs like, 'Hell no, we won't go.'"

"Exercising my freedom of speech when I got smacked from behind, some Nazi guardsman not liking the sign I was holding. Took his baton to the small of my back. I rolled and got up, asked if he went and served, and didn't wait for his answer, just smashed my sign over his head and put him on the ground."

"In the name of peace, huh? Same way you kicked that guy in the nuts, thinking he worked for Lonz."

Denny ignored her, saying, "Then there was this guardsman, guy was rough-handing a coed at a Berkeley protest. Pushed her on the pavement and had his club on her throat when I grabbed him off. Turned to help the chick up and got pepper-sprayed and hauled in that time. Charged with assault and instigating a riot."

"You do time?"

"I missed my court appearance," Denny said.

She glanced over, waiting for more.

"Hitched up the coast instead, considering the best way to skip across. Not like I could plead at the consulate or some immigration office. Anyway, I crossed at this marsh, coming out on this Zero Avenue, hitched the rest of the way uptown. Stayed in a Y, then a couple of flops till I met with Wilson in the Hare Krishna food line, a brother on the dodge. Let me crash with him and his buddies in this three-room flat."

"Then you found the gig driving for Lonzo . . ."

"That came a little later, but that's basically my story." Denny steered into Smithers. Flat-roofed two-stories, a Shop-Easy, Edwin's RCA advertising its annual sale, get a color TV on layaway, a drug store with a Coca-Cola billboard on top, a hotel called The Sandman with a flashing vacant sign. Pulling into the Esso, Denny got out and had the attendant pump in a couple bucks of regular, thinking he'd ditch the van, no point filling it. Then, driving up the block, he kept watch for a ride worth stealing, same time looking for a place to eat, saying, "You still craving that burger?"

"Suitcases full of cash, and you want to get me a burger."

"Order what you want." Pulling next to a Studebaker, a place called The Logjam. Its neon flashed open. He could see the Wagonaire's door locks were down. Too much trouble and too many people around.

"Gonna wait here," she said, looking through the window at the place, counter service with some mismatched stools. Not worth getting out in the cold. Telling him, "And get me fries."

Denny pulled the keys from the ignition.

"Coffee, black," she said. "And how about you leave the keys, could use some tunes?"

"Hum." Pocketing the keys, he got out and walked around the van's nose.

Reaching across, she honked the horn, laughing at the way he jumped.

Giving her a look, then a finger. Bobbi blew him a kiss.

Looking up at The Logjam's board, he ordered a grilled cheese, burger with the works, a couple orders of fries, a Coke and a coffee. Paying with one of Lonzo's bills, juggling the cardboard tray, he went out, expecting her to honk again, getting back in the driver's door. The two of them using the dash like a counter, passing salt and ketchup packets. Bobbi blowing the sleeve off her straw at him.

Pot funk and that fishy smell, both too hungry to care about it.

Denny pointed at a poster taped to The Logjam's window, reading, "Revival of the Smithers Harmonettes. Playing tonight."

"Harmonettes, huh? Think they know any Van Halen?"

"Can hang around and find out?" Squelching a burp when he finished, felt good being full, collecting their trash, he got out, stepping past the hood, tossing it in the bin out front of the place. Bobbi jarring him with the horn again.

"There you go, drawing attention." Denny getting back in.

"Should've seen you jump." Laughing at him, Bobbi told him it was worth it.

Denny looked out at the town, the Sandman Hotel up the street, couple more homespun places to eat, a corner bar. "Could get a room, ditch the van, lay low a few days, catch a hot shower. Give me a chance to score another ride."

"Not all you gonna catch, a place like this." Bobbi saying she was holding out at least for a Best Western.

No point arguing. He swung back on the highway, a sign showing an airfield ahead on the right. Pointed to it. Bobbi telling him again she wasn't getting in one of those flying death traps. Denny switched the radio knob, Ray Charles doing "The Right Time." He was starting to say the man had God in his fingers when another cruiser showed in his sideview. He checked his speed. The black and white just a half block back, looked like it was keeping pace.

The town lay flat ahead of him, the two-lane going straight, giving him no place to run. Putting on the blinker, Denny took a lazy turn past the Kingdom Hall, the place not open, no cars around it. No idea where he was going.

"Said we're not staying." Bobbi tipped up her ball cap, looking around.

"Be cool. We got company." Denny giving a little gas when he was out of sight behind the hall, catching sight of the cop car making the same turn. Pulling into the gravel lot around the side, he gunned it to the far end, pulling behind the place, hoping for an exit that wasn't there. "Shit." He stopped and threw open his door, told her to move, and hurried around the back.

Bobbi slid off the seat, grabbing the suede jacket. Denny was yanking open the rear doors. Pulling out the Guccis. Shoving one at her, he tucked the other under an arm and was running, ducking behind the place selling flooring. Bobbi cradling her Gucci like an infant, running behind him, past a row of birch, neither hanging around to see the cruiser pull around the side of the Kingdom Hall.

"Now what?"

"Gonna get you that new ride you wanted." Denny trying to keep the panic from taking hold.

Not looking back, she kept up, followed past the kiddie playground, a sandbox, slide and a swing. Denny stopped by a telephone pole, partly hidden by some cedars. Catching his wind, out of sight of the Kingdom Hall. Reaching in his pocket for the inhaler, he put it to his mouth.

Bobbi looked like she might throw up, but he kept going past the trees and onto a residential street, all the houses looking the same. Knowing she'd follow.

He was thinking a move ahead. The only things left in the van were a pack of Razzles, a half-finished Coke on the dash. Nothing for the evidence locker. Skirting the playground, he had them moving down the street of trim lawns and boulevard trees, every house with a single garage out front. Getting them past a trailer parked on the street. Somewhere a dog barked. Past a side street, he stopped and looked back again. His heart jumping when a car came the opposite way around the crescent, its headlights on. Realizing it wasn't the cops. A woman in a Cortina drove past and smiled at them, then pulled in a driveway a couple houses back.

Denny hooked Bobbi by the arm, held her upright, told her to look easy, giving a smile to the woman getting out of the car. Both of them catching their wind, both huffing frosty breath. The housewife popped her trunk and smiled again, said something about this weather, reaching for a couple of grocery sacks, carrying one under each arm to the front door, her teen daughter coming to the stoop in her socks, helping with the bags, the woman going back to the trunk for more, giving Denny and Bobbi some small-town chit chat, "Cold enough for you?"

Denny agreed it was. "Hope we're going the right way, looking for number forty-two?" Denny hoping there was a forty-two.

"Oh, you mean the Erskins?" She lit up. "Fred's . . . *hmm*, likely at All Seasons, less he's still in bed with that bug. Darn thing's been going around."

"Thought he got past it," Denny said, making it up as he went.

"And Maddy, let's see, she could be out back, it's early, but she's been talking about getting in her Dusty Millers. Can't keep that girl from digging in the dirt, you know." This woman talking with that small town way of knowing everybody's business.

"That's for sure," Denny said, smiling at Bobbi. "Was hoping they were picking us up, but I guess we got our wires crossed."

The woman frowned, scooping up another grocery bag and a case of TaB, saying, "Well, if they're not in, Fred usually gets off about five. Meantime, you're welcome to come on over. I can put on a pot, and you can make yourselves at home. Be glad for the company."

"Well that's real nice of you . . ." Denny said, like he was hoping for a name.

"Margaret Perkins, but just call me Margie." She kept smiling, asking what happened to their luggage, the bungee cords around the cases.

"They've sure got some rough handlers at CN." Denny remembered seeing a station on the map, judging by her nodding head he got it right, CN made a stop here, saying he wanted to go and file a complaint at the ticket counter.

"Gucci bags, you know?" Bobbi threw in, guessing this woman wouldn't know designer from clearance.

"A darned shame, that's for sure. Bet they'll make good, folks at the depot are decent," Margie said, showing she knew everybody, still smiling as she went into the house.

The teenage girl hadn't reappeared. As soon as Margie turned and the screen door closed, Denny dropped his case on top of Bobbi's and told her to keep walking. And he was moving.

"What the fuck —" Bobbi juggled, keeping the top case from falling off.

Across the lawn in a few strides, Denny slipped behind the wheel of the Cortina, the key in the ignition. Turning it, he shifted the stick and backed out, chirped the tires and picked Bobbi up down the block. Piling the twins on the back seat, she jumped in the passenger seat.

Denny had it moving before she got her door closed, pealing around the block, glancing back at Margie coming out her door. Feeling bad seeing the woman standing there dumbfounded. Hoping her insurance was paid up, he sped out of there before the cops rolled around the block. Looking at Bobbi, saying, "This Mercedes enough for you?"

"Not what she meant by make yourselves at home."

"Yeah, sorry about it, but it was Margie or us." Pulling back onto the Yellowhead — Bobbi saying they should have got that pot of coffee to go — he rolled back past the Kingdom Hall, watching his speed, feeling bad about taking the woman's car. A second cop car sat parked next to the first, its lights flashing, a bunch of cops standing by the Dodge van, one checking under the driver's seat, another climbing in the rear doors.

Rolling past the nine-hole course and the sign to the airport.

"Let me guess, north?" Bobbi's heart still jumping, feeling like she might throw up the burger and fries.

"Margie'll be ringing the cops, and we need to be gone."

He didn't slow till Moricetown, telling her to roll up another doob, could use some more mellowing.

Couldn't see why not, Bobbi took the baggie, pushed in the lighter and had the joint ready when it popped.

No Best Western, no chain restaurants, nothing like civilization until they rolled past Hazelton, just a few rooftops and a few stop signs, and that was it.

Denny felt better for every mile he didn't see gumballs flashing in the rear-view. A highway junction coming up, he eased into the Texaco on the northeast corner and got out, asking the attendant to fill it. No telling when they'd see another station, Denny thinking they'd stick with the Cortina for now; at least its heater worked.

The sky was leaden, the temperature dropping. The attendant was a short guy, middle-aged, swiping at his runny nose, wiping it on the back of his pants, saying, "Looks like we're in for a bitch." Then looking down, tapping a work boot at Denny's front tire, saying, "You got chains, mister? In case you don't, can let you have a set half off. This late in the season, letting 'em go cheap."

"Good of you, but we're nearly there."

"How about your oil, want it checked?" The finger sawing under his nose again.

"Naw, it's fine, thanks." Denny expected Margie was the type to stay on top of regular maintenance.

Bobbi got out, saying, "You point me to the little girl's room?"

The attendant nodded to the side, and Bobbi held a hand across the roof, saying to Denny, "The keys."

Denny not wanting a scene, tossed them to her. Palming them, she winked at the attendant, saying, "That or he might take off with the twins."

The attendant looked in back, didn't see any kids, told her the bathroom key hung just inside the glass door. "Pink one's for the girls."

"It matter if I go blue?"

"Not to me. Cleaned both this morning."

Denny watched her go.

"Got twins, huh?" the attendant said, looking in the back seat again. "Got two boys myself, three years apart." The numbers flipping on the pump's display as he filled the tank, finally clunking to a stop.

"What she calls the luggage, on account they're the same, twins. See? But naw, we got no kids." Denny getting the cases from the back seat, putting them into the trunk. Wanting them out of sight.

Taking out the nozzle, the attendant reset it, telling Denny, "Looks like three-fifty."

Turning up his collar, Denny paid him a five, took his change, feeling a wet wind out of the north. "Man, sure cold, huh?"

The attendant shrugged, said that's why he mentioned the tire chains, then, "Where you folks from?"

"Prince George, just up visiting family. Sister's got a kid, a boy." Denny looked at the intersection, deciding to keep going west. A pick-up with a winch on the bumper pulled to the pump, coming from that way, the driver getting out, a toothpick at the side of his mouth. Oily ball cap and a flannel shirt over a beer bulge, the driver stood with a leg up on his running board like he was proud of it. Nodding to Denny, telling the attendant to fill it, asked which way Denny was heading, looking at the skinny tires on the Cortina, saying he ought to get chains.

"So I been told." Denny nodded to the west, saying he was going that way.

"Not your day then. Lumber truck dropped its load, got logs all over the place. Mounties shut her to a single lane."

"We make it through?" Denny didn't like hearing there were Mounties.

"Yeah, if you don't mind delays."

Three to five years' worth. Denny nodded, guessing that's what stealing the Cortina would get him. No way he was driving past more Mounties. Looking at the fork, deciding they'd go right.

Bobbi crossed back over the lot, telling the attendant the men's room was nice, getting back in.

Twisting his mouth into a smile, the attendant wished them a safe trip, on account of doing it with no chains. Denny nodded to both men, started the Cortina and turned north at the T, the marker calling it Highway 37, telling her what the pick-up driver told him.

She stuck a cigarette in her mouth and popped in the lighter.

"You know, Bobbi, getting tired of you getting us noticed."

She looked over, took the lighter when it popped, asked what he was talking about.

"Called Lonzo, told him he snores, practically saying I was in on it. Honking back in Smithers, making me jump, had everybody in town looking over."

"I do things for kicks sometimes. And what's with you anyway?"

"The crack you just made about the twins, and using the

men's. Drawing more attention, the kind people remember when somebody comes asking questions."

"You're turning into a bore." Making a face at him.

"You do something like that again, I'm gonna pass you a take-out cup, can pee in that."

She lit up and blew smoke at him.

"Lonzo's got people looking, and the guy at the station'll remember crap like that, you using the men's." Denny coughed, telling her to crack her window.

Bobbi opened her window a half-inch. "Had one of those things with a blue thingie in the bottom." Bobbi blew smoke at the windshield.

"Called a urinal cake."

"Why'd they call it a cake?"

"You're asking me?"

"So, you stand there, aim at it and what's it do, gives off a scent?"

"How about next time you just use the ladies'?" Suppressing a cough, reaching his Medihaler, taking a puff. More patches of snow showed among the pines, dark clouds looking heavy. Trying the radio, he didn't get a signal.

Bobbi leaned her head against the glass, looking at the pines going by. Denny kept his eyes on the road, thinking of the last letter Dale wrote, how he'd been out on patrol with the heavy packs, four days of keeping low in the bush, scouting for pits of Punji stakes. Dale suffering from the jungle rot. Wrote about leeches dropping off the trees, damn things smelled the patrol coming through the bush, falling on them and filling up on Marine blood.

"Kitwanga, that how you say this town's name?" Bobbi looked at a marker, a cluster of buildings of board and tin coming in view. "Nothing looking like a Best Western."

It was a dozen more miles before they came to a place called Gitanyow.

"Where they come up with these names?" Bobbi looked at the closed service station, one pump out front. A sign that read: Gitanyow, Eat and Get Gas.

Full dark when the snow started, big flakes drifting slow, Denny's eyes feeling heavy when they came to Meridien Junction, the road splitting. Remembering she didn't drive, plus he wouldn't trust her to drive while he caught a nap. Betting she'd turn around and head south. Just had to keep himself awake till they found someplace to stop for the night. He pushed open his door, got out and went around the tailgate, standing so she couldn't see him.

Facing the ditch, Denny thinking it was as cold as the parent-teacher trip to Mount Eddy back in grade school, him and Cousin Nort wearing parkas and crossing some frozen creek instead of using the bridge, the ice not as thick as it looked. Being a kid from Berkeley, Denny knew shit about ice, just had enough sense to keep a distance between him and Nort. His cousin not possessing such sense, went for safety in numbers, getting too close. Both of them plunging through. Denny remembered that icy rush and the panic that had him thrashing and clawing his way up onto the ice, pulling Nort out of the hole, the two of them crawling to the opposite bank. Denny never wanting to go in the water after that, never learned to swim. Walking back to the lodge with Nort, their pants frozen by the time they got there, Denny standing his up, thinking later he should have kept them on till after his old man finished strapping his ass for being so dumb.

•

She was reading the junction signs, one arrow pointing left to a place called Ripley, the other North to Alaska. Could scoot across the seats and drive off, leave him holding his pecker, except where to. Noticing the keys missing from the ignition, the son of a bitch not trusting her. Popping open the glove box, she reached inside, found a plastic insurance folder, Margaret Perkins' name on it, a pack of Kleenex on top and a Twix underneath, practically frozen. Bobbi put it under her thigh, thanking Margie.

He got back in and stuck the key in the ignition, smiling at Bobbi. The engine catching after a couple of tries. He nodded at the signs. "The Nootka Hotel, rooms from under ten bucks."

Giving him a look like she might shoot him, she took the Twix from under her thigh, tore into the wrapper and took a bite.

"Where'd you get that?"

"Glovebox."

"Got another one?"

"Uh-uhn." Taking another bite.

"How about sharing?"

"Go ahead and try." Patting the bag, reminding him about the Beretta, she munched into it, going, "*Mmm.*" Tossing down the wrapper, she took her pack and lit another cigarette.

Cracking his window, Denny swore. Bobbi betting he wouldn't allow himself to cough, wouldn't give her that. Following the arrow that pointed west, he kept driving.

"Worst thing about Lonzo, the guy was a bore and he snored," she said. "But he had money, lots of it, a warm bed and a heated pool."

He put the puffer in his mouth, pressed the top button, sucking in medication.

"How about you stop that?" she said.

"What, breathing?"

"Acting like poor you." Bobbi blew smoke at him, then put a foot up on the dash, above the Mark II chrome strip. She could only imagine the Mark I.

The gloom of a million pines, a gray peak cutting above the low cloud bank. And snow falling. Bobbi saying, "You start singing 'Winter Wonderland,' I will shoot you, I promise." She patted her bag.

"Be doing me a favor."

"See, there you go again, poor you."

•

Headlights came over a rise ahead of them, coming their way, Denny getting a hopeful feeling, like there was civilization ahead. Seeing it was a cruiser, black and white with a light bar on top. Smiling over as the cop passed. The Mountie glanced over. Denny checked his speed, doing about sixty. Seeing the cop hit his brake lights.

"Shit."

The cruiser pulled to the shoulder, Denny guessing the cop was calling in their plate, about to find out it was stolen. Going over the rise he gave it all the gas he dared, the Cortina slithering as it picked up speed.

Stamping the butt in the ashtray, Bobbi turned in the seat, watching out the back.

... *eleven*

Heavy snow danced in the headlights' beams, Denny switching the wipers to high. A lot of snow on the ground here. The piece of shit Cortina lacked any getaway guts, its ass end wanting to slide out. The cruiser was gaining, red and blue flashes from the light bar, the screaming Plymouth bearing down. Not going to shake him, Denny barely able to keep it on the road.

Swishing around a bend, the Cortina going like a Disney ride, the shoulder heaped with plowed snow, separating the road from a gray, swollen river. Bobbi clawed at the dash as Denny sideswiped the plowed shoulder. The cop flew around the same bend, still gaining. The Cortina hopped the next rise, Denny keeping it in the lane. A lake to the west, covered in white. Couldn't touch the brakes on the downslope, nothing to do but steer. Skidding into the bank, the Cortina struck something on the driver's side, a country mailbox taking out a headlight, Denny fighting to keep it from spinning out.

Her feet planted, Bobbi braced a forearm against the dash, her other hand clutching the door handle. Feeling for the seatbelt that got jammed between the cushion and seat back.

Roaring up on his bumper, the cop was going for that PIT nudge. Swerving, Denny tromped the pedal, trying to keep the cop from making contact. The road curved, and there it was, the clank of metal on metal, the cop getting the tap. Sending the Cortina on a carny ride, Denny losing control over the steering. Spinning, the small car launched onto the snowbank, not enough weight to dig in. It bucked over the hump of the bank and struck something. In a blur, Denny was thrown forward, striking the wheel, seeing it as a Johnny on the Spot, the hulking shape knocked backward. The sound of crunching boards. Several other shapes loomed in front of the car. Denny realizing it wasn't a shitter he hit, these were ice huts that had been pulled off the lake.

Bobbi was hunched over with her elbows up, covering her face and head. Kept them like that, even after impact. Denny looked out back, saw the cop car sliding out behind them, lights and the howler still going.

Backing a few feet, he pushed the pedal, and the Cortina plowed forward, Denny tasting blood in his mouth, his forehead wet, maybe sweat, maybe blood. Steering onto a snowmobile track the ice fishermen laid down, he got the wheels lined on the packed-down tracks, steering onto the lake, snow falling harder.

"You okay?"

"Oh, fucking great, yeah, you?" Bobbi sat up and licked at her bleeding lip.

In the rear-view, the cop was out of his car, had his sidearm in his hand, stomping over the plowed snow, his shoes sinking deep, putting him off balance, moving between the ice huts, shouting and waving at them. A second cruiser arrived from the opposite direction, its lights flashing, too. Denny kept his wheels on the packed track, heading out on the frozen lake, dark pines lining the bank. Snorting blood, he felt a stab in his chest.

The second cruiser backed up and plowed up onto the shoulder, the cop humping the bank, getting stuck there, its headlights aimed up, lighting on the thick falling flakes. Then the two cops were running past the ice huts, coming on foot.

No idea where to get off the lake. Nothing but falling snow, the white powder they plunged through, the dark around them. His wheels missed the track, the deep snow slowing them, Denny fighting to get them back on it.

The shadow of another ice hut came through the falling snow, the snowmobile track ending out front of it. Denny turned the wheel and missed hitting the hut. The Cortina off the hard track again and plowing deeper snow. Feeling the tires spin and dig in, he pressed the pedal, making out the dark patch ahead on the white blanket. Didn't know what it meant. Heard the swishing sound against the undercarriage. Denny seeing the sign on a stake:

THIN ICE

"Out!" Throwing open his door, he stepped into the slush. Ankle-deep, the water as icy as that time with Nort, Denny felt the panic, wanting to get away from the car, but forcing himself around to the back. He yanked at the trunk, but couldn't get it to pop. Needed the keys dangling from the ignition. Ice cracked under his foot, and Denny grabbed Bobbi as she came around the back, catching her wrist, tugging her away.

Twisting to get free, she yelled, "Get the twins. The twins!"

He pulled her to the ice hut. Looking back, no idea where the cops were, seeing nothing but the falling snow. Couldn't see the shore or the patrol cars with their flashing lights.

"The twins, we can't leave them," she yelled.

Feeling the cracking of ice under his feet, he tugged her. Getting behind the hut, he looked out, couldn't see ten feet through the falling snow. Gripping her arm, he pulled her, ignoring her protests, guessing which way to the road, watching for the shadows of the cops. A dozen strides and he lost sight of the Cortina and the ice hut, trudging with Bobbi in tow, feeling the icy wet at his feet, the numbing cold, then finally seeing the flash of cop lights and the red glow against the falling snow. Finding their way back onto the snowmobile tracks, he let it lead them back to the road. The wind had picked up, howling, whipping snow angling and stabbing at their faces. His eyes were slits. Couldn't feel his feet in the sneakers as he pulled her along. Bobbi had stopped fighting, clutched onto his arm, letting him shield her, guiding her off the lake.

Moving toward the flash of blue and red. Alert for the two cops. Scrambling onto the plowed bank, one hand on her arm, fingers of his free hand digging into the snow, getting them over. One cruiser sat high-centered on the plowed berm. The other was on the road, flashers still going. Denny went to it.

"The fuck you doing?"

"How you feel about Plymouths?" Denny shoved her, told her to get in, then got behind the wheel, thanking Christ the key was in the ignition. He got it started, looking at the controls.

Shutting her door, Bobbi looked at him, saying, "The fuck's wrong with —" and screamed.

The cop charged over the berm and leaped for the car,

his arms out wide like he was flying, landing against its side. Denny punched down the door lock, jamming the stick in gear and mashed the pedal. Two hundred pounds of cop in a parka and fur hat threw himself again, landing on the hood with a thump, yelling about them being under arrest, punching his gloved hand at the windshield, the other hand grabbing for a wiper blade, something to hold on to.

Denny hit the gas, then slammed the brakes, the cop sliding off, yelling and pounding.

Putting it in reverse, straightening out on the road, Denny drove past. The cop getting up and yelling behind them. Denny adding distance.

Not slowing till the windows started fogging, Denny telling her to find the defrost. Finding the toggle switch, next to the police scanner with its mic, Denny switched off the light bar. Then switching on the headlights, he rolled west on the white highway.

Thinking he did alright getting them out of there, saying, "Guess we traded up." What of him wasn't hurting from the collision was burning or numb from the sub-zero cold. He couldn't be sure he hadn't pissed himself, that part of him had retracted.

"Dumb, just fuckin' dumb. You left the fuckin' money."

Denny looked back, knowing nothing could be done for it.

She was yelling at him to turn around.

Giving it some gas, careful on the white road, the needle up to twenty-five, and Denny kept it to the center.

Bobbi turned and looked out back, said he was driving like her grandma.

Nobody else on the road, nothing but pines, and Denny driving with no idea what lay ahead. Snow crunching under the tire chains.

"Know it's sixty-five, right?" Bobbi glanced at the speedometer, Denny doing half the limit.

"Don't know shit about your metric system, but I know about ice."

"I got another one: What's up with a guy, starts out with a Caddy, a half-million in the trunk, trades it for a fishy van, goes to a piece-of-shit Cortina, leaves it and the money on the ice and takes off in a cop car?"

"Less shit from you'd go a long way." Denny picked it up a bit, edging the needle past forty, the Plymouth feeling solid enough.

"Always talking like you know what you're doing, but here we are."

Looking at her, he was thinking he'd never hit a woman, couldn't do it, not even this one. Looking past the cop scanner, saying, "How about see if it's got a regular radio, try and find us some tunes. Maybe some 'Hazy Shade of Winter,' or 'Whiter Shade of Pale.' Or how about 'Girl from the North Country'?"

Understanding she was pissed about leaving the money back on the ice. The cops likely back there by that hut, counting it. Denny pushed it to fifty, the tire chains biting down and putting distance between them and the lake, those two cops likely trying to get the other cruiser off that berm, wanting to give pursuit.

"So, now what?" Bobbi folded her arms, huddled in the suede.

A voice crackled over the police radio, scared the shit out of both of them, it was a woman's voice asking for Sergeant Kendall.

Looking at her, Denny reached the handset.

Bobbi shaking her head no.

Thumbing the mic, he put on his Jack Webb, saying, "This is the city, middle of no place. I work here, I'm a cop. I carry a badge."

"Henry?" The voice on the radio.

"It was Tuesday, March tenth, maybe the ninth; it was cold in no place, we were working the night watch out of homicide division, checking for roadkill. My partner's Bill Gannon, the boss is Captain Trembly . . ."

"You on the sauce, Henry?" The woman's voice crackled.

"My name's Friday," Denny said. "Joe Friday, badge seven-fourteen. Who the fuck's Henry?"

"Not funny, Henry. Not a bit."

Bobbi started to grin, like she was getting a new appreciation of him. Grabbing the mic from him, she dropped her voice, saying, "The story you are about to hear is true. The names were changed to protect the innocent, you dumb cow." Handing it back, reaching her bag for a smoke. Couldn't believe she just did that.

Laughing, Denny switched off the mic and hung up the handset. A slope to the north, the road winding to the west. A couple of lights and the silhouettes of wet rooflines, guessing this was another no-place town.

Bobbi saying, "Cop who jumped at the windshield, think he's Henry?"

"Never want to find out. Man was pissed, all I can say." Stopping at the top of the slope, he pulled it over and looked at the shapes of this sleeping town through the windshield, the snow lessening, spotting the glass in big, wet drops.

"They catch us, gonna nail you for impersonating Jack Webb and me the other guy." Getting out, Bobbi looked around. Guessing aloud it was wood smoke she was smelling.

A lamp outside a dark trading company, a field out back blanketed white, goal posts at either end. Outlines of several more buildings beyond it, a northern town in sleep.

"Come on." Denny crunched snow underfoot, going down the middle of the street, feeling the gravel under the snow.

"The fuck where to?" Bobbi looked, a cluster of lights ahead, fields of nothing with the dark of the woods beyond it. Like no town she'd ever seen.

"You wanna guess how long before the cops get it unstuck? Gonna follow our tracks, lead them right here."

Putting on the ball cap and pulling the collar of the suede jacket around her neck, she held it closed, looking around, nervous.

Left the cruiser with its doors hanging open, the dome light on. A porch light showed outside some storefront, the place dark inside. A vacancy sign out front of a hotel on the opposite side, its office dark, too. A place up the street called Klondike Kate's with its porch light burning, dim lights inside and people sitting in the window. A Pacific Coach tour bus parked along its side.

"Think they got coffee?" she said, her body shaking.

Reaching in a pocket, he handed her a couple dollars, saying, "Go on in, order us some."

"What about you?"

"Gonna hang back. The cops come, they're looking for two of us, right?"

"Where you gonna be?" She squinted, not trusting him.

"Be looking for another car." Glancing at the hotel, the place called The Ripley, the building was painted yellow. Balling his hands into his pockets, Denny tried to keep his teeth from chattering, saying, "Go in like you're one of them, a tourist. Blend. And don't forget the cream and sugar."

She thought about it, holding out her hand. "Keys." Bobbi twisting her mouth, her teeth chattering.

"They're in the cruiser." Denny smiled and turned toward it. Then back to her, easing his hand forward, hesitated like she might bite him, then gently wiped some blood from the corner of her mouth.

... *twelve*

Leaving loafer tracks in the fresh snow, she stamped her feet when she got to Klondike Kate's, live music greeting her, some bluegrass number. Bobbi walked into the warmth, instantly felt like she needed to pee again, looking around for the restroom, guessed her hair looked like hell under the ball cap, wet shoes, the bottom of her bell-bottoms wet. The suede jacket two sizes big on her, felt like the fringes were frozen. None of the tour bus folk looked her way, sitting at tables and talking to each other as Bobbi walked past the bar to the ladies'.

•

Watched her go into Klondike Kate's, a place of wood beams and paneled walls, hurricane lamps on plastic tablecloths, the kind with the checks. Better than a dozen people sitting in groups, talking. Tourists off the bus, maybe excited about getting snowed in. The bus driver in matching blues, a cap on his head, sat alone near the window, elbows on either side of a plate.

Nobody paying attention as Bobbi walked through the place, draped the suede jacket on back of a chair and headed for the washroom, said something to a couple in passing, making like she was one of them. The placard out front said the music was coming from the Repeat Offenders, tonight only, with Minnie Winks on the mic.

Guessed the music was alright, Denny dug in a pocket, had less than a hundred left. Trying not to think of the half-million out on the ice, he walked back up the street, thinking of his next move, willed his teeth to stop clattering, looking for his next ride. Walked by the tour bus and over to The Ripley. Clamped his teeth, thinking a shot of scotch would do the trick, that ninety-proof burn all the way to his belly.

Could be the cops got to the Cortina by now, or maybe she dropped through the ice. He tried the office door, knocked on it and waited. He wanted to kick it. It was only about eight, and except for Klondike Kate's the town was locked up tight. Keeping an eye up the road for the cops, knowing they'd be along any time. Denny leaving a trail on the snow-covered two-lane, all the way to Ripley. Keeping to the shadows, he walked, trying other doors, looking for a car or some place they could hole up. The night was getting colder, and wind was blowing from the shadow of the mountain looming high over town to the north.

No street lights, a few porch lights, here and there another glow from a window. He could see the cruiser up the road, its door still hanging into the street. The snow started again, thick flakes drifting same as before. Crossing the street, Denny moved along the storefronts. Stepping on a stoop, a dead-looking place called Grillo's. The sign called it a public house, then under it Gallery & Crafts — genuine ivory, soapstone and jade. Haida art in the window: a bear carved out of wood. Denny guessed the watering hole took the tourists coming off the Pacific Coach, plied them with drinks, then sold them art.

Nothing but quiet wrapped the town, snow crunching under his sneakers, no feeling left in his toes. Going around the side of Grillo's, the place with no windows down the side and all the hip of a legion hall. A couple of pick-ups sat in the back lot dusted in snow.

A porch with a light above the side door, a couple of fresh footprints going up the steps. Denny went to a short-box Fleetside, brushing snow from its side window. The door opened and the dome light came on, Denny sliding onto the cold vinyl, left the door open, one foot hanging out, rubbing and blowing on his cupped hands, getting his fingers to work. Middle of reaching under to pull the ignition wires when the side door of Grillo's opened. A white-haired guy stepped out before Denny could swing his leg in and shut the pick-up's door.

Waving a lazy hello, Denny got out and eased the door shut, looking pleased with himself. Walking to the rail, he put on a smile. Betting this town had never seen a car theft.

Reaching a pack of smokes, the white-haired guy used his boot to sweep some of the powder from the stoop. Looking and saying, "Figured you for Gert."

"That his truck?" Denny stopped at the bottom and leaned on the rail, could smell the Canadian Club on the guy.

"Yeah, old Gert Kohn." The old guy tapped one from the pack, offering it to Denny.

Denny waved a hand, said he didn't smoke. "Walking by and saw the dome light from the street, figured it wasn't the night for needing a boost." Playing the good Samaritan, opened the door, reached a hand in and switched it off.

"You're right about that." Glancing up at the night sky, the old man in shirtsleeves, didn't look bothered by the cold. White hair maybe, but this guy had thick hide. "Sure Gert'll appreciate it, that truck's like his wife, know what I mean? Though I can't say why he went Chev when he shoulda gone Ford." Stretching out his hand, saying, "Name's Mose Grillo."

"Like on the sign." Denny shook the man's rough hand. Denny saying his own name, not sure why he didn't make one up.

"Yeah, nice meeting you, Denny."

"Same. Got a nice place, huh?"

"Not bad. Picks up in peak season, rest of the time the backroom's the hangout, place the boys play cards when they don't want the company of wives or the old folks over at the hall playing bingo. You with the tour bus, I take it?"

"Yeah, looks like we got snowed in." Denny going along.

"Putting you up at the Ripley then?"

"The hotel, yeah. And you, you the artist carved the bear in the window?"

"Me, no," Mose chuckled. "I got no talent like that. Just the dealer, the guy in the middle."

"Travel brochure didn't mention getting snowed in."

"Just showed you pictures of nature, mountain peaks, glaciers, wildlife, stuff like that."

"And maybe something about northern lights," Denny said, guessing they had them up here.

"Well, good thing for Gert you came along," Mose said. "Man's got his mind on that poker pot."

"Fellas playing cards now, huh?"

"You live in Ripley, you drink, shoot the breeze and you play cards."

"Sounds like a lot of places."

"Well, you're welcome, sit in if you want, have a drink. Sure Gert'd like to pour you one, way of thanks."

"Well, that's okay, Mose. Tour folks're gonna wonder where I got to."

Mose looked at the sky again. "Won't be going anyplace tonight, that's for sure."

Blue and red lights reflecting off the boards and snow between the buildings made up his mind, Denny saying, "Well, guess a hand or two can't hurt." Guessing the cops at the lake got the other cruiser unstuck, followed his tracks in the snow to the stolen one, and now were patrolling the main drag.

Flicking the butt into the snow, Mose turned for the door handle, letting Denny go first. "So, let's go see about that drink?"

"Guess a short one can't hurt." Going through the door. Lonzo's cash in his pocket. Could picture Bobbi waiting for him with coffee, hanging out at Klondike Kate's. Stomping his sneakers on the mat, he went down a hall, a fire in the back room, a table with half dozen guys sitting around it, stacks of poker chips, beer bottles, bowls of snacks in the middle. Double doors opened to the gallery out front, the place all closed up. Framed movie posters lined the back walls: *A Clockwork Orange, The Sting, The French Connection.* A pair of Big Eyes on the washroom doors, one a boy, one a girl. Nothing that looked like Native art back here.

Rough-cut faces turned to him, tough-looking men. Denny guessing it's how you look living up in this hell of a place. Nobody looking like an artist.

"This here's Denny," Mose said, explaining he shut off Gert's dome light. Clapping a round-faced guy on the shoulder, saying he ought to be more careful.

Gert made a face, said he always switched it off, talking in a clipped accent, German or Swiss.

Pointing around the table, Mose introduced Denny to the Clay Landrys, senior and junior, the old man with a bird-face and pinched looks. The son with a broad nose and deep dark eyes, had some Haida in him, looked kind of like the guy who played C.W. Moss in *Bonnie and Clyde*. Across from the Landrys sat Jack O'Dey, his hair greased back. Looked like he hadn't shaved in a couple of days.

Mose dragged a metal chair from under the *Clockwork Orange* poster, the Landrys making room between them.

Mose ushered Denny to sit, took his own chair, saying, "Whose deal?"

"Yours." Sliding the cards, Gert got up and went to the Big Chill fridge, pale green and humming in the corner. Fetched Denny a Molson, explaining white was a buck, red was a deuce, blue was five, green a ten-spot. Denny reaching in his pocket, flattening some bills on the table, sliding them forward and buying in.

Jack O'Dey giving him his chips.

"Not my night so far," Clay Jr. said, getting up. "Bladder's on a losing streak, too, caught a chill or some damn thing."

"Comes from whizzing off the porch." Jack O'Dey grinned, saying to Denny, "Man pees for distance." Watching Junior go to the can. "Thinks it's like an Olympic event. Fact, bet you walked right through his latest world record."

"On account you were hogging the can, in there near a half-hour," Landry Jr. said over a shoulder, going and closing the can door.

"How about we just play." Clay Sr. said, like he was tired of these guys picking on his dumb-minded kid.

Shuffling the deck and dealing the hand, Mose called it Follow the Queen, dealing two down. Jack, Gert and old man Landry tossing in white chips. Denny following the lead.

Mose dealt the up cards, Denny getting a queen, waiting his turn and doubling the ante. His next card was a wild ace. Sipping beer, Denny raked in the win, thinking it could be his night. Heat felt like heaven coming off the wood stove, his fingers and toes tingling, first time he'd been warm since leaving Toad Hall back in Whistler.

"They gonna miss you at Kate's?" Mose checked his down cards, turning up a pair of queens.

The rest of them tossing down their cards, everybody out.

"Probably don't even know I'm gone, the way they talk, can't believe those people." Denny with a pair of tens, no wild cards, counting on his luck holding, upping his bet.

"Come up, check out our glacier, huh?" Gert looked at him, this guy walking in from a blizzard wearing city clothes, claimed he shut off his truck lights, beating them at cards.

Gathering up the cards, Mose shoved the pot Denny's way.

"Yeah, that and maybe some northern lights." Denny slid back one of the white chips.

Landry Jr. came back from the can, zipping up. "Summer's the time to come, when the lake at the north end of the glacier busts its ice dam, water flooding the Salmon River the way it does. Ask me, that's worth seeing." Going to the side table, taking a box of Dippy Canoes, he shook some in a bowl. Setting the bowl on the table, telling Denny to help himself. "Got the Salty Surfers, you prefer 'em?"

"Naw, these are good." Scooping a handful, Denny washed them down with the Molson's, watching the cards fall.

Pouring a CC chaser, Gert slid the glass across, saying, "Keep you warmer than that jacket." Dealing the next hand.

"Thanks. Guess I started walking, didn't feel the cold so much. Just was tired of hearing the same stories up on the bus. Glad to get away from it, meet you fellas."

The older Landry picked up his smokes, watching him, offering the pack.

"No, thanks." Denny caught the look between the old man and Mose, something going on. Guessing they weren't buying what he was selling.

"Any gals on the bus, you know the kind I mean?" Clay Jr. said, checking his down cards, smiling up at Denny.

"Well, yeah, maybe one or two."

"Way these cards are treating me, may as well head to Kate's, show some tourist gal my welcome package."

His old man shot him a look.

"Yeah, Clay boy, you're a player alright," Gert said, grinning, dropping in his chip.

The older Landry giving Gert a stare, anteing up.

"See, the way I figure, they got that cramped head on the bus," Clay Jr. said. "The ladies not liking to use it, all that sloshing, squatting behind the rear axle. See what I'm saying?"

Denny chased more whisky with the last of his beer, saying, "So, you hit on them coming out of the can at Kate's."

"Right. See, Kate's got nice johns, keeps them clean, pipes won't freeze up so ladies can do their business."

"We going to talk all night or play?" Older Landry looked up from his cards, like he was ashamed of his son. "You get on then, boy. And when you're done over there, you go on home, hear me?"

"I ain't drunk, Pa."

Palming some more Dippy Canoes, the only thing he'd eaten since Smithers, Denny checked his down cards, guessing Bobbi was mingling with the tourists over at Klondike Kate's. Likely wondering about him.

"They put you up at the Ripley, you said?" Jack O'Dey looked across the top of his cards, cowboy hat tilted to one side.

"Yeah, assigned us all rooms, doubling up where they could. Not sure which room I got," Denny said, looking through the doors to the gallery, catching the blue and red lights strobing along the wall by the fridge, guessing the cops were making a second sweep.

"Not the northern lights you come to see, huh?" Mose said.

"Maybe the Doob's got another moose on his hands, a big rack gone wild in the streets," the older Landry said.

"That or Deputy Dummy lost the keys to the station house again," Gert said, chuckling, his belly jiggling.

Playing his hand, Denny thinking he needed to get back to that lake by daylight — praying the Cortina was still atop the ice, and that the Mounties hadn't dared to get close to it on the thin ice, not knowing the stakes — Denny needing to get in the trunk before the cops came up with a plan, like going back in the morning and wrapping a chain on that bumper. Saying to Mose, "Only seen photos of northern lights, *National Geographic* or someplace. Got to see 'em for myself."

Putting on his coat, Clay Jr. calling it the aurora borealis, saying, "Ask me, summer's the best time."

Mose had been looking at Denny, the friendly out of his voice, saying, "You want, we can go on, shoot more shit about northern lights, moose in the streets, all that, but me, I'd just as soon you get to it and tell the real story."

The others turned to Denny. The blue and red lights flashing through the front window. The sound of a car door shutting.

. . . *thirteen*

Denny wasn't feeling the cold now. His second drink and another winning hand, Denny had raked in the chips, saying to Mose, "What makes you think there's a story?"

"Guy walking around back middle of the night, dressed like it's springtime. Cop car up the street with its door hanging open, but no cop around. You getting out of Gert's ride out back, looking like you got a hand in the cookies, handing me the Shinola about turning out his dome light. Then we got the Mounties cruising by, with their lights flashing. I don't know, you tell me?"

Old Landry gathered the cards and dealt two down, looking at Denny, saying he wouldn't mind hearing it himself.

Eyes down at his cards, Denny glanced around the table, all eyes on him. He heard the back door open, hoping it was Landry's kid, giving up on the pussy hunt at Klondike Kate's, the sound of boots stamping snow on the mat.

Nodding at Denny's glass, Mose said to Gert, "Better hit him again."

"Might come to that." Gert grinned at Denny, reached across for his glass, sticking his fingers inside the rim, tipping the bottle and pouring a shot, looking past Denny's shoulder, was asking Mose about the cop car up the street. Denny hearing the boot steps behind him. Two Mounties walking to either side of him. Parkas and beanies with POLICE on the front, pants with the yellow stripes.

Tucking his gloves under an arm, the male cop looked around the table, saying, "How you fellas doing tonight?" His cop eyes stopped, looking down on Denny.

"What's up, Henry? Another moose on the loose?" Mose smiled up at him, then around the table.

Henry Kendal put on a good-natured smile and nodded. Saying hi to Gert and Jack, then old Landry, then Mose. Slapping the leather gloves against the table edge, looking back at Denny. "Don't know you, do I, son?"

"Not from around here, that's what you mean, Officer? Come to see your glacier, hear it's a sight." Denny nodded up at the female cop, saying, "Ma'am." Her name tag making her Mikki Cook, officer-in-training. "Good to see, letting women on the force now. Me, I'm all for it."

"Well, that's real good to know," she said. "You with the tour group then, that right?"

"Denny's with me," Mose jumped in. "Up here for a visit, his first time."

"From the city then?"

"Yeah, big one with the bright lights," Mose said.

"Hoping to show him the glacier and nature's theater," Clay Jr. said, coming back in the back door. "'Course, you ask me, the best time for northern lights's September, and best place's Norway." Clay Jr. walked back to the table and said to Denny, "Though some might say Iceland."

"All good, Clay," Henry Kendal said, putting a hand on young Landry's shoulder, telling him to grab a seat. "Not why we're here."

"Legend's got it the lights are on account of some hole

the spirits pass through, on the way to their true heaven, you hear of that?" Clay Jr. went on, not sitting down, but reaching the CC bottle and pouring himself a shot.

"Not here about the lights tonight," Henry Kendall said, getting impatient with him.

Looking at Denny, Clay Jr. said, "Fact about the glacier, she glows blue at night, I mention that, hell of a thing to see."

"So, what brings you, Doob?" Mose turned in his chair.

Henry smiled, Denny guessing the cop didn't like the old man using the nickname, like he was being disrespected. Looking back at Denny. "Gonna tell us he's staying with you, I bet, Mose?"

"Sounds like you got your mind made up, Henry," Mose said.

"You mind if he talks for himself," Henry clapped the gloves against his palm. "That be alright with you?" Turning to Denny, asking his last name.

"Denny Barrenko. And like Mose says, I'm staying with him, Sheriff."

"Denny Barrenko." Henry Kendal nodded, making note. "And it's Corporal, we got no sheriff here."

"Sorry, Corporal then."

"When did you say you got in?"

"Come on, Doob," Mose said. "Told you, he's with me. What else you need to know?"

"Well, some answers would do fine," Henry Kendal said, then back to Denny. "So, you come off the tour bus then?"

"Not your old self tonight, Doob." Mose turned more in his chair, looking at the cop like he was concerned.

"Day I got to tell you police business, Mose, guess that's the day I start calling you mayor, huh?" Henry Kendall smiled at the female officer, keeping it friendly. "Till then . . ."

Gert and Jack smiled, too. Clay Jr. leaned in and explained to Denny about Mose's failed election bid a year ago, only took eighty votes.

"We're all just wondering what brings you in, the whole force," Jack O'Dey said from across the table.

Walking around the table, Denny watched as Mikki Cook stopped behind Jack, ran a couple fingers across his Brylcreemed hair, saying, "Well, road out there's slick as seal shit tonight, Jack, all the way to Smithers." Looked at her fingers, wiped them on his shoulder, and finished going around the table, saying, "Chased some fools in a stolen car, right out onto Meridien."

"That so, huh?" Jack said, palming some Dippy Canoes. "Best be careful, going on that thin ice, miles from nowhere."

Resting her hands on the table between Denny and Mose, she looked over at Jack, Denny sure he saw something passing between them. Reaching across and picking up Jack's glass, she said, "Can take care of myself." She downed the shot, banged the glass on the table. "Figured you knew that already, Jack."

Leaning across, Jack checked it for lipstick marks, saying, "Any time you need one to steady your nerves, you just come on back, girl." Tipping his hat.

"You know I'm on duty, Jack. Rules I got to follow." She turned to the sound of someone else coming in the back door. "You boys ought to get somebody to wash some glasses. Ask me, this place could do with a woman's touch."

Leaning close to Denny, Henry said, "Gonna ask one more time about the tour bus, son. You come off it? And be careful how you answer." Turning to the back door, seeing who was coming in.

"Told you, Doob," Mose said. "He came on the train, from over in Prince George, up from the big smoke. Can check it out if you want."

"Asking him, if you don't mind, Mose," Henry said.

"Was me picked him up," the new man said, coming from the hall.

Denny could see blond hair gone gray, combed back off the man's forehead, saying it sure was coming down out there. Calling it winter's last hurrah.

Henry turned to him, saying, "You sure about that, Dalt?"

"You mean, am I sure winter's done?"

"Mean about you picking this fellow up?"

"Station right on North Railway. Busy like a cattle drive today, am I right?" Dalton looked at Denny, not knowing his name.

"Sure was packed in," Denny said, looking at the new man.

"There you go, Dalton went and picked up Denny, like I told you," Mose said, getting back to his cards.

"Hard to figure folks coming north this time of year." Dalton shook his head, pulled a chair from the wall, sat next to Gert, saying, "Now, somebody pour me a drink, huh, let me win some of this boy's city money."

Henry Kendall looked at the lying faces, then back to Denny. "Your boarding pass, you got it on you?"

Denny thinking a moment, saying, "Conductor came round and collected it. You want, I got ID?" Leaning to the side, he made like he was getting his wallet.

"All these fellas vouching, guess that's good enough." Henry nodded to Mikki Cook and he started for the door.

"Not yourself tonight, Henry," Mose called after him.

"Chasing a car out on Meridien, the sons of a bitches doubling in the blizzard and making off in my cruiser, kind of thing's got a way of pissing me off."

"You leave the keys in it, huh? Well, sorry to hear it, Doob," Mose said, not looking sorry. "Goddamn embarrassing if you did, but, you got it back in the end, thank God. How about the one on the ice?"

"Turns out it was stolen from out front a house in Smithers, lady unpacking her groceries when it got jacked. Only the second time something like that's happened over there. But hell, well, it ain't over."

"Don't go beating yourself up, Doob, what with the blinding snow and all. Coulda happened to anybody."

"You hear about the mad trapper?" Clay Jr. said to Denny. "Happened over by Rat River. All these Mounties going after one old man."

Denny saying he didn't, and Henry Kendal slapping the gloves in his palm. "Wish I had time to hear it again, kid." Rolling his eyes and nodding to Mikki Cook, the two of them walking to the door, going out.

"Friend of the people, old Doob," Mose said to Denny, then, "Whose shuffle?"

Dalton bought in, stretching a hand to Denny saying his full name, Dalton Benning.

Denny giving his full name, shaking the hand, looking around the table, sizing up his new friends, not sure why they covered for him.

Jack dealt the hand, and chips landed in the pot.

"Think they'll get it off the ice?" Mose watched Jack deal the four up, tossing in a blue chip.

Seeing the bet, Dalton wondered aloud where the carjackers got to.

Mose looked at Denny. "You in?"

"You bet." Denny dropped in a blue, glancing around.

"Thin ice past those huts. A marker plain as your face," Mose said. "I say she goes down by morning."

"Yuh, a spring out there, down forty, fifty feet," Clay Jr.

said. "Brings in the squawfish. Lucky it didn't drop right through, the two of 'em in it."

"Can't believe the Doob getting his car swiped," Old Landry said, calling it and turning up his down cards. "Dumb as nails, that boy."

"Not as dumb as you think. And me, I got to wonder what's in the car, maybe the trunk," Mose said, turning back to Denny. "Guessing who left it might come back for it, whatever it is."

"Pair of jacks, ace high." Denny laid down his hand, looking around the table.

The rest of them tossed in their cards, Denny raking in the chips.

"Looks like your night, alright." Mose tossed his down, too.

. . . fourteen

"So, you got lucky, found the car and made the call. But, instead of doing what I said, you went on your own." Lee Trane glanced up at the neon sign: The Last Spike. A shithole of a restaurant and store with nobody in it, a lone gas pump out front. Some kid waitress peeping out the front window, pretending to wipe a table, minding her own business.

"It's what Lonz—"

Lee Trane stepped close to Dex, and the big man stopped talking. Several inches taller and about twenty pounds on Lee Trane. Ape arms and a skull from the time when man used stone tools. Standing out front of the gas pump, Lee faced these two clowns with their car locked, their keys thrown away by Denny Barrenko. Him and Bobbi Ricci getting away in Lonzo's Cadillac.

"Come on, Lee, I know what you said, but they'd a got away. Had to do something — the two of us." Dex turned to his partner, not wanting the shit to land on him alone.

"Trouble's right there, Dex. You figured. Did things your way." Lee gave a tight smile. "Let the draft dodger kick you in the nuts, tough guy like yourself."

"Suckered me. Didn't think —" Dex put his hands wide, like what else was he supposed to do.

"That's right, you didn't."

"No offense, Lee, but Lonzo said, You see 'em, you grab 'em." Dex looked at his partner, saying, "Feel free, jump in anytime, Flip."

"Man's got a point, Lee." Flip just shrugged.

"Trouble is, this man's an idiot. What's the matter, don't like how I'm talking to you, Dex?"

"Not making me happy, no." Dex frowned at Flip, then set his jaw, turning back.

Swinging his foot, Lee landed the kick. Shoved Dex aside and had his piece out, caught Flip reaching inside his jacket. "How about it, Flip, you happy?"

"I'm good." Flip showed his empty hands, looking at Dex sinking to all fours, second time he was on his knees, the man groaning, maybe going to throw up again.

Crouching down, one eye on Flip, Lee put a hand on the big man's shoulder, said to Dex, "Next time I say something, you listen up, huh?"

Dex nodded, couldn't find his voice.

Rising up, Lee stepped away, not wanting this mope throwing up on his brogues.

"The guy tossed our keys. Could use a lift," Flip said.

Going to his T-Bird, Lee opened the driver's door. "Call up Lonzo, tell him. Maybe get him to send roadside service." Getting in, he tapped his shoes together, knocking off any gravel, swung his door shut and drove off.

...*fifteen*

The aroma of fried heaven hung over Klondike Kate's potluck, Denny breathing in the Canadian bacon. Hadn't eaten anything but Dippy Canoes and Salty Surfers since the grilled cheese and fries back in Smithers. Bobbi not sharing the Twix bar.

Stepping in behind him, Mose Grillo tugged off his toque, stamped snow from his boots, flattening his white hair with the palm of his hand, looking around the place like he owned it.

Kate was doubling as waitress, looked over and called Mose an old dog. Her pale blue uniform with some shape under it, her hair tied back. Mose headed for his table at the back, sitting with his back to the wall, the small stage across from him. Kate coming with a menu, offering it to Denny.

"A couple of lumberjack stacks, hon," Mose said.

Denny gave back the menu.

"You'll thank me later. Flapjacks, pair of easy-overs, couple links and peameal strips, hash browns on the side. Everything a man could want."

"Lumberjack, huh?"

"You don't want links, Kate'll sub in ham or extra strips, eggs anyway you want. And do it with that million-dollar smile. Won't you, darlin'?"

"Way you tip, gets you a smile anytime you want." Kate bumped his chair with her hip, turning to Denny, telling him the special came with buttered toast and refills on the coffee.

Denny saying it sounded pretty good, taking in the dark walls with the trophy heads over the bar, a serving counter with a pass-through to the kitchen. A tacked poster promised nightly entertainment. The Repeat Offenders playing all week. Then his breath caught in his throat. Catching Bobbi coming in the front door behind a couple of women, wearing that fringed suede jacket too big on her. The two women had tourist written all over, both with parkas, matching white toques with maple leaves, one with a Minolta on a strap. Shedding their outer layers, they hung their coats on hooks by the door, taking a table by the window. Shrugging off the suede, Bobbi in the same clothes she was in yesterday, the turtleneck and bell-bottoms, she slung the jacket on back of her chair, looking around, past Denny, doing it like she didn't know him.

Mose followed Denny's gaze, caught his eyes sticking on Bobbi, saying, "Not bad, nice rack, huh?"

Denny pointed to the mount closest to the window. "Thing looks like it's staring, glass eyes following me."

"Not the rack I meant." Pointing to the mount, Mose said, "Eyes are acrylic. Twelve-pointer Kate bagged with a bow last year, on the backside of Otter."

"Play cards, drink, fish and hunt, what you do up here? Even the ladies?"

"Do lots of things," Mose said, pointing to the band poster. "Even do it to music."

"They any good?"

"Do a couple by Jimmie Rodgers, Carter Family, Lefty Frizzell, like that. Mostly folks come wanting to hear what's on the radio."

"Country, I bet?"

"What we call honest music."

Denny thanked him for letting him crash in the back room of Grillo's. Had a funny smell to the cot, but he was warm all night.

"You need it another night, not a problem." Mose looked thoughtful and added, "Fact, got nothing but room at the house. A couple miles from town."

"Wouldn't want to be no trouble. You and your wife — you married? I mean, a place like that, sounds like you would be."

"I'm a lone wolf. Except when I feel like company. And I got a gal comes by, tidies up the place. Sometimes I think about patting her rump." He winked.

Denny nodded, glad Mose hadn't asked again about the real story, but expecting he'd get back to it. Dropping a sugar cube in his coffee, he stirred it around, stealing another glance Bobbi's way. The throbbing behind his eyes from last night's heavy drink not letting up, more than he was used to. Settling his nerves after the Mounties came in with their questions and looks. From what he found in his pockets this morning, he'd lost most of Lonzo's cash on hand, following the queen, then curling up on that cot. Denny searching his mind, trusting he hadn't let his tongue go loose, saying anything about the twins in the trunk of the Cortina. Couldn't remember much after the Mounties left, drinking to take that big edge off.

Klondike Kate's had looked closed by the time the game wrapped up. Denny hoping that Bobbi made out alright, then telling himself that girl always landed the right way up, and he was quick to fall into a boozy sleep. Coming awake when Mose was shaking him, asking if he was ready for breakfast. The two of them walking in tire tracks through the unplowed snow of the main drag, making their way up the block to Kate's.

Topping his cup with the cow creamer, he considered the odds of the Cortina still sitting on the ice. Could be the Mounties were back out there now after last night's storm, venturing on the ice and trying to get a chain on the bumper and dragging it off. If the car went down, then what? Well, he could come back in warmer weather and dive for it. Ripley hardly being a spot on a map, maybe he could hole up here, wait for the thaw, Denny knowing Lonzo had people looking, but who would come looking way up here?

Remembering Lee Trane from the days he chauffeured the old man around. Lee with the black-eyed gaze, a guy who never said much. Aldo the bodyguard had told him that Lee Trane was a piece of work. Didn't have Aldo's size, but Aldo said a badger wasn't big, either, made up for it with a mean streak. Told him Lee served with some infantry outfit during the Korean War, moving on Heartbreak Ridge, sent to take out the bunkers and hold their position, waiting on the Sherman tanks. When that first night fell, Trane left his rifle and crawled up the ridge with just his trench knife. Came back before first light and dug in with the rest, cleaning the blade, saying he'd gone off killing time. The outfit dug in under fire all the next day, waiting for the tanks to clatter in. Lee crawling off on his own again under nightfall.

"You with us, Denny?" Mose asked.

"Yeah, right here." Denny looked at him, then back to the window, Bobbi Ricci laughing at something one of the women said.

"Thinking about your car?" Mose said, sipping his coffee, watching him.

"The special comes with toast, right?"

"Toast, the least of your worries."

"Makes you think I got worries?"

Kate swung by with two platters stacked high, asked Mose if he heard about the Mountie chase, some stolen car getting lost out on the ice.

"Yeah, old Doob came in last night, mentioned it." Mose shook his head and chuckled, picking up his fork. "Chased the car out there on foot, you believe it? The car thieves sneaking around him in the snow, taking off in Doob's own cruiser."

"Enjoying this, huh?" she said, bumping her hip into his chair back.

"Ought to be something in the Mountie manual, you go in hot pursuit, you don't leave your keys in the car." He speared a link and took a bite, winking at Denny, big greasy grin on his face, giving Kate a pat.

"You're plain awful, Mose Grillo," Kate said, play-slapping his hand away and walking to the table by the window, her order pad at the ready.

Denny dabbed toast in his egg, watched Bobbi order. Kate pointing at something on the menu, nodding and walking to the pass window, sticking the order on a pin.

"Boys tell me they're taking wagers at the bingo," Mose said. "A buck a bet, picking the time the car goes through the ice. One who bets closest to the minute wins the pot."

"Nothing better to do, huh?" Denny caught Bobbi glancing past him again, then turning back to her conversation. From her look, he guessed how pissed she was.

"What I can't figure is, why pinch a Cortina. I mean, aside from the Dodge Dart, no worse piece of shit on the road." Mose stabbed his fork in his egg, put some in his mouth, waved the tines in the air, saying, "Okay, you get in a spot, you take whatever ride you can. I get that. But, given a choice, I'd be keeping an eye for an Imperial, something with legroom and some getaway power." Looking across the table like he was hoping Denny would open up.

"That spot you're talking about. Don't get time to worry about legroom. More like looking for something with keys in it." Denny thinking this guy was like Bobbi, thinking luxury had something to do with jacking a car.

Mose nodded, sipped some coffee. "Had Gert take a ride out before light."

"To the lake?" Denny feeling the alarm, trying not to show it.

"Doob's out there as we speak trying to get a tow truck close enough to snatch it back." Mose leaning back, laughing.

"Ice won't hold that." Denny doubting a tow truck would make it that far out from shore.

"No tow driver I know of dumb enough to find out."

"So, why you call him that, the Doob?" Denny took a forkful of eggs, changing the conversation.

"Known him since the one-room school. Rail of a kid with more pimples than friends back then, easy to pick on, you know. But, the name came long after. When he was on the force, he nailed young Landry on a pot bust. Was just a rookie then. Did his surveillance and figured the kid dead to rights, showed up at the Landry place with a warrant and back-up, standing there with one of those rams, you know, for taking the door down. Went in and searched the place, turned out Junior was in possession of one joint. Doob finding it like a bookmark in the June *Playboy*. Some twigs and seeds under the mattress. Been called the Doob ever since."

"On account of one joint."

"Right. But you call him what you want, the man's the law in the middle of this no-place, and he's got you figured for the car on the ice, plus the joyride in the squad car."

"You don't like him much."

"Been kind of a game between us. Man always figures me and the poker boys are up to something. But since the one-joint raid, the local judge'd think twice before issuing him another warrant." Mose finished what was on his plate, saying, "Got a spring down there, bottom of Meridien, what makes the ice thin over that spot. Why the fishermen put their huts near it, ones you hit. It's the warm water attracts the trout."

"And you figure it'll fall through."

"Already did, just before first light." Mose looked in his eyes, letting him sit with that. "Down there to stay. Cost more to haul the car up than it's worth. The way the insurance'll look at it."

Denny looked at the jam caddy, deciding between the marmalade and grape jelly, Kate coming around again, asking how everything was.

"Good as always, doll." Waiting till she left with their empty plates, Mose leaned across, saying, "Anytime now, you want to stop jerking my chain, boy, maybe we can do some business."

Denny picked grape jelly. "Makes you think I got business?"

"Any time now, gonna realize you need my help."

"That right?"

"Only way you'll get what's in the trunk." Mose looking him in the eyes.

Denny kept up the poker face, taking a sip from his cup.

"Wondering if you can trust me?" Mose eased back.

"Wondering why I'd need to."

"On account I can get down there, and you can't. Top of that, you forget it was me, the reason the Doob didn't drag your ass in."

"Thanked you for it, that and the cot. But I'm guessing you did it on account you think there's something in it."

"Just my nature. But you wrap your mind around needing my help, you just got to ask." Mose finished his coffee, sitting back, satisfied. "Well, you think on it. Just wouldn't take too long. Not to add pressure, but let's say the Doob comes off the ice and gets it in his mind to go see that housewife, one with the stolen car. That woman points her finger, IDs you, won't matter much what I told him."

Finishing his cup, Denny caught Bobbi getting up from her table, passing behind Mose to the ladies'. Not looking over at him.

"Kate comes 'round asking, could go for a refill." Denny pushed his chair back, saying, "Got to hit the head."

Mose pointed his bread knife to where it was, went about buttering his toast.

•

"What the fuck . . ." Bobbi said, grabbing him by his shirt-front — Denny looking surprised, like maybe he thought she was going to kiss him. Talking between clamped teeth, she swung him into the routered letters on the john door.

BUCKS AND DOES

"You got any idea the shit you put me through. The fuck were you?"

"Went looking for a car, saw the cops coming and one thing turned into another." Denny put his hands on hers.

"And who's the old guy?" Bobbi not letting go of her grip.

"Guy who saved my ass from a night in jail." Denny lifted his hands, showing his palms, like he was surrendering.

"Why'd he do that?"

"What I'm trying to figure out. Maybe just being small-town friendly. How about you, you sleep someplace? Had me worried sick." Eyes glancing down, Bobbi not letting go of his collar.

"Making like you care."

"Come on. Give me some —"

"Cops came in asking questions, looking around this place. Bus driver did a head count and said yeah, we're all his flock. Called us that, his flock. Pacific Coach springing for hotel rooms on account of the blizzard, so I ended up bunking with Alice and Tammy over there." Nicking her head to the table out front, she kept her hold. "One with her hair up's Alice, got wallpaper in her living room with blue with gold stripes, other one's Tammy. Snorts, grunts and kicks her feet in her sleep, would give Lonzo a run. Before sawing off, she talked my ear off about *Queen for a Day*, her favorite god-damn show. You see that place, The Ripley House, one all painted yellow?"

"Hard to miss."

"Used to be a brothel when this was a mining town. Alice and Tammy can't wait to snap photos, go home and tell about it, staying in a place like that." Bobbi flipped her eyes to the ceiling. "So, what's the plan, genius? Gonna get our car back and drive north some more?"

"Working on something. Take it easy." Patting his fingers on the top of her knuckles, trying to get her to let go.

"This something involve your new friend?"

"Trying to see what kind of friend he is."

The two of them watched the coach driver come in, stepping over to Bobbi's table, saying something to Alice and Tammy.

"Guess the bus'll be leaving," she said, finally letting go of her grip, smoothing his collar.

"Maybe you ought to get on it."

"And leave you with my money, huh? Guess you'd like that."

"What I hear, car's likely at the bottom of the lake by now. Also hear the cops're looking for two men. You hang around, won't be much to figure out. Give me a number, and I'll call as soon as I get it back. Get you your share."

"Should've shot you when I had the chance." Bobbi walking back to her table.

·

Going back and sitting down, Denny spread grape jelly on a slice of toast.

Mose lit a cigarette, saying, "You mind?"

"Thing is I'm asthmatic."

Mose took another drag, blowing smoke to the side. "Asthmatic, that the lungs, huh?"

"The cousin of bronchitis, yeah, means I got trouble breathing."

"Comes from living in the city, all that smog." Mose dragged and slid the ashtray to the corner of the table, making an effort. Saying the smoke didn't bother him last night, when the Mounties came in snooping.

"Yeah, well . . . Let me ask you something."

"Shoot."

"Suppose there was something in the trunk, how you gonna help get to it?"

Stubbing out the smoke, Mose leaned back like he had all day.

. . . *sixteen*

"Beats the cot last night." Bobbi dropped back on the double bed, her head on the piled pillow, the springs creaking. Looking at Denny, saying, "What's this smell like? Cabbage, right?" Holding a pillow out to him, putting her nose to the other one, she tossed it from the bed. Propped up on her elbows.

"Got bigger things than cots and cabbage." Denny put the pillow down, looked out the window, the Ripley House, this one-time brothel painted yellow, with new wiring and plumbing since those days when it serviced miners, loggers and the crews from the freighters moored in the Tootega Canal, a couple miles away. Denny thinking, only so much Sherwin-Williams can cover up, all that history drenching its soul. New owner, Nils Skerritt, had hung a bronze sign out front of the office: "The Ripley House, formerly The Brothel." Nils making it a point of pride, tourists snapping photos of loved ones next to it — look, Ma, we stayed at a brothel.

The single room was up an outer flight of stairs, a wing of three rooms with a shared bath at the end, Nils posting a sign warning that the pipes may freeze up in the winter months. The mattress with its sway-back, the iron headboard against the paneled wall. A Morgan armchair upholstered in something pretending to be leather under the drafty bay window. The front of one arm taped over, the tape almost matching the leather. The dresser had the look of being dragged here behind sled dogs, its drawers scraped up and sticking. A couple of knobs missing, bolts showing through.

"Guy calls it renovated. Can hear the scrabbling inside the walls." Bobbi told him rodents freaked her out. Nothing like that back at Lonzo's, the master bedroom looking over the lit pool.

Denny stood at the bay window and looked across the empty street. Kate stood outside of her place, sweeping a dusting of fresh snow with a broom, knocking more from the sandwich board. The Repeat Offenders playing again tonight.

Getting a picture of the Cortina sinking to the bottom again, the twins in the trunk, all that money going down, Denny's mood sinking, too. Saying, "Think they're any good, the Repeat Offenders?"

"Caught a bit last night, chick singer's pretty good."

"Good as Boppin' Beppe?"

"Guess we can check it out. Seeing how we're stuck here." Bobbi twisted her mouth into something that wasn't a smile, more an accusation. "Make it look like we just met. Or hey, I can let you pick me up."

"Or how about you see me across the room . . ."

"Act like I can't help myself." Bobbi getting that thought again, like she should've shot him back at Lonzo's.

Denny told her what Mose said about folks placing bets at the bingo hall, the exact time the Cortina dropped through the ice. How the volunteer fire department was taking turns going out there with a stopwatch, marking the exact time. Some old lady winning the jackpot, two hundred and fifty bucks.

"So, it sunk?"

He just shrugged, looking out.

"Gonna need some money," she said after a while, adding the room was comped by the bus people, at least for last night. "Nils at the desk was quick to say checkout's at eleven. Looking for twelve bucks if I want it for another night. Told him I'd get it to him."

Denny looking at the cramped dive, putting a hand in his pocket, pulling the bills he had left. Didn't mention losing at poker. Counted enough for a couple more nights.

"So, how much you lose at cards?" Like she was reading his mind.

"Was up, then down, then up, you know . . . Had to build an alibi, right?"

"How much?"

"Important thing's to get to the car. Figure it out."

"You talking about swimming after it?"

"It sinking could turn out a good thing. Keeps it safe till I can dive down to it."

"And before Lonzo finds us."

"Maybe you stop calling him, could improve our odds."

"And you're going to dive, you with your inhaler thingie?"

"Straight down, come right back up." Denny saying it like there was nothing to it, hadn't paddled in a pool since he was a kid. "Just needs to warm up a bit."

"Ever do it — dive?"

"Like I said, straight down, come right back up."

"And what, I just sit around, slap at flies and apply ointment. And for money, hey, you can turn tricks, this former brothel."

"Mose mentioned some work."

"What kind of work?" Bobbi sounding dubious.

"Didn't get into it, but he owns a bar, doubles as an art gallery."

"You know something about art?"

From the room below came the thump of Stompin' Tom doing the song about ketchup. The sound of somebody clapping along. Walls paper-thin.

"You believe this shit?" Bobbi got up and stomped the floorboards. "All the good music out there, Gino Vannelli, Rick James, and this hick plays ketchup loves potatoes."

The music was turned down, Bobbi picked up and punched the discarded pillow into shape and shoved it under her head, laid back on the bed. Cabbage or no cabbage.

Looking at the armchair, he said, "Ought to think about sleeping arrangements . . ."

"Yeah, well, think again." Reaching the other pillow, she tossed it to the armchair and missed.

Denny looked at the chair, went and pulled the dresser drawers one at a time, hoping for a spare blanket, found one looking like it had been used for moving furniture, a couple holes eaten into it.

... *seventeen*

"Hedgehog, that for real?" Denny was interested.

"Not the buttons and browns you find at your local grocery."

"Other kinds, huh?" Only mushrooms Denny ever thought about were magic, and he swore off them years ago.

"Sure, you got your pines, chanterelles and morels, all growing wild," Mose said. "And it's foraging, picking's for banjos."

"Okay, you forage. And they end up in gourmet shops and restaurants, places paying to get them shipped fresh."

"That's it."

Kate's teen son manned the dish pit, wrapped in an apron and spraying water while Kate prepped for the dinner rush, chopping vegetables on a board, knife tapping like a drumstick, then setting glasses and napkins on tables. Moving in a whirlwind. The tour bus had pulled out, and another charter was due later that afternoon. Minnie Winks setting up for the show, tuning an acoustic guitar, adjusting some levels on an amp, doing a sound check.

"Trick is telling them apart, seeing most are poison." Mose watching the woman on the stage, eyes moving over her.

"Like in that Clint Eastwood flick, *The Beguiled*. You see it?"

"The what?"

"Doesn't matter. Look, I appreciate the offer, but come on, man, what the hell do I know about mushrooms?" Denny tore into a sugar packet, blowing across the top. "You got your guys, ones who know the woods, right? Can forage all day, know which one's poison." Denny waiting for it, Mose leading up to something.

"My guys got plenty to do. Look, you want the work, or you don't . . ." Mose waiting, watching Minnie blow into a mic. Then he looked at Denny, leaned close like he was confiding, admitting he'd had some trouble.

"Kind of trouble?" Denny biting.

"Got these local no-goods, could be Native, could be hill-billies, who the fuck knows. Do know they work the woods, do it like ghosts, go around robbing the camps, miners and even the tourists. Do it without a trace, not a goddamn foot-print on the ground. Got my boys keeping an eye, these sons of bitches robbing folks blind, right down to their food, clothes, take the tents, posts and pegs, everything. Even stripped the socks drying on a line, the last camp they pil-laged. Left no sign there even was a camp. The kind of shit we got to deal with up here."

"How about your law?"

"You met the Doob, right?" Mose shook his head, then leaned back, letting Denny take it in. "I send a crew to pick, got to send an extra man just to keep lookout." Mose with an arm over the back of his chair, gave a look in Kate's direction.

Kate getting the coffee pot, coming over and filling his cup. Denny putting a hand over his own cup, saying he was fine.

"Thanks, doll," Mose said, then back to Denny. "So this job, you want to hear the rest, or not?"

Denny gave a nod.

"First thing I want you doing, you're walking to Killik." Mose watching Minnie step off the stage, going to the ladies'.

"On the Alaska side?"

"Just a couple of miles in." Mose pointed a finger west.

"They got a mushroom shortage?"

"All you got to know, it pays fifty bucks and it doesn't come with questions."

"Something you could get Dalton, or the Landry kid to do. I right?"

"See, that's a question. And thought I explained it."

"Carrying what?"

Mose sipped his coffee. "Taking a bag over, doing it on foot. Bringing back a van."

"A van?"

"Just need you to keep this one on the road."

"Van loaded with the kind of weight they measure in jail time. Saw the way the Doob was eyeing me, right?"

"Mounties got no jurisdiction on the far side."

"Uh-huh. And what's in the van?"

Mose sipped, taking his time now, saying, "What's in that trunk?"

"Changing the subject now."

Mose just waited.

"Cash." No point playing. Denny thinking it almost felt good saying it.

Mose smiled, like he was getting somewhere now. "Kind of cash?"

"The kind that's enough. Now, how about the van?"

"Ivory."

"Like dope?"

"Like ivory.

"You mean like elephant?"

"This part of the world it's walrus. Some jade, some soapstone. Stuff gets sent to Indonesia. Gets carved up, comes back and gets sold to the tourists."

"That legal?"

"You want the work?"

"Want to know what I'm getting into. And, uh ..." Denny moving his mouth, rubbing his hands like it was part of the thinking process, then saying, "This kind of thing ... I'd say a hundred."

"For taking a walk and driving a van back?" Mose grinned.

"Crossing international borders, contraband, yeah, that's a hundred. And maybe that's light." Putting a hand to his chin, Denny thinking out loud.

Mose finished his cup, glancing over at Bobbi at the same table by the window, sitting on her own this time, same turtleneck and jeans, Mose saying, "That her, huh? One you were talking to by the can before."

Denny turning his neck. "That a question?"

Mose leaned back like he had him all figured out. The tattoo on his forearm showing, an anchor with a rope script wrapped around it.

Turning from Bobbi, Denny caught the tattoo and had a better look.

"'Rocked in the cradle of the deep.'" Mose showed his arm.

"That a sailor thing?"

"Was deckhand on the steamer *Northwestern*. Ship with worse fucking luck than you."

Mose stopped as Kate came around with the coffee pot again, splashing more in each cup.

"Signed up in '32, got hired on account of knowing how to dive. Sailed from Seattle to Cape Spenser, Gulf of Alaska. Place where she dropped her stern-post and rudder. Crew got pulled off, and the ship got towed to port and put in dry dock. Took up fur-trapping in Juneau awhile. Martens, mink and ermine. Wasn't any good at it and practically starved." Mose tapping the tattoo as he talked.

"Went back to being a deckhand, and next time out the captain plows a reef, clear weather with the lighthouse lamp burning, the keeper blowing his foghorn. God knows what went on in that wheelhouse. Would have quit but for the smuggling I got into."

"Tusks?"

"Whisky. From Seattle. Worked on the dive crew that got the hull patched up, got called up to quarters when somebody finked to the captain about my stashed whisky. Ended up the man at the helm was okay with it, so long as he got a taste. And the very next time out, the same ship's master was taking a taste when the *Northwestern* clipped the SS *Tacoma*, moored and tied to goddamn Pier 41. Captain was drunk as a skunk before we even cast off. When we hit, we hit so hard, my ass got thrown to the deck. Bruised my hip and fractured this arm. Worse than that, half the stowed bottles got busted."

"Shit luck alright." Denny listening, wondering where the old man was going.

"Then in '35 we sailed through some heavy fog, passing the light at Cape Smudge when we ran aground at Orange Point. Lost the whole stash that time."

"Drunk captain?"

"And a cursed ship. A bad combination. After that, we got assigned a new captain, a self-professed teetotaler. Not sure why I stuck around, but I took to supplying the army boys posted at Ketchikan. And those boys were thirsty like you can't believe. Had me turning a fine trade till the second time we sailed into port, the new captain swiping the Union Oil Dock, stone sober and plowing a couple of fishing boats and ending against an oil barge. What went on in that fucking wheelhouse, I do not know."

Denny laughed, the old man good at telling a tale.

"But, as luck would have it, the *Northwestern* came away with barely a leak, but what whisky didn't bust when we hit the dock was lost when we rammed the oil barge. The ship got laid up again, and being broke I took to foraging, learned it from a Haida woman, making enough to get by. Almost joined the Marines, except for some medic shaking his head at my flat feet. Closest I got to action was signing back on the *Northwestern*, maintenance crew this time. New owners had her moved to the Lake Union dry dock to be fit for service as a floating barracks.

"Putting you right back in the whisky business."

"Thirsty servicemen will not be denied, son. The *Northwestern* got her overhaul, and I got to sneaking my cases onboard, getting myself some deep pockets. Left Seattle on the Alaska route for the last time, serving on the same tin can that survived fourteen groundings, a near dozen collisions, smashed up half-dozen docks, dropped a couple of props, lost its rudder, lost its anchor, half-dozen crew killed and more injured, me included. Hundreds of jugs smashed. A cursed ship sailing some of the worst waters of the world. But, she made it that time, got herself dry-docked at Dutch Harbor, had a berm built around her hull. Electricity from her generators lighting the whole town. The navy took her over on account of the war efforts, and I kept on building my customer base, one whisky jug at a time. Would have retired flush if the Jap planes hadn't buzzed over. Aided by poor weather and worse navy judgement, bombed the shit out of Dutch Harbor, tore craters up the beach, blew up a bunch of buildings and just like that they were gone." Mose thinking back, making a face.

Denny leaning in, had to admit, he was liking the story. Maybe because it made him think of his brother, Dale. Away from home in wartime.

"Navy and Coast Guard got busy sandbagging the place, machine guns aimed at the sky, waiting for the Zeros to come back. Meantime, I got my skids off-board and into some half-built hangar, with the tarps over the works. Next morning they attacked again, buzzing off some nearby carrier, flying in low with the bombers coming right after, blowing the shit out of the place, hit some fuel tanks, along with the air station dock, dropped a five-hundred-pounder smack on my hangar. Our machine gunners doing no good.

"Soon as they flew over, I went running in, but was nothing left but busted glass and whisky bleeding in the ground. Next pass came right after, the Japs dropping a fat one on our foredeck. Was lying on the ground, watched it drop and hit. A sight to see, the Northwestern's hull busting and splintering, going up in a big fireball.

"Two of us went running in and pulling airmen out. Guys on-board having a lunch of pork chops when that bomb dropped in their lap. Goddamn thing igniting the fuel, the whole ship going up." Mose snapped his fingers. "One minute I'm sitting with a hangar of salvaged whisky, next I'm pulling coughing fellows out, along with the chief mate.

"When it was done, the chief insisted on repaying me for saving his ass. Couldn't get me decorated, me being a civilian, but he got me this." Showing the tattoo. "Got one of the surviving crew, a guy knowing a thing about doing ink." Pushing the sleeve right up, Mose turned the arm, let Denny get a better look. "Rocked in the Cradle of the Deep" in a banner around the flag, a sailing ship in the middle, an anchor at the bottom.

"That the end of running whisky?"

"Switched to penicillin the rest of the war. Navy boys with a good fear of the clap. Brought it in from Anchorage, shipped in milk bottles. Sold it by the ampule. Nice and small and no clinking bottles. Helped the Navy win the war on clap, warded off a pox epidemic."

"Doing your bit for the war effort?"

"After the Jap surrender, I got to know some boys up here growing the jolly green, a place called the Matanuska Valley. A decent strain with local demand, and I saw right off what those boys lacked was distribution. Found out Alaskan courts upheld this notion that constitutional privacy protection covered possession, cultivation and use of certain substances. Turned out nobody was real clear on what that meant or what denoted personal supply. To some it was a bag, others maybe it was a trunk load. Left a gray area, so I worked a way they could compress it, truck it out of the valley on logging roads, getting it down here by float plane, land them in the canal."

"You got a real eye for importing and exporting."

"Guess I do at that, but nowadays, it's just the ivory, just this side of legal."

"Just ivory?" Denny saying, trying to look convinced.

"That's what I'm talking about."

Sipping, the coffee long gone cold, Denny thinking this guy sure could talk, saying, "Still, it's gonna be a hundred upfront."

... *eighteen*

Tapping on the door, Lee Trane stepped back on the concrete porch and straightened the tie. Smiled through the screen door when the door opened, asking, "Mrs. Perkins?"

"Yes." Margaret Perkins sized him up — a man in his middle years, wiry with deep lines either side of his mouth, hair combed back and dark eyes. Lee knew he didn't have cop size or looks, saw her hesitate before unlocking the screen.

"I'm Edward Rush, insurance adjuster. Got a couple follow-up questions on your case," he said. Told her to call him Eddy, making the lines around his mouth deepen as he smiled.

"You with Mutual of Omaha?"

"The good-hands people, ma'am. They contract me from time to time, report on some cases." Lee holding out the business card between two fingers, the ones he had printed up at the Jiffy Print in Prince George, a storefront offering photocopies and instant printing. The man working the counter told Lee he could have the box of cards ready by end of day, any single color he wanted. Took an extra ten to get them done in an hour, blue and black ink. Lee telling the guy not to worry about the ink drying, thinking he'd only need one or two. Came back after the two-piece special at the Chicken Hut and picked up his cards, fanned them out on the car seat and dash, letting them dry on the drive to Smithers.

Got Margaret Perkins' name and address from the police report, his RCMP connection back in Vancouver.

Margaret Perkins looked at his name on the card, Lee telling her he was investigating a rash of thefts from here to Prince George, same m.o., the company suspecting it was the same couple working northern towns. Preying on the innocent. The police with only so much time to investigate car thefts, the insurance company wanting to delve a little deeper.

"There a chance of getting it back, my car? We just bought it six months ago."

"Well, we're always hopeful, Mrs. Perkins, but, of course, I can't make promises, other than I'll do my best, with your help, of course."

"Sure, anything I can do." Margaret Perkins unlatched the screen and led Eddy Rush to the front room. He watched her glance at the nice Ford with the whitewalls parked in the drive, taking it as a sign of his success rate.

Following her along the plastic runner over the shag carpet to the living room of matching armchairs and sofa around a glass coffee table, Lee pulled up the knees of his slacks and took a seat, looking at the line of photos on the mantle, the same girl at different ages in most of them. Commenting the girl was her spitting image, very pretty. Margaret lit up at that, said the girl's name was Cathy, and offered him coffee or tea. Told him she had a tin of Peek Freans.

Thanking her anyway, he got to it, saying, "I know the police asked about the two you saw, but if you don't mind

I've got a few of my own questions, anything you can give me. . ."

"Well, like I told Jeff and Don, the officers this morning . . . Fellow I was talking to was maybe mid-twenties, brownish hair, long, the way they wear it, you know? Don't think he shaved, not in a day or so. Denim jacket, casual, ordinary, no offense to him, but you know the type?"

Lee pictured Denny Barrenko without the cap and jacket. Saying, "How tall — about my height?"

"Maybe about six feet, my husband's size, without the . . ." Tapping her stomach, rolling her eyes.

"Bet you're a good cook, then." Lee smiled.

"So, it's my fault," Margaret smiled back, her cheeks blushing. Saying, "Pretty sure about the brown eyes, had a kind look, I remember that. That's what surprised me, that he could do something like that. Even offered them coffee while they waited. Said they knew the neighbors."

"Till he stole your car."

"Still can't believe it." Folding her arms in front of her chest. "Just brought the groceries in, you know." Her eyes starting to water.

He reached the tissue box under the lamp, passing it to her, saying he understood how she must feel.

"Thanks." Margaret tugged a couple of tissues and dabbed at her eyes. "Pot roast was still in the trunk. Had to order out."

"Sorry to hear it."

"Imagine, coming out and your car's gone."

"Can only imagine." Shaking his head.

"Could have struck me down. Just stood there looking at the empty spot, my mouth hanging open."

Lee nodded, wanting to move this along.

"I mean, who does such a thing?" Wiping her eyes again, she smiled. "Sorry, Mr. Rush."

"It's Eddy, and no need to be." He looked out the window. "How about the one by the road?"

"Didn't really get much of a look ... oh, where are my manners, got a nice tin of the Peek Freans. Didn't get left in the trunk."

"Oh, I'm fine, really, thank you, Margaret." The woman forgetting she'd already offered the cookies. Lee prompting her, "The other one ..."

"The other one, *hmm*, well, let's see. On the short side maybe. Had on one of those suede jackets, the kind with the fringes, think it was big on him. Maybe belonged to the other one. *Hmm*, and a ball cap, blue with a logo, remember because he had it pulled low like it was too big, too. And they were holding bags. First, I thought they were selling something door-to-door, you know?"

"What kind of bags?"

Margaret Perkins thought a moment. "Like luggage, I think. The one who came up asked about the Erskins, Fred and Maddy." She pointed to her neighbors' place. "Said they just came on the train, come for a visit. Remember commenting on the ropes around the luggage, like it had been damaged. Told Jeff and Don the same thing, no idea who they were. Not from around here, I'm sure of that."

Lee Trane made a note on his pad, getting up, then thanked her, told her not to worry about the claim, Mutual of Omaha was good for it. Then he stopped like he remembered something. "The one by the road, any chance it was a woman, in a man's jacket and ball cap?"

Margaret Perkins thought about it, raised her eyes like she considered it, said she guessed it was possible. Lee offered his hand, thanked her for her time, left Margaret standing on the stoop as he got in the T-Bird and drove off.

It was getting late in the day, Lee thinking of looking for a motel in town, call Lonzo and tell him what he found out. Then make another call to his guy at 312 Main, see if the missing Cortina turned up on any cop sheet.

. . . nineteen

"You try lying on this." Denny got up and arched his back, frowning at the chair, worse than Mose's cot. "Like sleeping through a game of Twister."

"You ever do it?"

"What, Twister?"

"Yeah, used to play, even did it naked once."

"Guess you want me thinking about that, huh? You with one foot on the red dot, hand on the blue, your tush in the air."

"It's a free country." She smiled at him.

He looked out at the water dripping off a few icicles along the eaves, shaking off thoughts of her bent like that on a Twister mat. The evening sky streaked pink. Nearly out of cash, he put his mind on the lake, no idea how he'd get to it, hardly any cars around here to steal. And Mose was talking like they were partners.

"Are you?"

"What?"

"Thinking about it?"

"About the lake?"

"About Twister."

"Thinking we got enough cash for two more nights in this place. So, I say we take turns on the bed, that being fair."

"Mistook you for a gent, you know, the kind that would curl up on the chair and not make such a fuss."

"What happened to women's lib? Tossing your bra in a bin and setting fire to it. Beating the shit out of Miss America."

She propped on an elbow, grinning, the handbag on the bed next to her. "Was a former runner-up, a total bitch who had it coming."

"You like having things your way."

"Always pictured you guys from California for cool, ahead of the curve, you know."

"Sorry to disappoint. But how about we share it, do a head-to-foot thing if you want?" Showing what he meant with his hands.

"Now you're being weird."

"What's weird? You go one way, me the other."

"And wake up with your foot in my mouth." Bobbi shook her head, still grinning. "How about we spoon?"

He hesitated like he had to consider it, then said, "That could work." Feeling a drum solo going in his chest.

"But first you're buying me dinner."

Looking at this woman who wouldn't share her Twix, saying, "Guess I could eat." Denny with hardly any money left, hoping Kate would extend them some credit, settle with her when Mose paid him the hundred.

•

A couple of hot-plate specials at Klondike Kate's. Sitting under the twelve-point buck, they both faced the stage. The Repeat Offenders with Minnie Winks getting set to kick it off. The warmth off the fireplace felt nice, a couple of split logs burning. The roast beef came sliced thin, a thick gravy, baked potatoes, the skin crisp, lots of butter and sour cream, cobs of corn with the grill marks, and soft rolls right from the oven. Kate dished up ample portions for the freighter crews who usually came in with big appetites and loud talk. Big tippers. The same went for the miners coming from the Grandluck, just as they did back when the brothel hotel offered more than a good night's sleep and clean towels.

A pat of butter softened and ran between the kernels, Denny mopping gravy with a roll. Looking over at her plate. "Figured you'd go for rare."

"You mean like I'd eat it raw?" Licking butter from her thumb.

"Got this image of you beating up Miss America. Can't get it from my mind."

"Past runner-up, a total wash-up who ran her mouth and telegraphed her punches."

"Man, I'd pay to see something like that."

"A catfight, girls pulling hair and ripping at clothes?" Bobbi thinking her own top could use a soak in the sink, wring it out and hang it on the shower rod down the hall. Could use some Secret too, wondering if the trading post sold antiperspirant and toiletries. Sticking the fork in her roast beef, she looked up at Denny looking at her. Saying, "You're thinking about it, huh? Me, with my clothes ripped off."

"Was thinking about the twins." Slicing into his baked potato, dropping on another pat of butter, then reaching the salt. Knowing he was blushing.

"Mine, my twins?" Bobbi pushed out her chest.

"You know what I mean."

"Wondering if I'm wearing one, a titty mitt." Bobbi playing with him, loved seeing his face go red.

"Told me you burned it." Fluffing potato with his fork, remembering seeing her getting dressed back at Lonzo's, down to her bra and panties. Saying, "'Sides, I got my mind on bigger things."

"Bigger? Like a D-cup." She was laughing at his darkening face, people turning to look.

"And who calls it that, a titty mitt?" Denny leaning in, talking low, telling her to remember what he said, about drawing attention.

"How about slingshot or foam dome. You ever call it that?" Bobbi settling down, realized people were looking over. Watching as Minnie Winks stepped into the glow of the stage light, taking the mic from its stand, saying who they were, the drummer getting on the stage, sitting on his stool behind the kit, two guys in cowboy hats strapping on Fenders, adjusting knobs on the amps.

The door opened and cold air rushed in. Denny glanced over at Henry Kendall, the Doob, swiped his boots on the mat, a thermos in his hand. Tugging off his cap, this one with the earflaps, the Mountie looked around the place, nodding hey to Minnie and the band, meeting Denny's eyes and giving him a wink. Going to the pass window, saying something to Kate doubling as cook and waitress on the night.

•

Henry came in for his customary shift coffee. Stepping over to Denny's table while he waited.

"Any moose tonight, sheriff?" Denny said.

The smile was good-natured, Henry nodded to Bobbi, remembering her from last night, with the tour group, the kind with looks hard to forget. A fringed jacket on the back of her chair, like the one Margaret Perkins described to the officers over in Smithers. Only trouble, Margaret Perkins swore it was two men. Hard to think of Bobbi Ricci as a man, a pretty face and that Linda Ronstadt hair. But put on the suede coat and a ball cap, tie back the shag and stand her a hundred feet down the driveway, and maybe . . .

No chance of getting either of them ordered into a lineup, but Henry was thinking he could snap a couple of Polaroids, send them to the Smithers detachment. Get Margaret Perkins to take a look. Henry asking, "You two meet here, huh?"

Smiling, she said, "Can't stand eating alone. And this one offers to join me. Even think he's going to pay." Bobbi smiled at Denny, then looked back to Henry. "No harm in it, I hope, Officer." Big innocent eyes.

"Not if he behaves himself," Henry said, playing along.

"Well, did start off by talking about burning bras and cup sizes. That a normal thing up here?"

"Actually, around here we call that a felony."

"Well, he looks harmless enough . . ." Leaning close to Henry, she whispered loud enough for Denny to hear, "But maybe kinda dumb."

"And doing it in plain sight." Henry smiled. "You sticking around then, Miss . . ."

"Bobbi. Bobbi Ricci." Setting down her fork, offering her hand like she expected him to kiss the top of it.

Henry gave it a light shake.

"Thought I'd stick around a few days, happy to get off that bus. Take in some of your icy sights." Explained how the crowd on the tour bus had become tiresome. Bobbi hoping to kick back and stretch out. Showing a leg from under the table, flexing the Oxford. Saying, "Denny here promised to show me some sights."

"Guy who's never been here before," Henry said.

"It's what gives it the kick, no?" she said.

"Show her the glacier, the northern lights, maybe some bears pawing salmon," Denny offered.

"Stuff from a brochure," Henry said.

"Bears, huh?" Bobbi said.

"Got them coming right into town, along with the moose, that right, Sheriff?" Denny said.

"Nothing to worry about, miss. We Mounties will keep you safe." Looking from one to the other. "Both of you."

"And we thank you for it, Sheriff," she said.

Henry went back to the pass window, Kate filling his thermos.

●

Bobbi watched Minnie Winks count down, kicking off the set with "Your Cheating Heart." Doing Patsy Cline proud, an expressive, powerful voice, leading the Repeat Offenders through some Donna Fargo and Tanya Tucker. A righteous version of Glen Campbell's "Honey Come Back."

End of the set, Kate came around, clearing dishes and asking, "Got room for some cheesecake?"

Denny quick to go for a slice, putting it on his tab.

Kate looking at Bobbi. "How about you, hon?"

"I'll just nibble on his." When Kate left, Bobbi said, "Think he knows something, the sheriff?"

"Maybe, but thinking's not knowing."

Kate came back and set down the cheesecake, a couple of raspberries on the side, asking if he wanted cream on top.

"Oh, sure he does," Bobbi said, waiting till Kate came and blasted the Reddi-Wip can.

Kate asking if Bobbi was sure about having her own slice.

"I'm always sure." Smiling and watching Kate go, Bobbi scooped some cream, then sank in her fork, getting a good scoop of cheesecake.

"Got some there," Denny said, pointing to the corner of her mouth.

Licking at it, she said, "That better?"

. . . twenty

CAUTION
WILDLIFE CORRIDOR

Silhouettes of bear, cougar and moose. The sign had Denny glancing past his shoulder, walking the gravel road, spruce boughs swaying with the breeze. The road to Killik was desolate and ran in the opposite direction of the Grandluck Mine, its miners coming along it every blue moon, going into Ripley for supplies, catching the potluck at Klondike Kate's. Nobody else using it much.

A hundred bucks to walk from Ripley to Killik, drive a van back loaded with jade and tusk and bone. Denny betting despite what Mose said, the Doob and his female deputy kept an eye on any vehicles coming from the Alaska side. Mose telling him the border crossing had been unmanned since '63, making it sound easy.

"Biggest thing, you got to keep an eye out for the odd grizz." Mose told him the tourists liked to get shots of the big bears in the rapids, pawing for fish. "Stick to the road, and you'll be fine. And word to the wise, stay the hell out of Killik."

"How come?"

"One thing, folks there go strapped."

"Like armed?"

"Been known to fire warning shots, mostly when griz-zlies come too close, fur smelling like wet goat. Couple times tourists've been shot at too, not slowing for the local kids playing in the street."

"They shoot at tourists? Warning shots, huh?"

"The speed limit's 'Don't stir no dust,' it's marked clear enough."

"Killik, huh?"

"Inuit word, means lightning or something. You go to the dock, get the van and drive back, all you got to do. You'll be fine."

"Take it over twenty, and maybe I get a blast through the windshield, huh?"

"Killik folk are salt of the earth, generally speaking. Meet up with 'em when they come for their mail."

"They come to Canada for their mail?"

"Yeah, the general store, how we do things. Sometimes they come for the bingo, too." Mose clapped Denny on the shoulder, saying some came to bet on the car going through the ice, then told him about last summer's pig roast, two hundred pounds of pork on a spit, middle of Killik's main drag, used a pothole as the pit. Canadians bringing the coleslaw, Kate making enough baked Alaska to go around. Canadians and Americans, and all their kids and dogs. Everybody getting along.

"Nice folks so long as you don't speed, huh?"

"Yeah, watch the limit, don't drink the snakebite and don't talk about taxes. And if you do chance going, do it on your own time."

•

The Killik Road wound south, passing a bulldozed parking lot. The lookout Mose had talked about was built of beams above the creek, its water below rippling into a pool. Signs nailed to trees warning of bear. Denny guessing they'd been put up to impress the tourists. Not seeing any bear, hoping it was too early in the season. The road twisted, the whistle of the wind, wagging the ghost moss hanging down. The scraping of his shoes on the gravel kept him company. After a mile he came in sight of the border station, Army Engineer Storehouse No. 5, a small stone building, a plaque claimed it was Alaska's first stonework building. A desk and chair through the narrow window, a faded *New York Times* on the desk, its headline about the slaying of an unarmed Vietnamese farmer, a tin cup like a paper weight on top. The station not much bigger than those ice huts out on Meridien. Denny bumping his hip on the swing gate of rust hanging open, a lock and chain wrapping its post. Passing the international boundary, unmanned for years.

Back in the U.S., he walked until he was in sight of the Tootega Canal, its dock pilings sticking up like broken teeth, the low tide laying bare the shining mud flats, mussels and algae clinging on the stumps and logs, a floating shed stranded and leaning in the muck. Mose had told him the waterway had been named for the ghost of an Eskimo woman who walked it end to end, the stuff of legends. The canal that never iced up, a log jam and a rusting freighter being loaded with ore, copper or maybe lumber.

Mose had gone on, how back in its heyday, miners struck a vein nine hundred feet down in No. 4 Tunnel. Killik and Ripley both bonanza towns back in the '20s. Tales of miners trading punches with the ships' crews, busting up and burning down both towns. A guaranteed dust-up every Friday and Saturday night, church service Sunday mornings. The watering hole on the Killik side catching fire in '22, '24 and again in '25, and finally the whole town burned the following year. Ripley going to the ground in '28, revived in the '30s. Then the hopes of the miners petered out in the early '50s. Bust following boom, then followed by more bust. Killik just a shadow of what it once was, down to a hundred voters, hardly rated a spot on the map. Its clocks running an hour behind the ones in Ripley.

The sporting girls that once resided there had packed up and left along with the miners, only one sticking around, getting hitched to the brothel owner on the Canadian side, back before Nils Skerritt travelled from the east, bought the place and brought along his yellow paint and dreams of making a nest for his own wife and kids.

A dim past with a dull future. Mose talked of some annual motorcycle run proposed by town council, a gang of throttle jockeys looking for a place to ride into town and party. Town council thinking it could spark the economy. Mose expecting the kind of sparks that could leave both towns in smoke and rubble once more. Bikers on the drink and the pistol-packers of Killik, all under the aurora borealis, with only the Doob and one female constable to step in the way of it ending badly. One thing was sure, Mose liked to talk.

Denny's thoughts shifted to diving for his money and getting out of there. Not sure how things would go with Bobbi, maybe they'd be doing more than spooning, maybe not. After leaving Kate's, he thought there might be more coming, but she got into bed fully dressed and was soon asleep. Denny curling up behind her, lying awake, hearing her even breathing.

Bobbi handing him Lonzo's Beretta before he set out that morning. Told him not to shoot himself in the foot. Denny feeling the weight of it in the pocket of Mose's parka. It did make him feel better.

The breeze pushed the boughs some more, and Denny checked over his shoulder — too late — setting a foot in what Mose would call scat. A squish of bear shit up to his laces, dropped from a thousand-pound grizzly. Horrible and rotting. Made a sucking sound when he pulled up his shoe. He scraped his sole like a mad man, wiping the side on a patch of roadside grass, spotting a bear track in the mud, with claws as long as his fingers. So much for the shaggy fuckers hibernating.

He quickened his pace, kept his hand on the Beretta in the coat pocket, the damn thing feeling small now. Wondered if the fear of being on the Killik Road was like being on patrol with the grunts moving on Da Nang, place his brother had been, walking single file through jungles, pants muddy and feet wet, every step holding the prospect of a VC can or a pissed-off viper. Worse than stepping in bear scat.

When Denny stepped in the hotel office, paying Nils Skerritt for the two nights, cash in advance, he'd watched the small TV at the end of the counter, a repeat of Cronkite reporting the evening news, giving an account how the VCs were training bees to attack U.S. troops, giant ones associating G.I. green with nectar. The VC hiding in their camo, charcoal and grease, tying bangers to the hives set above jungle trails, lighting wicks when a Yankee patrol came by, sending them swatting and running, easy targets for an ambush. Old Ironpants declaring the commies were running training camps for these giant bees, Uncle Sam developing chemicals, redirecting the bees to counter-attack. The most trusted man in America telling it straight, saying goodnight and giving the nation hope.

Denny had said to Nils at the hotel desk, "You believe that, about killer bees?"

"Americans, what you expect?" A little late, but Nils caught the red, white and blue in Denny's eye. Saying he knew lots of the Americans over in Killik, some of them were fine folk.

Thinking about his brother, Dale, again on that road, with the First Calvary moving on Da Nang. His ghost eyes in the last photo he sent home, the letter telling about going in-country on a sixty-day tour, how he couldn't see ten feet most of the time, scouting for bunkers under elephant grass, swinging a machete to clear it. Wading hip-deep with the M-60 on his shoulders. Heat, sweat and flies loaded with malaria, goddamned leeches everywhere there was water. Dale writing there was nothing like a dry camp, some place he could dry his socks, write his letters home.

The next letter told of Cobra gunships, the *whop-whop* sound they made, laying the grass flat, their star shells lighting up the bush. Dale part of a crew sandbagging a fire-base, spanning concertina wire around the quad-50 dusters. Only time he slept easy was under those gun barrels. Sharing his thoughts on getting back to base, joking about holding some smiling Coca-Cola girl in his arms. Denny guessing his brother just wanted to come home. Praying for him every night, knowing there wouldn't be any hero's welcome, soldiers being branded baby killers, taking public blame for what the officers called duty. Didn't matter, when Dale did come home, the family flew the stars in the window, Mom and Dad crying about it at first, then not talking about it, both with the same ghost eyes. The patrol had taken his tags, eyeglasses and helmet with the ace of spades in the band, sent it all home.

Had to get out of the house after that, Denny going to the rallies, letting Uncle Sam know what he could do with his stars and stripes. Not sure why he told Bobbi about the protests.

Over dinner, Bobbi had wanted to know if it did any good, all that burning draft cards? Told her he felt good about it, how he needed to make a stand. Not wanting her to feel sorry for him, he changed the subject, saying, "So, this spooning. You thinking back to back or head to foot?"

"Wasn't thinking about it at all. But how about we just do it normal. Like I said, I don't want your foot in my face."

They smoked another joint, Bobbi finishing it after he started coughing again, the two of them going back to the room, Bobbi going to sleep on that sway-back bed, with her back to him. Denny remembered she said she used Prell, but he couldn't smell it in her hair now. Lying behind her, hearing her breathing. Hardly slept at all.

•

The wind whistled along the road, the wall of a mountain showing its veins of white, the low cloud rolling and catching on its peak. Walking the center of the road, with just that sound of swaying boughs and his soles scraping the gravel. Everything green and wet, the promise of spring coming. Seeing past the trees, Denny looked along the pier, the float-plane tied to the end of it. A flurry along the treeline had him jumping — thinking bear — his hand on the Beretta.

Rodent eyes looked from under some low branches. Guessing that's what a hoary marmot looked like, its head poking up, sniffing the air. Walking on, he hummed "Fortunate Son," looking out at a couple of log jams and a freighter being loaded with ore. A van sat parked across from the pier, gray with its windows mirror-tinted. A beater farther up the road with "RENT ME" painted down the side. Then he saw the guy in the floatplane, legs hanging from the plane, the guy looking his way.

•

Cowboy boots out on the pontoon of the de Havilland Beaver, Caleb Hawkes had a chevron mustache, aviator shades, a headband holding back the hair, a Haida necklace under a denim jacket. A single-prop Beaver, white with a blue stripe running nose to tail. "Holy Smoke" painted on the fuselage above the stripe.

Blowing cold coming along the open water didn't seem to bother him, Caleb saying, "You're the new guy, huh?"

"That what they say?"

"You're late." Caleb pointed to the Beretta in his hand. "Mose give you that?"

Dropping it in his pocket, Denny said he forgot he was holding it, said he just saw a bear, about a hundred yards back, then extending the hand. "I'm Denny, by the way."

Slow to shake the hand, Caleb said, "We do it again, this dance, it's eight sharp. Keep me waiting, and I lift off, not taking risks 'cause you can't be on time. You got that, my man? Oh, and on the Killik side, we run on U.S. time, an hour different than Ripley. Saying it in case you ain't heard."

Denny nodded, said, "You want to hear sorry?"

"Might be nice, 'cause even up here, we all got shit to do." Caleb grinned like he was letting it go, reaching behind the seat, saying, "Figured old Silvertip maybe got hold of you."

"That another cop?"

"Bear, the size of a Buick, known to wander the road, maybe the one you spotted. Mose didn't tell you, huh?"

"Guess it wasn't a selling point."

"Got a taste for tourist, partial to draft dodgers."

"Guess Mose has been talking, huh?"

Caleb grinned.

"Well, you keep doing it, talking like that, might want to take off the shades," Denny grinned back.

Pushing a backpack out of the way, Caleb flipped a cooler lid behind the seat, fishing out a dripping Labatt's, popped the cap on his belt buckle, beer fizzing on his jeans. Looking along the government tie-up, he held out the bottle, a peace offering. "Well, here, let me show you my good intention. One thing you don't want is me taking off the shades." Looking over the top of them, showing his bloodshot eyes, serious at first, then making a joke out of it.

"Eight in the a.m." Denny taking the bottle. "Guess I can make it."

"Heard about the getaway on the ice, and how you stepped up to the Doob." Caleb reached for another bottle and popped its cap.

"Man's just doing his job."

"Whatever Mose told you, take the Doob for real. Man keeps a sharp eye, knows what's going on in his town." Wedging the bottle between his thighs, Caleb reached in his top pocket, straightened a joint and fished for a lighter. Getting it lit, he took a pull and held it out, saying through the exhale of smoke, "Here you go, a little taste of Alaskan Thunderfuck, good as it gets."

Denny glanced to the freighter, its waterline high and red, its crew up on its deck. Taking a pull on the joint, saying, "Mose said something about the Doob's dope raid, the one time the man botched it up."

"Yeah, a long time back. But Mose and his company's sure got some history with the Doob. But wasn't nothing to do with dope raid, really. Was a woman."

"That right?"

"Yeah, Kate, the one runs the cafe."

"Woman scrambles a mean egg." Denny trying to picture either man with her.

"Yeah, that's the one." Sipping beer, Caleb changed gears, and went on, "So, he's got you making runs — you not sure what you're into. Bet he's talking about picking mushrooms, partnering to dive down to your car, get what he thinks you got in the trunk."

"Word spreads, huh?" Taking a toke, Denny suppressed a cough, waited for the fog to start in his head. Said he had a bag of pretty good weed back at the hotel, his girl holding onto it. Felt funny calling her that, after one night of spooning, but it felt kind of good at the same time.

"Happens in a small town. Everybody knowing you're hanging around till you get what's in the trunk of the stolen car, one that sank, one that everybody at the bingo hall's been betting on. Shit, man, you're a local celebrity, a regular Monty Hall. You brought the game show to town." Caleb took the joint back, toked and chased it with a mouthful of beer.

"Thunderfuck, you name it?" Denny said, draining the bottle — that numbness moving up his legs, starting to understand how the strain got its name, guessing Rubin Stevens down in Whistler would give it a thumb's up — focusing on the backpack Caleb had on the passenger floor,

"That what I'm taking back, Mose hinting it was bone or stone for carving?"

"Man says all kind of things." Grinning, Caleb nodded to the van at the foot of the pier. "Don't know what he told you, but I loaded a bunch of bags while you kept me waiting." Pinching the roach, he sucked on it, then held it out, looking at the van at the end of the pier, then at the joint, passing it, saying, "Dudes in Matanushka Valley claim it's on account of the climate, soil conditions making the shit what it is. Everybody wanting a taste. Got no idea who came up with the name. Maybe Mose himself." He reached behind his other ear, took another rolled one and handed it to Denny, saying, "You make it back, you bring this to your lady. Let her try my joint." Winking at him.

Not sure if he liked this guy or not, Denny tipped up his beer, feeling the spreading numbness going to his head. "That what you do, fly in the shit for Mose?"

"Just an importin'-exportin' man. Fly it here, fly it there. Take to the air, anybody with the cash upfront."

"Driving a van-load of shit over the border, I don't know, man ..."

"Man's paying you a hundred bucks, right?"

Denny nodded. No secrets up here.

"You don't do it, he'll get somebody else. But you say you're gonna do it, and then you do it. Not a good one to piss off, our boy Mose."

"Gonna banish me from picking mushrooms?"

Reaching another Labatt from the cooler, Caleb held it by its stubby neck. "Man takes you to a burn area, where the black stumps smell like ash, tells you how it's the best soil for it." Snagging one for himself, using his church key on the belt buckle, popping both. "Pick your way through the ash, and end up looking like a coal miner, back sore as hell, but you stay on the man's good side, and you stay out of Doob's jail. Least till you work things out."

Denny looked at him, taking that in.

"Well, it's a choice. Anyway, I got to fly the sky, my man, got more folks waiting," Caleb patted his pockets for the van keys, holding them out.

Denny hesitated.

"Like I said, you don't do it, man'll get somebody else. But, you walk back, instead of driving the van, just remember about old Silvertip."

Denny tapped the Beretta in his pocket, taking the jingling keys.

"Let's have a look." Caleb held out his hand, looking at his pocket, Denny getting his meaning, taking the pistol out, passing it to him.

"Just gonna piss a bear off with this." Handing it back, Caleb reached for a map pocket, pulled a long-barreled .44 Magnum, a Ruger with the wood grips. "Show him you mean business."

"I'm good." Denny hefted it and passed it back.

Putting it back in the map pocket, Caleb told him to suit himself and climbed across the seat, asking him to cast the line and shove the pontoon. Settling behind the controls, he checked the primer knob was unlocked, worked the wobble pump, getting fuel in the system, working the primer knob, getting the pressure right. Checking the oil cap, clicking the master switch, pushing the mixture forward, hitting the start and mags, the engine kicking and the prop spinning. Eyeing the oil pressure gauge, oil and cylinder head temperature gauges. Letting her warm up, calling, "Park it out back of Mose's and leave the keys in it."

Denny watched him work the controls, the engine revving louder. Thunderfuck clouding up his mind, the weed as good as anything Rubin Stevens grew. Walking down the dock to the van at the end, he glanced at the crew busy on the freighter, leaving Caleb to warm his engine.

... twenty-one

"Said his name, Moses, right out of the Bible. Old kook with white hair knocks on the door and says to let you know he's ready," Bobbi said.

"Mose, not Moses."

"How he's diving to get our money. Says to me, 'Didn't he tell you?' Imagine, you not telling me you agreed. And you and me supposed to be partners, two of us spooning. Imagine, me not shooting you and leaving you bleeding on Lonzo's rug."

"Relax. I didn't agree to shit yet." Denny went to the window, sipping the glass of water he got from the bathroom down the hall, water looking cloudy.

"Then how about you tell me all of it." Bobbi sat on the bed and crossed her arms.

"Mose figures he can dive down for it, only way we'll get it back."

"Meaning we're going from half to a three-way split." Bobbi looking unhappy.

"Man used to dive in his navy days. Says it'd be tricky doing it in the cold."

"Sure he'd say that, and you believe it." Bobbi got a picture of Denny in snorkel and fins, a dumb mask on his face. "Second thought, I bet you'd drown in a kiddie pool."

Not far off. Denny hadn't told her, along with the asthma, he couldn't swim. "You got a better idea, I'm right here."

"So, we let Mose make the dive, or I end up standing out front, picking up johns, this one-time brothel, while you go pick mushrooms, talking about someday diving for it. That it?"

Denny thinking it could be worse than that. Saying, "We got Lonzo looking, and a lawman knowing we stole the car, digging for proof." Denny glanced out again, the same moment saw the Doob walk into Kate's, his thermos in his hand.

"So, what stops Moses from doing it on his own, keeping it all for himself?"

"Water's too cold right now. Anybody going down won't be coming back up."

"Let me guess, he told you that?"

"Okay, you don't trust him."

"This guy I hardly met."

"So, we tell him he's in. It warms up, say in a couple of weeks, and I make the dive, beat him to it." What Denny needed was another car, drive to the lake and check around on his own, then there was the problem of getting his hands on some diving gear. Remembering the beater car he passed, parked on the outskirts of Killik. "RENT ME" painted in house paint down its side, along with a phone number. Finishing his water, he set the glass on the window ledge.

"Sign at Kate's says they got an advisory, supposed to boil water before you drink it." She smiled, sweet.

Denny looking at his empty glass.

... *twenty-two*

"The man came by looking for you." Mose leaned on the desk in the gallery, kept his voice low. Glass cases of carvings of bone and jade and ivory, the carved bear in the window, paintings on the wall. Double doors to the backroom closed.

"What man?" Denny felt the fear kick up, thinking it was Lonzo's guy, Lee Trane. Taking the chair across from the desk, not sure about setting his beer down on the polished surface, waiting until Mose did.

"The Doob. Had one of those cameras with him, makes prints on the spot. Ask me, he's gonna snap your good side and send it to the Smithers detachment, get the housewife to make the ID."

"Can't just do that, got to have probable cause, right? Got to charge me with something first."

"Not fussy on rights up here. Doob's got a bug up his ass on account his cruiser got jacked. Doesn't matter I vouched for you. The way a cop's mind works." Mose drank from his glass, looked like he enjoyed watching Denny squirm. "He gets his snapshot ..."

Denny looked at him. "But you got an idea, huh?

"Well, with the morels poking up, can get you in the back woods, start you picking, keep you out of sight. Works out because you need money anyhow. And can get you making another run, see our pal Caleb."

"Can use another hundred."

"Fifty this time."

"I cross the border, risk running into the Doob and this bear Caleb was talking about. For that, it's a hundred."

"Silvertip, huh?" Mose leaned back and grinned. "That man and his stories. His way of having fun. But hey, you worried about wildlife, you keep your piece handy."

"Beretta's just gonna piss him off, what he told me."

Pulling the Colt from his bottom drawer, Mose checked the safety, set it on the desk, let Denny have a look. "My just-in-case piece."

Everybody up here walking around armed, even the Canadians. Denny hefted it, twice the weight of the Beretta.

Mose saying, "Seven rounds, single-action, magazine-fed and chambered for .45s. Standard-issue for the armed forces back in the day. But as far as bear up here, you just got to say *hah!*"

"*Hah?*"

"Yeah, loud like that. *Hah!* Tlingit woman taught me that. That or clap a couple of stones together. Works on moose, too. Except in rutting season, bull comes tearing through the bush with them antlers down — worse than any bear, and not much you can do, even with this."

Denny didn't think knocking stones would work on Lonzo's people, either. He set the piece back down.

"Anyway, you keep out of sight and get your mind on the diving we got ahead."

"'We' — like your mind's made up, huh?"

"Told you, a guy like you won't make it halfway down. Needs somebody who's done it."

"And that's you?" Denny looking at this man, gray streaks saying he had to be fifty easy, wondering if he could make it down, pop the trunk and make it back up with the twins in hand without popping a heart valve.

"I'm all you got. Willing to go down before the thaw."

"And taking a cut."

"I want half."

"There's three of us, I told you that."

"I risk my neck while you and the girl sit up top in a rowboat. For that it's half."

"Quarter-million just for getting wet." Denny catching the tattoo showing from Mose's sleeve, the anchor, a rope and the words. Mose turning up the arm, letting him see it.

"The *Northwestern*, where I learned diving."

"Yeah, already told me."

"That's right. Served on her till the Japs blew her to hell. Pulled them sailors out, just sitting down to their pork chops and peas. Nobody drowning on my watch."

"Said it was beached."

"Bombs blew it to hell, had the water coming in from all sides." Mose slapped down a hand next to the Colt, saying, "We row out, it's me going down, the only way you get what's in that trunk." Mose pulled the sleeve down over the tattoo.

No point saying more, Denny was back to thinking of the car with "RENT ME" painted on the door, parked outside of Killik. Next run to the docks, he'd dial the number and ask about it. Maybe find out from Caleb where he could get some dive gear.

. . . twenty-three

Denny tucked the Beretta in the pocket of Mose's coat, wool with the big buttons, the smell of mothballs. Looking at the fur cap with the earflaps like Doob the Mountie wore. "Likely get my head blown off, get mistaken for game." Denny handed it back. "But I'll take the gloves and boots." More clothes than any kid from California ever had on. Going through the closet in the storeroom, Mose letting him borrow what he needed.

Walking the Killik Road, passing the lookout with an eye out for bear above the rapids, double-stepped past, forgetting Mose's warning about not running from a bear. Well past the lookout, he slowed and caught his breath, settled himself by thinking about spooning with Bobbi, up against her that second night. Was she was thinking about it too, taking things to another level?

Passing the empty checkpoint, the same newspaper on the desk, he kept on, the canal coming into view, a crew working topside of a different cargo ship, different stacks and flag. The Beaver tied to the end of the Tootega pier.

•

Caleb watched Denny walk down the slick pier, careful of his step. Sitting in the cockpit, he made a show of checking his watch, saying, "Nearly got it right that time."

"Man cut my pay by half, lucky I showed at all." Top of sounding pissed, Denny looked like he'd seen a rough night.

"Need of money sure makes you do it anyway, huh?" Reaching behind his ear, the headband and hair hiding a joint, Caleb promised it would take the edge off.

"This the Thunderfuck?"

"Only kind we got." Handing Denny a beer.

Reaching in his own coat pocket, Denny took out a bent joint of his own, saying it was a Rubin Stevens, like it was high fashion, Calvin Klein or Ralph Lauren, calling it Whistler's finest.

Caleb sliding his joint back behind his ear, watching Denny light it and take a drag off it. Blowing out smoke, passing it, and saying, "So, how long you been doing the flying?"

"Since I got out." Taking a long haul.

"You mean like doing time?"

"I mean like the Marines." Caleb took a double hit.

"Infantry?"

"Dropped off the grunts who didn't dodge, no offense."

"Maybe I was 4-F."

"Yeah, maybe." Caleb saying it, but looking like he doubted it.

Letting it pass, Denny took a short drag and coughed it out.

Caleb saying, "Dropped our boys from Hueys and pulled them out."

"My brother was over there, one of those guys on patrol."

Something in Denny's voice told Caleb the answer, but he asked anyway, "He come home?"

Denny shook his head.

"Sorry to hear it." Like there was empathy in it.

Denny tried taking another toke, started coughing, handing it back. Chasing it with some suds. When he got his voice back, he said, "So, you fly charters and run some shit, it's how you get by, huh?"

"Yeah, that, and now and then I contract for this logging interest, fly in their people. Guys who wear suits and ties, dying to shoot something, or catch a fish they can stick up on the wall. Top of that, I volunteer on the scooper." Caleb took the joint back. "You know what that is, a scooper?"

"Got no idea."

"Twin-engine water bomber. A big Canso we call the Dump Duck, the way we douse wildfires up here." Explaining about the floating fuselage, how the crew used lakes as run-ways, taking off and coming down, skimming the surface, scooping 1,200 gallons into its belly. Four props lifting the Duck up, flying over the treetops and dropping the load on the fire zone, then going back for another scoop.

"This shit's not bad," Caleb said, meaning Rubin Stevens' pot, then going on about dropping lake water on a forest in flames, what it was like saving thousands of acres from going up in smoke. "Had a bad burn last fall, the far side of Otter," Caleb wagged a hand toward the mountain, the peak showing in the gray distance. "Forest service guys figure some camping asshole got it started, for all I know one of the charters I flew in." Caleb shrugged a shoulder, offering the joint, saying it's where Mose's mushrooms would be growing.

That creeping feeling starting in his feet, Denny shifted his legs and wriggled his toes. Waved off the joint.

"Some asshole tosses down a butt, not enough sense to step it out, you grasp that?" Caleb handed him another Molson, Denny saying he didn't remember finishing the first one.

Slapping a pocket for the church key, Caleb used his belt buckle, getting beer suds on his pants again. "Unlike my time in 'Nam, I got nobody putting me in crosshairs, trying to shoot my ass down."

"Long as you don't misjudge the distance between you and the treetops."

"Yeah, there's that." Caleb laughed. "But I tell you, I miss it, the action over there. And don't get me wrong, I feel for your loss, man. Real sorry for the guys I knew, anybody dying in that place. But something about it, like one minute you're in some camp, bored to death, and the next you're in it. And you feel you're going to die, but you feel so alive. Guess I don't expect you can get it, man."

Pinching the roach, Denny tried an easy puff, admitting he didn't, then asked, "The van all packed up?"

"I just got here ahead of you." Caleb pointing to the boxes stacked behind the Beaver's seats.

They walked the dozen boxes marked "Wild Alaskan Black Cod — guaranteed fresh" to the panel van. Denny guessed that Mose wasn't bringing in fish, paying him fifty bucks to drive it a few miles, town to town.

Caleb saying, "Could be tusks or jade in the boxes, maybe blow, maybe hard candy. Sometimes it's best you don't know."

•

When they finished loading the van, Denny went back along the pier and helped Caleb cast off, standing and watching him take to the sky, lifting off the canal. Not sure how the man did it being high.

Walking down the pier again, Denny got a feeling, like he was being watched. Likely just pot paranoia, then he thought he caught sight of bumper chrome past the tree boughs, along the Killik Road. Thinking that Mountie had his number, keeping an eye on him. And he got an image of Mose tipping the Doob, something to get Denny out of the picture, lock him up long enough for Mose to dive for the sunken money, have it all for himself. Delusions that could be the pot talking. But, at the bottom of the pier, he walked away from the van, heading the opposite way into Killik, thinking he'd find out about "RENT ME," and he was curious about this place where folks walked strapped and shot at passing motorists.

A boom town gone bust with the mountain looming over top of it. A couple of locals walked the muck street, weathered faces smiling at him. Nobody looking like they might take a pot shot at him. The road sign strung between a rock wall and the first rooftop, welcomed him to Alaska, Denny guessed he could spit the length of the main drag, maybe if his mouth wasn't so dry.

"RENT ME" sat parked alongside a rickety two-story today, moved from where it had been only a few days back. Denny took it as a good sign, meaning it was in running order. He stopped out front of a premise that looked to be on its last gasp, the only place he could see with its door open. The sun showed from behind some cloud, glinting off the rusting standing-seam roof, porch boards rotted out, no sign outside the place. Careful not to slip in the muck out front, water pooling from a detached downspout.

It had the look of a gift shop with the appeal of a dark attic; above the smell of funk and dank he caught the welcome hint of coffee. Thinking he could use a cup, and maybe a Snickers, he stepped in. The woman behind the counter was old, maybe she was Haida, black hair in braids and a weathered face. Looked surprised to see him, maybe she didn't see a lot of tourist trade this time of year.

"You got a pot on, or a pop cooler, something to drink?" His mouth was dry, throat scratchy from the weed, Denny reached in a pocket, pulling out a couple of bills, showing he could pay.

Reaching under the counter, the woman set down a shot glass, reached a bottle in a paper bag and poured two fingers. Sliding the glass across without a word.

Denny looked at it, then at the waiting woman, raised it and took a sniff. Didn't have a smell to it. The little woman looking at him, expecting him to drink it. What the hell. Downing half in a friendly gesture, he felt it drop, his upper tract feeling like the bombardment of Khe Sanh. Couldn't help his eyes watering.

"You don't spit it on the floor, I'll go fix you a fresh pot." Her face creased into a smile, her gum line hosting wide-spaced and bent teeth.

"Deal." All he could do was breathe the word, waiting a moment, then he downed the rest.

"Smooth, but with the right kick, ain't it so?"

"Yeah." His word a whisper. Blinking away the tears, hoping he wouldn't go blind, saying, "This stuff's safe, huh?"

"Use copper and silver solder, nothing with lead. Always pour off the first bit, and steer clear of the methanol. What you get is no smell, no color, then you do the spoon test, you know, light it on fire?"

Blinking. Denny understanding the fire part.

"It goes red, then you got lead. It goes yellow, well . . . then you'd be blind by now. Blue's what you go for. Meaning a good batch, like what we got here." Raising the bagged bottle and pouring into his glass, saying, "One more for the road."

"Gonna be hard to find the road." Thinking if he didn't go blind. He dashed the rest back, the after-hit not so bad this time, but still blowing a mouthful of air he could light on fire, thinking if he had any more he'd go in search of Silvertip, looking to do a little mano a mano, with or without the Beretta. Managed to find his voice, saying, "Now, I sure could use that coffee."

"A deal's a deal." She smiled, reaching a wood match from a pocket, striking it on her thumbnail and dropping it in his empty glass. Went up like a napalm *whoosh*. The old woman cackling, saying, "It's how you really know it's any good." The smile scrunched her eyes into slits. "Sure you don't want to go for three?" Holding up the bottle in the bag, ready to pour.

"Just the coffee, please." Thinking he had to get the van of salmon boxes over to Mose's place and collect his fifty bucks. Feeling he could die in a place like this, thinking who would notice? Watching the old woman go to a rough-cut table at the back, taking an empty pot off a two-burner and going behind a sea-shell curtain in back.

Left him looking at the shelves of hand-carved Yupik dolls. Some with bits of fur, leather and beads glued on, a plaque claimed they were crafted by locals. Denny wondering if Mose supplied the whalebone, tusk and jade. A stack of Hudson's Bay blankets on the lower shelf, striped and smelling musty. A bushel of beaded moccasins in various sizes and colors next to it. A totem a foot high with a carved eagle on top.

When she came back out with the pot, the old woman said she was Daisy, then, "How about a holster for your rig there?" Nodding at his coat pocket, the bump of the pistol.

"I mean you no harm, ma'am."

That got him another show of zigzag teeth, Daisy reaching and tipping the twin barrels resting under the countertop. Looked like a sawed-down Mossberg.

"Hope that's in case of bear?"

"And for folks returning merchandise."

Denny smiled back, saying, "Heard about this one bear, Silvertip, you hear of that one?"

"Guess you met Caleb Hawkes, then." Looking into his bloodshot eyes, grinning those teeth. "Man sure likes to spin his tales. And so you know, you do shoot a bear in town, you pay for removal. We got bylaws, son."

Denny remembering about the tourists speeding through town getting shot at, along the pot-holed muck road. Saying, "Good to have laws."

"Mostly we got common sense, knowing if we shoot at over a thousand pounds of bear, we're just gonna piss him off." Setting the coffee pot on the counter, she hobbled to a shelf by the window, reached past a carved seal, for a couple of fist-sized stones and clanked them together. "All you got to do. *Click-click*'em. Good on moose, too."

"Heard about doing it with stones. Really works, huh?"

"Beats shooting at them." She nodded at his pocket. "Had a moose over on Mina a while back, bucked the bumper right off Freddy Bean's Plymouth. Wouldn't've happened, he hadn't honked the ooga horn at it. Shoulda used the stones instead." She stepped to a display on the far side of the door, took a burlap holster hanging from a rack above some carved soapstone: a bird, a leaping fish, an Inuit raising a harpoon. Clapping dust from it, she handed it to him, said if he was going to walk around packing, he ought to do it like the locals. Said it was five bucks.

"A holster, huh?" Looked rotted and felt sticky, had a leather loop closing on a metal post, a hand-tooled belt.

Denny slung it on over the coat, took out the Beretta and slid it in, the burlap flap closing snug over it, the leather thong fitting over the pin.

"Fits good."

"This the only one you got?"

"How many you need?" Daisy looking down at his sneakers. "Keep you from shooting your toe off." Mentioned she had some mukluks, too, proper footwear for 'round here. Went and showed him a pair. Looked like half-moccasin, half loose-fitting boot, a patch of fur wrapped around it, with some beads on the toecap.

"I'm good for now. How about you take three bucks?" Meaning for the holster. Denny looked at the coffee pot, thinking she expected to haggle.

"Said five, sure I was plain about it." Daisy poured coffee in a tin mug and set it in front of him. "You want it city or country?" Caught his dumb look, saying, "Your coffee, how you want it?"

"You got sugar and milk?"

"City, then." She reached behind her, put down a couple of stained sugar packets and a jar of Coffee-Mate. Told him it was half a buck.

Adding sugar, Denny blew across the top and sipped. Surprised the coffee was pretty good. "What say to four?"

"Six."

"Price is going up."

"How it works. The more ticked I get, higher the price gets. Drinks on the house, like I said, on account you didn't spit up. A deal's a deal, and the price is the price."

No haggling then. Denny reached in a pocket, laying down a ten of Lonzo's money.

"Canadian, huh?" She frowned at the bill. Adding another splash from the bottle in a bag, topping up his tin.

"Money's on par."

"Somebody on the Canadian side tell you that?" Showing her teeth again, telling him he'd have to come back for his change. Daisy needed to take it to the bank, not sure about the exchange these days.

Denny thinking there was no place that looked like a bank in either town, maybe a dozen buildings in Killik. Guessing there'd be no change, and no sense arguing about it, he asked about the car he'd seen parked outside of town, "RENT ME" painted on the door.

Pointing toward the shack leaning against hers on the north side, she told him to take the outside flight of stairs and watch out for the third step, mentioned some rot. Told him to knock hard on the door of the flat under the tin roof. "Fella's name's Mickey Rocket."

Forgetting he had the holster outside his coat, Denny thanked her, said he'd be back for his change, then stepping past the puddle by the door, seeing his reflection ripple in the muck water.

·

Rapping on the door, Denny waited. Looked like he woke the guy up, barefoot and skinny in a housecoat. No doubt Mickey Rocket was nursing a hangover, his eyes wet and red, reeked of last night's disco drinks. Denny stepped back, a safe distance from the morning breath.

"Here asking about your car?"

"What?" Mickey rubbed his forehead, made a sound in his throat, leaned forward and spit off the landing.

"One with 'RENT ME' on the door. Interested if it runs."

"'Course it runs. Bit of peeled paint is all, but under the hood she's top notch." Mickey was coming alive to the prospect of renting it, scratching his head and going to find the keys, shoving his bare feet into ratty sneakers. Not bothering with a coat, leading the way down the stairs, saying, "Just did the plugs and filters." Negotiating the muck ground, he kicked a tire, showing it was good. "Don't let the looks fool you, friend." Mickey Rocket hooked his fingers into a claw and scratched at his scalp, asking Denny's name.

Denny gave it to him and followed him around the Corvair. Thinking he should have used an alias.

"Yeah, sure, lots of life in her, Denny." Mickey went around the hood, pulled the driver's door back, the metal complaining.

Smelled like rodents lived under the bench seat, Denny climbed in. Mickey handed him the key. Denny putting it in the ignition, shifted to neutral, surprised it fired right up, the Corvair's rear engine rattling out its exhaust note.

"Sounds, I don't know . . ." Denny hearing some knocking, breathing the banger's exhaust.

"Just runs a bit rich, is all. Guarantee she's set for the long haul though." Mickey waving the blue cloud away with his hand.

Denny pressed the brake, not getting much resistance, the tail lights reflecting in Daisy's side window, half of the four brake-light bulbs out. "Needs some lights, huh?"

Mickey shrugged. "A town this size, who's gonna rear-end you?"

Guessing Mickey didn't do a lot of business, no receipt book, a cash-deal-with-a-wet-handshake kind of place. Almost sorry he knocked on the guy's door, Denny asked, "How much for the week, providing it makes it?"

"Fifty even, taxes in," Mickey said without blinking.

"Talking about renting it, not buying it. And you got no taxes here."

"You heard my price."

"Mickey Rocket tries harder, puts you in the driver's seat, huh, and lifts your wallet at the same time. Ought to get a billboard?" Switching it off, Denny got out, made like he was leaving.

"You keep talking, maybe the price'll go up." Mickey not buying the act.

"Okay, throw in a full tank and I'll go forty. But she conks out on me — 'RENT ME' turns into 'FUCK ME' — and I'm coming for a refund." Denny put a hand on the butt of the Beretta.

"Nobody holding a gun to your head, friend — not like you're doing to me. And it's fifty, and get your own gas."

Frowning, Denny went to the trunk lid, fumbled around with the release and popped it. He pulled the dipstick, oil on the stick looked like tar. "Last time this got changed, when Nixon took office, huh?"

"I use heavy oil, additive makes it look that way, what we use up here."

"Good to know." Denny bent and wiped his hand on a sprout of last year's grass, then went around the four corners, toe-tapping the rubber. "This thing got a spare?"

"Already on it." Mickey pointed to the driver's front, no hubcap and one of the lug nuts missing. Told him about the eight-track he wired in, was right under the driver's seat. Called it a feature.

Denny reached his cash, held out twenty-five bucks. "Get the rest when it makes it to the end of the week."

Mickey grumbled about it, but took the money, turning up the stairs, looking cold without a jacket on.

Damn thing rode like a grinder, a shimmy in the front end, the clutch slipping between first to second. Waving as he passed Daisy's, hoping she'd remember his change next time he came, rolling down the main drag of Killik, the kid with the hockey stick pointing and laughing at him. The steering column shaking like it might come loose in his hands. Denny thinking he'd pull into the only station in Ripley, extortion price of thirty-five cents for regular. Stopping behind the panel van parked by the pier, he scanned around, then got out and popped the Corvair's hood, chanced going to the van, got out the other keys, loading the salmon boxes from the back of the van. Filling the trunk, the rest having to go across the back seat of Rent Me. If the Mounties were onto Mose's operation, they'd be looking for the van coming into Ripley, not expecting this piece-of-shit Corvair.

Drove into the morning light, squinting past the freighter in the canal, back to the Canadian side. Steering Rent Me around a pothole the size of the craters from mortar rounds Dale wrote about in his letters. Rent Me's exhaust giving that funky drift, leaking into the interior. Cranking down his window, Denny's mind flashed to the letters Dale mailed early on from boot camp, the Arkansas drill sergeant yelling he was his mother now, veins sticking from the man's dark neck. His brother writing that the yelling was meant to keep Dale alive where he was going. The sarge ordering him to his knees, scrubbing the latrine floors, peeling spuds in the mess. Getting yelled out of bed at 0500, forcing him to do a hundred push-ups before day-light, cleaning and breaking down his carbine, racing uphill with a full pack. Last one up the rope did five extra laps. Jumping the boards, belly crawling through mud, keeping his rifle dry. The abuse to his body shaping him, sure to save his sorry ass under enemy fire, the sarge making an army man of him, a killing machine.

Dale died the first month into his tour. It was a straw village the recon squad patrolled, keeping eyes sharp for Chuck. Dale the only one to step in the pit of sharpened bamboo left by a retreating squad. Killed in a place he didn't belong. His mother's sobs still woke Denny from sleep now and then, remembering the way her eyes looked dim, just giving up on living.

When his own notice came, Denny felt the anger rise, wanted to walk into that recruitment office, speaking his mind. Doing it for Dale. No way he was getting shipped back, getting buried next to Dale, become another flag in the window, putting his mother through that again. Turned out he would have been 4-F on account of the asthma, anyway, Uncle Sam having no use for guys like him.

Singing out Rent Me's window, that song from a few years back, one Dale liked about the eastern world exploding. Violence flaring and bullets loading. Denny thinking how much he hated that Johnson, and hating Nixon more. And the rest of those fuckers behind their diplomatic walls, sending somebody else's boys to die doing their shit.

The Chev Blazer flew around the curve, head on at him, trailing dust, black and white with a light bar and bull bars. Denny swung hard to the right. No way to tell if it was the Doob. Denny fighting to hold it to the road. Sure the cop would have turned to give chase if he hadn't slid into the ditch, busted him with the trunkload of whatever was in the salmon boxes.

All for fifty bucks.

Tromping his foot on the gas, rear tires spit gravel out the back, and he chugged down the center. Nearly in Ripley before he slowed. If it was the Doob, maybe he made the car, praying he didn't have time to make the driver. Weighing how much of it he should tell Mose, Denny parked Rent Me out behind Mose's gallery, went to the door, relieved to find it locked. He'd have to let Mose know the van was still parked by the pier. Pocketing the car key, he walked over to the brothel hotel, still high, trying to settle his nerves.

. . . *twenty-four*

"'Case I got to draw, get it out fast." Denny holding the coat back, showing her the holster. Thinking about Lonzo sending people. Third week of March — only been three days since breaking into Lonzo's place — wondering how long till it warmed up in this goddamn place. Couldn't get out of here fast enough.

Bobbi considered the holster, tipping her head, saying, "Got the look of my grandpa Jim's colostomy bag." Sputtering a laugh.

"Not what I was going for." Denny didn't tell her about running the cop off the road, held that back.

"You been smoking?" Bobbi sniffed.

"Yeah, a toke or two."

"You leave me here and you go party."

"Left you the pot. Plus, it wasn't any party, trust me." He reached in the coat pocket, pulled out a couple of joints Caleb shared.

"Homegrown?" Bobbi reached for them.

"Caleb calls it Thunderfuck."

"You're making that up."

"You light up, you gonna find out."

Bobbi got a match, struck it, saying, "Thought you were getting us a car?"

"Right outside." Denny making a sweep of his hand.

Going to the door, she had a look out at the Corvair parked out front of the office. "RENT ME" in red on the faded door. "You high when you stole it?"

"What's it say?"

"'Rent me' — you're kidding, right?"

"'Less you see a Tilden around, that's it."

"The thing's a beacon. A piece of shit with graffiti."

"I got any chance of getting to the lake, getting our money back, that's the car." Denny took a toke off the joint, not saying he'd be gone by first light, scope out the lake, thinking he was going to do it without Mose. Without Bobbi, too. Then he was back to thinking about spooning with her.

"It gets worse by the car," she said, sitting on the bed, reaching for the joint. "Hardly wait what's next."

•

Switching off the lamp, Denny lay back, listening to her get undressed, stealing a glance, catching her silhouette, the bed riding as she climbed in.

Punching her pillow, saying, "Well, sleep tight."

Guessing that was plain enough, he tried putting his mind on the lake, some forty miles to the east. Any kind of life for him was in Mrs. Perkins' trunk, fifty feet down in ice water. Denny longing to be back in Berkeley, away from this ice-and-snow place, these people walking around with too many clothes on, hats and gloves and big boots. Too many of them armed. Cronkite had talked about the war ending soon, rumors about resisters getting pardons and getting back to their families. Something Wilson and the card-burners had hoped for in that Eastside flat. Every one of them wanting to go home.

He breathed, trying to catch that scent of Prell, subtle and natural, but it wasn't there. Bobbi raised up and punched her pillow some more, saying, "Damn thing keeps going flat."

"Mine's like second base."

"Second base. You mean like back in high school when you made out, getting to second, trying for third."

He turned to her, could tell she was grinning.

"You never forget something like that, first time a guy rounds your bases."

Taking a chance, he reached, cupping his hand around the back of her neck, saying, "You ever shut up?"

"Admit it, you been thinking about it." Bobbi turning to him, too.

Drawing her close, he felt her breath on him. "Back when I was driving, you in back, me in front. Thought maybe there was a look between us."

"I don't know what you're —"

He kissed her and it happened, no more words passing between them. And sometime after that he drifted to sleep — the two of them spooning again, her in front, him in back — and he dreamed about drowning, but there was something peaceful about it.

... *twenty-five*

Forty miles, the tires slipping around every curve in the road, muck thrown up and sounding against the rockers. Denny thinking he should have taken Bobbi's Boppin' Beppe eight-track, the Pioneer deck rigged under the seat, held there by a twisted coat hanger. No radio signal out here. Just pockets of snow showing now and again along the miles of pines. Denny back to singing the words he knew to some Creedence.

When Meridien Lake came up on the right, Denny slowed, careful not to bottom out, and pulled into the gravel lot, surprised to see the Ford 150 backed down on the roughed-in ramp, green and cream with a homespun trailer, its wheels rusting. An ice hut laid on its side, the thing no bigger than a Porta Potty. First thought, it was Mose or one of his guys, here making a move without him. Turned out the local was a wizened guy, going bald, stoop-shouldered and rawboned, slinging a nylon rope over the hut, tying it off. Said he was Wim Dickens, offering his hand.

Shaking the calloused hand, Denny asked about the fishing. Wim saying he was the last one to pull his hut off the ice, the only one who'd been going home with any trout on the stringer the last week or so. Looking out at the lake, the ice breaking up in spots, he told Denny it had been a lousy winter of fishing. For most of them, it had hardly been worth dragging the hut out and augering the holes.

"Was thinking of wetting a line," Denny said, trying to look disappointed.

"Well, you ask me, could try off that point, maybe hook into a whitefish or if you're lucky a dolly," Wim said. "Come April, the rainbows and cutthroats'll be up, of course, can't say how they'll be biting. Worth a try before the flies eat you alive, though. Maybe fool 'em with a plug, something like a shad." Wim pointed along the western shore, a gravel bar showing, the mouth of a stream just beyond it, pointing to some spots.

"Yeah, how about bears?"

"Them, they bite most any time of year." Wim's bad teeth showed behind the grin.

"Place around I can rent a boat?"

"You got no boat?" Wim looked at Rent Me, finished fastening the yellow rope to his trailer frame. This guy from the city with a rented jalopy, no boat and no gear, but coming fishing.

"Just scouting it out, getting the lay, you know?"

"You want, can quit pulling my chain, son." Wim smiled. "You're here after the money, that car going through the ice, or you think I ain't heard?"

Denny smiled.

"One the cops chased out there." Wim pointing to the spot. "Right where it went through."

"Heard about that, stolen car out on the thin ice, the Mounties pursuing and the thieves making off with the cruiser. All anybody talks about."

"Fools drunk or crazed on the LSD. Lucky for them it was snowing. Stole a patrol car, joyriding their way to Ripley, and left it sitting with its door hanging open. Nobody seeing who done it."

"Got crazies even up here, huh?"

"Folks're mostly hardworking, on the decent side ... Something like that happens around here, you can bet it ain't a local. Was standing right here, watching a perfectly good car sunk to the wheels with the ice sagging under it, headlights like they were dying. Hard to believe it stayed up as long as it did. Mounties tried to get it hauled off in time, but nobody was willing to drive out and tie up to it, the ice getting thinner every day. Folks came out and just stood in this spot, making bets and watching it sink. You hear about the bets at the bingo, when it would go through?"

"Yeah, so you were here, saw it happen?"

"Standing right here. Sounded like a groan on the ice, then the front end tipped down, ass end went up, then *ker-plunk* — she was gone, right about ten in the a.m." Holding out his hand, Wim showed the tip angle, how it happened. Looking back at Denny, saying, "You come a little late for it, but a little early for the fishing." Wim smiled, this guy with no boat and no gear, then pointing along the shore. "Path through them trees. Comes to a deadfall, a hundred and fifty yards or so, there's an old rowboat, some local kept there one time, tipped belly-side down, maybe forgot about it or moved away. Not in much condition, but guess nobody'd mind if you decide to borrow it."

"Good to know."

"I were you, give her a kick before you flip her over. Never know what's under there besides the oars." Wim winked, looked like he enjoyed doing that to tourists, catching that look of doubt. Cinching the rope, he shook his head, wondering aloud what Mickey Rocket clipped him on the rental. Then looking up as a cruiser pulled across the top of the ramp, blocking the exit.

"Well, now . . ." Wim looking like the day was improving.

Henry Kendall stepped out, nodded to Wim, called him by name, then to Denny. Reached a Polaroid camera off the seat, opening its case, saying to him, "How about you say cheese, son?"

"I got a choice?" Denny looked to Wim, then back to Henry.

"Always a choice." Henry smiled, slinging the strap around his neck, saying, "Now, let me ask you one: You in Killik early this morning?"

"Why you asking?"

"Nearly got run off the road. A car coming the opposite way, looked like a wreck. Tell the truth, wasn't time for a good look, not more than a blur, but maybe it was this one."

Denny saying, "How do you mean nearly?"

"What?"

"Said you nearly got run off the road." Denny trying for a look, somewhere between innocent and dumb.

Ignoring that, Henry did a once around Rent Me, checking the car over, then stepped back in front of Denny, lifting the camera, setting the exposure wheel, saying, "Smile if you want, but this picture's gonna tell a thousand words. Or, we can skip it if you want to 'fess up now and hold out your wrists."

. . . *twenty-six*

"Man just drives up with his camera and takes a shot." Denny explaining where he'd been, telling about the Doob showing up on the boat launch, popping the flash in his eyes.

"Meaning?" Bobbi said, sitting up straight.

"Meaning we got to make a move."

"Last night, you said you got to wait out the cold. Worried about hypothermia. Now you want to jump in."

"The woman's gonna ID me."

Bobbi looked at him — the guy whose fault it was in the first place — the money ending at the bottom of the lake.

"I called up this place Caleb mentioned, Skip's over in Prince George. Guy's got some gear, says it's used but calls it top-notch. Thinking maybe I drive out, get the stuff, go to the lake and row out to the spot."

"Talking like Mike Nelson, the guy from *Sea Hunt*." Bobbi thinking of Denny in the water with a dumb mask and fins, not coming up with the money.

Denny saying he bet Lloyd Bridges knew how to swim.

"You don't do it, then Mose does it. And maybe cuts us in. And maybe he doesn't."

"Mose is for Mose." Denny stuck his feet in the sneakers, said he was going to the can, a good place to think. Standing by the open door, she watched him walk along the outside hallway, looked down past the dark office. Rent Me parked out front. Bobbi thinking the Doob knew just where to find them. Lonzo's man, Lee Trane, was looking, too.

Combing her hair when he came back in, the same bell-bottoms and turtleneck she'd put on at the bottom of the stairs, the night they ripped off Lonzo. Bobbi thinking she was starting to smell ripe. Saying to him, "What I say won't matter, so, yeah, how about you leave me some cash, so I can eat? And you go see this guy about the gear, and go get our money."

"And if Lonzo's guys show up . . ."

"Then I'll take care of myself."

Didn't look like he liked it, but he handed her half of what he had in his pocket, weighing his odds of getting in a card game over at Mose's, win what he needed for the diving gear, the guy on the phone in Prince George told him a hundred. "A few hands and I'd have it."

"How about we go with a sure thing." Bobbi taking his hand, leading him to the bed, thinking they could go to Kate's, get dinner, but first . . .

•

The stew special at Kate's was real good, came with hot biscuits right out of the oven, both of them finishing as Minnie Winks stepped to the stage, the colored lights coming on. Plugging a mic cord into a small Vox amp, adjusting the gain, she introduced The Repeat Offenders, guitar, bass, keys and drums, guys ready to play, no matter how big the crowd. Working through a set of Hank Williams, taking the chains from her heart, going to Lynn Anderson, then doing justice to Eddy Arnold's "It's a Sin," an outlaw number by David Allen Coe, another one by Waylon, then "Hello Walls" by Willie, a request for some Mac Davis, singing about putting Texas in the rear-view mirror, moving to an old shaker by Chuck Berry, finishing with Jeannie C. Riley's "Give Myself a Party," doing a Bobbi Gentry encore.

Kate swung by the table and set the tab in front of Denny. After a tip, he had forty left, handing Bobbi half. Back in the room, she turned up the heater, sat on the bed and said maybe she ought to go with him. "It's my money, too."

"How about you think how we're gonna spend it. You know I'm coming back, right?"

"'We,' huh?"

"Yeah, thinking we're a we thing, at least we could be. Just need the trust part."

"Guess I'm gonna find out, sitting here and waiting."

Denny crossed to the bed, leaned down, kissed the top of her head. Saying, "How about Montreal? You been there?"

Said she hadn't.

"It's got the Métro, and decent nightlife along Ste. Catherine and de la Montagne, theaters, restaurants and bars, the way I hear it. Maybe we'll check it out."

"You been?"

"Guy I lived with in the flat, Wilson, told me about it, said it's the place, except maybe in winter."

"Wilson, one of your draft dodgers?"

"Resisters. 'Dodger' says we ducked something, 'resister' says we stand for something."

"Like not getting shot?"

"More about our rights."

"Peace, baby." She held the two fingers, saying, "Heard somebody call it a chicken track, the peace sign."

"Nothing chicken that time I marched with Jerry Rubin."

"Guy from the Grateful Dead?"

"Different one. A student march from Oakland to Berkeley. We got stopped by the gestapo blocking the road and pointing rifles our way, some with bayonets, all with that look in their eyes."

"Like they'd shoot a bunch of students."

"You forgetting Kent State?"

"Yeah, a real bummer. But at Berkeley . . ."

"Just saying they had that look, sighting down their barrels. A bunch of us standing our ground before turning around."

"Showing you weren't chicken."

"Something like that. Another time, was at this Mobe protest when a guy in the crowd tossed some shit at us and a fight broke out. Gestapo in riot gear jumped in, swinging sticks and tossing protesters in the can. Didn't matter who started it. A dozen of us spent the night, had my fingertips inked, got off with a first-time warning." Denny shook his head, thinking back to it. "Next time, I was waving my sign at the Federal Building: 'Drop acid, not bombs.' Some newshound filming it ahead of the rush of the Nazi guardsmen. One of them getting knocked to the ground, hit with the sign I was carrying, looked like it anyway. The clip making the six o'clock news."

"Still showing them you're not chicken."

"Showing me it was time to split."

"So you came north."

"What with the cops knocking on the front door, yeah, I went out the back. Hitchhiked to —"

She waved him off, pretending to be bored. "Already heard it." Drawing a big breath. "So, think you'll go back?"

"When Nixon grants amnesty, yeah, maybe."

Not sure how she felt about him leaving, going back to the States, she swung the conversation to some rock concert she heard about, set to happen in the Ozarks, seemed a million miles from Ripley. "Already like thirty bands on the bill: Eagles, Bachman-Turner, Marshall Tucker, Jeff Beck, Springsteen, a bunch more. Could be another Woodstock. Maybe, you and me . . ."

"Risk jail for music? Yeah, that sounds about right."

·

Bobbi lit another joint and dragged on it, Denny taking a couple of hits, telling her he'd been to a couple of Ken Kesey's acid tests. Seemed she liked to hear about the Golden State.

"The guy who wrote the cuckoo book?"

"Yeah, had some good times with the Fish and the Dead playing, one with the real Jerry guy, only they went by the Warlocks then." Telling her how Kesey was *harawonking* on the harmonica, messing up some Woody Guthrie song. All the while, the Pranksters squeezed feedback through the sound system, Cassady walking around tossing that hammer in the air, no idea how nobody got hurt. Everybody having a good time, high on something. Told her how Country Joe insisted the Fish go on last, on account of "Not So Sweet, Martha Lorraine" made it on Billboard.

"The crowd not giving a shit who went on," he said, "the Warlocks not giving a shit, either, getting on the stage and jamming till like three, giving Joe and the Fish the stage, two, three people left hanging around to do the Fish cheer. Know that one, 'Give me an F.'"

"Yeah, heard it on the Woodstock album." Bobbi asking about other places she'd heard about, like Winterland and the Avalon.

"Saw the Airplane both places, back when Grace joined, the time of *Surrealistic Pillow*, the first time they played 'White Rabbit,' the band called The Great Society then. Caught a double bill at the Avalon with Butterfield. Janis and Big Brother at the Cow Palace. And let's see, the Stones at the Fillmore, Humble Pie at the Carousel, Moby Grape and Peanut Butter Conspiracy on the same bill. Good times."

Bobbi saying it sounded like the place to be.

"There was so much going on all the time, it'll take the rest of the seventies to get over the sixties."

Bobbi nodded her head, liked his stories, saying, "But, this Alaskan Thunderfuck, you made that up, right?"

"Told you, it's what's Caleb calls it."

The two of them close on the bed. Bobbi held the smoke down in her lungs, took his hand and turned it palm up, flicking ash on it. Smiling at him.

Brushing it off his palm, he took the joint back, taking a last toke, coughing.

"Be good we had some wine to chase it down." Getting up, she swayed to some unheard music, raising her arms and moving her hips. Saying right now he needed to get his mind out of the past. Unbuttoning her top, she dropped it on the bed, helping him get into the moment.

Denny watched her do it, this woman who beat up Miss Runner-up.

Standing in front of him in her panties, Bobbi with a good buzz, saying, "Before you take off to the lake again . . ." Taking a pull on the roach, exhaling smoke, she said, "How about you thunderfuck me?"

Getting up, he reached her, put his hands on her hips and danced her to the light switch. Flicking it off, letting his eyes adjust to the dark, seeing her in the glow as she drew again on the roach in her mouth.

. . . *twenty-seven*

Clay Jr. and Casey Hopper sat on either side of him. Denny was bored of hearing about the pool at the bingo hall, the talk of the town still being the car going through the ice, a bunch of hicks.

"Wanted to get another bet going," Clay Jr. said, sitting at the same chair in Mose's back room, obviously feeling the booze, reaching for the Fritos, spilling some from the bowl. "Betting you wouldn't make it to the canal."

"Betting I couldn't walk a couple miles?" Denny holding back from elbowing Jr.'s wide nose, couldn't miss from there. Thinking he should have stayed in bed, spooning. But he needed to win a few hands, make enough money.

"Didn't think you'd get past the lookout and old Silvertip."

Dalton Benning and Jack O'Dey sat across the card table, grinning, too. Couldn't hit all of them. Denny saying, "Silvertip, that bullshit story you guys feed the tourists."

"Bear's got a taste for tourist alright. Salmon's just the appetizer." Clay Jr. went to the cooler, hauling beers up between his fingers, the bottles dripping from the ice. Denny taking one, Clay Jr. set down the rest, the others reaching in.

Dalton Benning tossed in a chip, saying, "How about we play cards?"

Denny considered his hand, slid a white to the pot.

Dalton snapped open a beer, raised a couple more chips.

"I'm out." Jack O'Dey slapped down his cards, yawning. Clay Jr. and Denny slid in more chips, Clay Jr. laid down his hand, a pair of aces, Denny showed his three nines. The night starting the right way.

A couple hours and a half-dozen beers, he was tossing in the last white chip. Flat busted, he got up, bumped Jr.'s chair, on the way to the can, lifting Jr.'s wallet from the shallow pocket of the windbreaker on back of his chair, the thing practically falling out. His body blocking the view, and nobody seeing him do it. Junior busy explaining to Dalton and Jack about this chick he saw over at Kate's, a hot number in a suede jacket. In the can, Denny counted what was in the billfold. Pocketing half, he tucked the rest back, dropping the wallet on the floor under Jr.'s chair as he went to sit down. Nobody the wiser. Finished his drink, stretched his arms and said, "Hey, that your wallet?" Then called it a night, going out, revived by the early morning air. Crossing the street, Rent Me's door creaking as he pulled it open, got onto the cold, crinkly vinyl seat.

Maybe Bobbi would be pissed, him just driving off without another word, but forgiveness was sure to flood her eyes when he walked in with the twins, saying something to her like, "Look who's back."

Sliding the heater's lever to the right, he drove out the town road, out of Ripley and east on the 37. Hoping Doob wasn't doing the early shift on highway patrol. Pushing in the eight-track he took from Bobbi's bag, Boppin' Beppe coming to life in the deck Mickey Rocket had wired under the seat. Denny singing harmony to "Dream Lover."

. . . *twenty-eight*

"Found them like I said I would," Lee Trane said into the phone.

"Took longer, doing it alone," Lonzo said.

"I'm way up in Buttfuck, middle of no place where the air's cold and thin, and I'm freezing my ass off. Why it took longer than you figured. Not living the dolce vita like you."

"Not how you say it." Lonzo saying it the Italian way.

Lee looked at the handset. *This guy for real?*

"So, you got eyes on them?"

"Hope to, tomorrow."

"Tired of hearing tomorrow, Lee, I got to tell you. The reason I sent those boys, one you kicked in the nuts."

"You sent two clowns who let them get away. You know I do it alone, and you know I get it done." Lee Trane held the rest of it back, remembering who he was talking to. "Report I got, Mounties up here chased a stolen car out on the ice few days back, some lake north of here."

"Ice?"

"Yeah, they got ice, everywhere you look. What's not ice is snow. Son of a bitch switched your ride for a van, someplace called Lillooet, then kept driving north, switched rides again, some other place called Smithers."

"The woman with him?" Lonzo not calling her Bobbi anymore.

"Got to be her. Car on the ice got swiped from the Smithers woman unloading her groceries. Went and had a chat with her."

"And you're sure it's them?"

"On account of my chat, yeah." Lee kept it at that.

"Gonna send Aldo, give you a hand."

"You send him, you can count me out. Nothing I'd like more, get the hell out of here. Where nightlife's a flashing Coca-Cola sign, place that's got no women, but you want a drink, they got plenty of ice."

"This car still out on it, on the ice . . ."

"Doesn't matter. They got chased on the ice by the cops, left the car and ran on foot, circling around in a blizzard and swiping the cop's cruiser. Drove to this place Ripley."

"How am I supposed to keep track of all these places? Where they are now?"

"That's what I'm saying. Place called Ripley."

"Okay, you call me soon as it's done. *Pop. Pop.*"

"Thought you want the woman back?"

"What woman?"

Lee Trane heard the dial tone in his ear. Stepping from the pay phone, looking up at the flashing Coca-Cola sign. Walking back to his T-Bird, slush building around the fenders and spokes of his wheels.

... *twenty-nine*

The top guide was missing off the old fiberglass rod, a Cardinal level-wind on its reel seat. The tackle box held a bunch of hooks, lead sinkers, a book of matches, a twist of line and a plastic bobber. Nils Skerritt, the guy at the desk of the Ripley House, told Denny he didn't have much time for fishing these days, let him borrow the stuff yesterday.

Temperatures were climbing, the early sun easing away the winter. A four-hour drive to Terrace, the roads clear of snow, and no threat of more. Denny asking at a truck stop for directions, making it by noon, finding the place called Skip's.

Going to drown or end up with the money. Mose warned him if he tried it on his own he would drown, no question about it. His only chance was to wait, go pick morels and drive the van with tusks and jade from Killik, make enough to pay for the hotel room at the brothel. Let Mose make the dive and pay him half.

Skip turned out to be a burly guy, standing behind his glass counter of the pawn shop. Going in back for the gear, he laid it on the glass counter, showing Denny the Viking Voit Lung, the forty-cubic-foot tank all charged up, and a Body Glove with no holes.

"Not like I imagined it on the phone," Denny said, looking disappointed, saying, "Give you a hundred."

"Yeah, maybe except for inflation, sure you heard about it." Skip felt with his fingers, showing the six mil of sponge neoprene, showed how it sealed at the ankles, wrists and along the zipper. Went in the backroom again and came back with a pair of Water Dogs and a mask. Said he was throwing them in. Said one-fifty was his bottom line. Asking when Denny planned to go diving.

"Sooner than you think."

"Sure if you're crazy. You cut yourself underwater, gonna bleed out before you notice the cut, water's too cold. Got to give it . . . say, another six more weeks or so."

"Yeah, seeing I'm here now, and it's off-season, let's go back to a hundred even."

"Hundred's giving it away." Skip studied him, like he was wagering whether to tell about some other phantom customer he had on the ropes of negotiation — Skip looked to be schooled in the art of buying low and selling high — and owning the only place around with dive gear, Denny waiting him out, letting him know a hundred was all he was going to get. Skip trying one more time. "Tell you what, at one-forty, I can let you have a decompression meter at cost."

Denny saying he could do without it. No idea what it was. Putting the hundred on the counter, unfolding it and smoothing it flat on the glass, saying, "It's up to you."

"One thirty, and I got a dive watch and light, yours, all at cost."

Denny waited, tapping fingers on the bills.

A big sigh, and Skip counted out the bills, ended up helping Denny carry the gear to his trunk.

Stopping at a one-pump Esso, Denny had the guy pump in five of regular, giving him his last bill, hoping he had enough fuel to make it back. Found a nickel in his pocket, bought a Milky Way, the gas jockey saying the price of candy bars was going to double any day now. "A dime for a candy bar, you believe it? A dime for the dailies, too, thirty cents just for a pack of smokes. Hell's the world going?"

"Going crazy, you ask me," Denny said, convinced he wouldn't need to worry about nickels and dimes after tomorrow.

"How a man's supposed to get by without turning to crime . . ." The guy shook his head.

"Maybe I ought to rob this place." Denny looked at him, this guy trying to decide whether he was joking. Wondering what he'd do if Denny peeled back Mose's coat and showed the Beretta in the holster.

The guy grinned, figuring it was a joke. "You do, let me know, I'll give you a hand."

Driving off, Denny bit off the top of the wrapper, tore it away and chewed the Milky Way slowly, making it last, driving back to the lake, thinking as soon as he got Lonzo's money, he'd put himself in a nice Mustang II. Thirty-two hundred bucks for the two-door with the 2.8L V-6, four-speed manual. Highland green like the one in *Bullitt*. Didn't matter it cost more for the fastback with a 390, that baby'd lay a patch of rubber a block long and turn some heads. Didn't matter about getting shit gas mileage or the Arab oil embargo he read about.

The lake showed like a mirror through the pines. Rent Me's dash clock was stuck on 9:12. Denny guessing it was nearing four o'clock when he got there, the day waning, Boppin' Beppe looping one more time.

Pulling onto the launch, he bottomed out hard enough to eject the tape. No sign of anybody else on the lake. He tucked Rent Me off to the side of the ramp, out of plain sight of the two-lane, pulling up the parking brake to keep her from rolling in the lake. About to spend the night curled on the seat, set to get an early start. The car heater the only thing between him and the morning stiffness that was sure to come. No spooning tonight. Telling himself for a half-million, let the cold bite.

He played it through his mind: row out, put on the flippers and kick his way down in the cold dark, using the dive light, pop the trunk and grab the twins, kick his way back up, break the surface, a case in each hand. Nothing to it, didn't need to know how to swim, just had to kick and know up from down. Drive back for Bobbi and get the hell out of this place. Yeah, Montreal was looking good, get there and get lost in the big city. Change his name and looks, maybe dye his hair, walk into a Ford dealer and count out the cash on some sales guy's desk. Point to the one he wanted.

Checking the Beretta, he got out and locked the door, a city habit. Leaving the diving gear in the trunk, he took the rod and tackle, waved at a cloud of tiny flies, made his way on the thin trail Wim Dickens had talked about, stepping over wet and mossy stones, careful of the rod getting caught on the branches all around him.

The hull had moss like a beard along its bow, yellowed grass in tufts along the gunwales of the row boat. Didn't like sticking a hand underneath, he was surprised by its weight, using both hands and putting his back into flipping it over. Guessing it looked alright, he shoved it stern first to the water's edge. The sun dropping, the flies disappearing, the cold was the only thing biting now. Setting the tackle box on the front seat, the rod in the bow, he pushed the paddle wrapped in hockey tape against a rock and shoved off, paddling to where he guessed the Cortina had gone down. The cry of a loon echoing across the lake, the breeze rippling the surface. Looking down into the dark, he hoped to make out the roof of the car, but the sun had dropped low behind the tips of the eastern trees. Swishing his hand along the surface. Yeah, it was cold.

Running the monofilament through the rod's guides, he opened the rusty box and after a dozen tries, his cold fingers getting the line through the eye of the hook, he tied the lead jig to the line, a black one with a feather skirt. Casting it out, he heard it plonk, letting it sink and twitching it. Reeling it up, he slung it back out, letting it sink to a ten count before cranking the handle. Shrinking into Mose's coat, he paddled around, getting the feel of being out here, trolling the line behind the stern, looking down, the water dark as ink.

The drag complained and the line tugged. Denny pulled up on the handle, guessing he was snagged on bottom, a hope like maybe it was caught on the Cortina. The line peeled, making a V in the water. Pulling back, he cranked the reel's handle, whatever it was was greedy for line, Denny pulling up on the rod, gaining back line, a fish thrashing on the surface. When he lifted it over the gunwale, the fish flopped in the bottom of the boat, splashing in the water that had leaked in. Didn't matter what kind it was, it was supper-sized.

The sun dropped beneath the trees now, the shadows getting longer, and the night chill coming on strong. Stepping off the bow and onto the shore, he dragged the boat partway back onto soft muck. Taking the fish to the water's edge, he snapped back the head, then poked a finger into the anus, ripping flesh to the belly, scooping the innards and tossing them out with a splash, doing it the way he remembered when he went fishing with cousin Nort when he was a kid. That loon crying across the lake. Rinsing the cavity, he set the fish on the boat's seat. Gathering kindling dry enough to burn, he took the sticks and fish and went to get the lighter from the car. He planned on having his supper on the launch, then he'd sleep in the car, dive in the morning and be a half a million richer before he even stopped shaking.

The canopy of pines led him back along the trail and opened to the launch, the muddy tracks where he parked. Rent Me was gone. It took him a moment and a thousand heartbeats, and he dropped the kindling and the fish, pulled the Beretta, replaying it, sure he locked the doors, shaking his pocket, hearing the keys.

Everything around him was dead quiet. Denny turning in a circle, ready to shoot anything moving. Then he ran out on the empty 37, hearing his own footfalls, breathing hard before he stopped — nothing but the silence — thinking of what Mose said about some Natives robbing camps, taking everything, right down to the socks and underwear hanging on a line to dry. Walking back to the launch, he stood there a while, was aware of his foggy breath, his cold toes and fingers. Going back down the trail, the fish hanging off a finger, the Beretta in his other hand, he pushed branches out of his way, stumbling on a root, knocking his head on a tree trunk. Finding the rowboat in the near dark. He kept his ears sharp for any sound, set to shoot whoever robbed him and left him out there. Sitting on the bow of the rowboat, feeling the cold and wet through his pants, not sure of his next move. Hanging onto the thought, the money was out there, out in the dark, under the water, waiting for him. The goddamn loon sounded like it was laughing from across the water.

Hadn't eaten since the Milky Way. Middle of fucking nowhere. Leaning against the hull, he pushed himself up. Fumbling around for kindling, he cleared a spot in the small clearing, piling a few sticks, remembering the book of matches in the tackle box. Three left, he hoped they weren't too damp, getting the last one to strike. On his knees, he blew to get some dry needles to catch, adding some twigs and cupping his palm around the tiny flame. A small circle of light grew, allowing him to find more twigs. Teepeeing some sticks over the top, he got it smoking and catching. What he could do with a mouthful of Daisy's grain alcohol, make the flames *whoosh*. When it was crackling, he skewered the fish on a stick that was long enough and held it to over the flames, waiting and turning it, letting the skin brown. The cooking meat smelling good. Careful pulling off pieces off the bones when it was done, he ate them hot.

Tugging off his boots and socks, he set them close to the fire, held his bare feet as close to the flames as he dared, the top of his feet feeling the cold, the bottoms warm. Draping the limp socks on his last stick, he held them close to the flame, watched the steam coming off, the wool smelling rank, the same socks he'd been wearing since tiptoeing through Lonzo's place.

Who steals a man's ride and strands him out here? Thinking again it had to be the damn locals Mose talked about. Slipping his feet into the warmed socks, he pulled on the boots, grateful for that moment of warmth.

Thinking of Bobbi back in the hotel room, likely wondering what happened to him, like maybe Lonzo's man caught up. He pictured her at Klondike Kate's ordering the chili special, some of that garlic bread with plenty of butter, catching a set of Minnie Winks. Reaching around the withering circle of light, he tossed in the last of his twigs.

Denny seeing the shimmer over the lake, the aurora borealis, a swirl of green going to blue to yellow and back to green. Looked at it a while, then tipped the rowboat against a deadfall leaning out from the shore. He watched the fire as it died, then he rolled under the hull, the ground damp and hard. Setting the Beretta next to him, he found a spot with the least stones, shrank into the coat, pulling it around his ears, tucking his hands into the sleeves and curling up his knees. The night sounds closed around him, and he folded his arms around himself, lying awake a long time, dropping into an uneasy sleep, snapping awake to every night sound. A couple of times he listened in the dark, promising anything that came for a sniff around the rowboat, he'd shoot it and empty the clip. Trying not to think of Silvertip.

Man, if he ever found out who took the car . . .

. . . *thirty*

The guy's name was Snuffy Waldon. The man driving the same model of van Denny had jacked in Lillooet, but this one not smelling bad in back. Picked Denny up thumbing on the 37, Snuffy calling it the Glacier Highway, Denny getting in and shivering from the cold. Asked if he minded, Denny taking a grateful drink from his thermos, the coffee not hot, but doing him a lot of good.

Told Snuffy his car crapped out, didn't want to explain about Rent Me, didn't want this guy thinking why he was really here. Nobody going to feel sorry for a car thief getting his rental car jacked. Lied that he left the Corvair with its trunk up over a disabled engine, just a few miles east of the lake. Spent the night in the cold.

"Out here all night, huh?" Snuffy said, looking over at him.

"Yeah, the night a million miles long, and cold like you can't believe."

"Funny I missed seeing it, your car back there, but good thing I come along." Snuffy making his weekly run to Ripley and Klondike Kate's with cases of Libby's, tins of Campbell's and jugs of Heinz, a rack of paper towels and sacks of potatoes and onions, all stacked in the back.

Denny looked in back, the sacks got him thinking of the ones Dale had written about filling with sand. Officers ordering grunts to do it, telling them the sandbag was a grunt's best friend, would save their asses from sniper fire and mortar shrapnel, the grunts bitching about the work, but filling them like they were told. Scooping bags full of laterite and sand they dug for their bunkers, did it every time they set up base, dog-tired, the officers watching them do it. Dale had written he was working in zombie mode, getting four hours of sleep at best, most of it with one eye open. Dumped the sand out again when they broke camp in the morning, stacked any bags that were still good, without holes in them, and the men tied their boots, picked up their rifles and packs and moved on, filled the sacks again at the next encampment. Started out the sacks were made of cloth, the guys on second tour telling Dale about it, better than the plastic ones they had during Dale's vacation, slipping around when the grunts tried to stack them, easy to punch in holes and made for an unstable wall. Dale writing how soldiering was nothing but a repeat of actions, walking the same-looking jungle trails, fording swamps with your rifle held overhead, applying ointment on bites and bumps, living in a new foxhole every night, looking the same as the one from the night before, taking orders from the assholes you called sir, the ones walking near the back of the line. Dale writing how all that sometimes felt worse than dying.

"Ain't a local." Snuffy gave him a look, said it like a fact, not a question.

"Yeah, I'm just visiting."

"Funny place to do it, visiting." Snuffy jogged around some roadkill, saying, "Somebody maybe I know?"

Like I know who you know, Denny thinking it, saying, "Well, if you know Mose Grillo, then yeah."

The man slapped the wheel, his voice rising, saying, "That old son of a gun, sure I know him? Old Mose. Who doesn't?" Bobbing his head. "You relations? Kind of look like him." Taking off his cap with the earflaps, about forty and gray, receding hair and putty for skin made Snuffy look sixty.

"Not related, no, we're more like poker buddies, guess you'd say."

"Then you know to watch when he's dealing, right?"

"You bet I do. Guess you've sat at that table, too."

Snuffy giving the wheel another slap of the hand. "Man ran for mayor, he tell you that?" Chuckling, his Adam's apple bobbing up and down.

"Yeah, heard about that. Better luck next time, right?"

"Luck for who? God save us all." The man laughed. "Found myself in more'n one of his all-nighters, yeah, that's for sure."

"That right?" Denny seeing it would be a long drive to Ripley, saying he was still hoping to get in some ice-out fishing, catch a Dolly or two on the surface this time of year, this guy Wim Dickens telling him about some local lakes. Holding back telling him about the trout he caught last night, not wanting to put himself on Meridien Lake.

"Well, Wim's your man. Sure knows his fish. Him and me go way back. Fact, was me and Mose tied the cans to Wim's bumper, the time he got hitched." Snuffy going on, "Didn't work out for him, but, yeah, fella sure can fish, about as good as Mose plays his cards." Reaching a pack of smokes under his visor, he offered him one, then he thumbed in his lighter, going on, "Yeah, that lake we passed, Meridien, got a few with size, mostly lakers down deep." Asked Denny if he heard about the car dropping through the ice, the one the cops chased.

"Yeah, all anybody talks about. Had a bet going at the bingo."

"Damn fools, the crooks I mean, ditched it next to the 'THIN ICE' sign. Who drives that close to a 'THIN ICE' sign? Guess the snow was coming down thick, maybe couldn't see it. And luck be a lady it was snowing the way it was, the crooks running from the Doob, stealing his patrol car." Snuffy laughed. "Yeah, heard everybody at the bingo placing bets about the car sinking. Any idea who won it?"

"Some nice old lady," Denny said.

"Anyway, if I know anything, he's gonna keep looking, the Doob, I mean, along with that girl Mountie he's got, the two of them cack-handed and half-assed, but they won't let it go. Ask me, they ought to keep to scraping up roadkill, what they know best." Snuffy laughed some more, speculating how the crooks circled around on the ice and took off in the Doob's cruiser. "Them two likely high on that flower power, you know?"

"Got that up here, huh?"

"Leaks up from the city."

... *thirty-one*

"Look like you could use one." Setting his bottle on the Beaver's floor, Caleb Hawkes reached the styrofoam cooler, pulled one, uncapped it and handed it over.

Saying it was good going down. Denny had been in the same clothes too long, that rumpled look and smelling of wood smoke. He unbuttoned the coat, said he hiked from Ripley, just felt like a walk. Looking back down the pier in the early light.

Not sure why he made the trek, Caleb knowing Mose didn't send him out to make another run, guessing Denny would tell him in his own good time, Caleb smiled, seeing the holster. "Been to see Daisy, huh? Hear you rented the car, too."

"Thing about this place, everybody's in everybody else's business." Drinking some of the beer, Denny gave him the short strokes, about going to the lake and getting his car jacked. Stranded in the cold all night, then catching a ride back in Snuffy's van. Told him he'd helped unload the van at Kate's, then walked past the brothel hotel, not ready to explain things to Bobbi. Walking the Killik Road to the canal, nobody paying him to do it this time. Taking a chance Caleb's plane would be tied to the pier.

"Well, you got one thing right. Here I am." Caleb not getting into the business he had with a couple of the crew on the freighter now being loaded.

"You hear of tourists getting their camp stripped, leaving nothing behind?" Denny looked at him, ducking under the wing brace. Relaying the story Mose had told him about no-goods robbing camps.

Caleb thought a moment, then saying, "Happened to a charter of mine a year or so back, this couple come up to do some fly-in fishing, Tull Lake, ten miles in the bush. Left them to set up their camp. When they got it done, they canoed out and got caught in a squall. Waited it out and paddled back to camp and strung a clothesline and hung their wet stuff. Sky cleared and they went back to canoeing, getting a nice stringer of trout, came back for a shore lunch and found the camp stripped clean, right down to the wet socks and undies on the line. Everything gone. Spent ten days like that before I flew back and picked them up. Shoulda seen the bug bites."

"Who'd do that, take everything down to a man's undies?"

"Was the woman's undies, but yeah, beats me." Caleb reached in a pocket, took out a Baggie, guessed Denny could use it and got to work rolling one.

"Had my dive gear in the trunk." Denny waving his hand, said he was fine with just the beer.

"You got a habit of leaving shit in the trunk, the way I hear it." Caleb lit it, dragged on it, saying, "All that true, about the money?"

"Every dime of it."

"Most folks keep it in a bank." Caleb lighted up.

"Not that kind of money." Denny got into it and told how he'd worked for Lonzo, the type of man he was and how he drove the man around. Explained how old Lonz had it coming, about breaking in, taking the man's stash. Told how Bobbi showed him where it was, saying, "Take me with you."

Caleb heard him out, nodded, then saying, "So, you figure this Lonzo's coming for you?" Pushing the joint at him.

"Don't think it, I know it." Denny waved it off. Told him about Lee Trane, what he knew about the contract man.

Caleb insisted with the joint, saying, "Do you some good."

Denny looked at it, had a small hit, coughed and passed it back. Then he told him about the two guys at the diner on the way up here, the guy he kicked in the nuts, sure they were working for Lonzo.

Caleb was impressed, saying, "Kicked a man in the stones on a hunch, huh? Well, good on you. Shows you got some pushback in you."

"No doubt in my mind we're being hunted. And now I'm wondering if I got followed out to the lake, had the car and dive gear swiped. Leaving me out there to die. Or it was Mose, making me think it was phantom camp robbers."

"Maybe sounding a bit paranoid, but tell the truth, I can see it: Mose getting you to pick mushrooms on the other side of Otter, get you in that burn area. Give him a chance to make the dive on his own, you not knowing about it."

They were both quiet a while. Caleb smoking and looking out along the canal, then back to the mountain, saying, "Was a bitch putting that one out."

"What one?" Denny looking at him, the man's eyes glassy.

Caleb pinched the roach, getting the last of it, explaining about fighting the big fire last fall, how he crewed on the Dump Duck, the water bomber swooping down, filling its big belly and making its air attack. Something that made him feel alive.

"Told me how you put it out."

"Was more about knocking down the hot spots, containing it, keep it from spreading, you know. Making it safe for the guys on the ground."

Denny nodded, drinking his beer.

"Lost five hundred hectares before we got her put out. You know hectares?"

"Bigger than acres."

"Yeah, the size of a high school running track. Acre's less than half."

Denny asking what it had to do with getting the rental and his diving gear snatched.

"Only good thing after a burn like that, Mose and his guys go off picking mushrooms. At least what they put on their tax returns." Caleb watched Denny slipping off the coat, looking at the holster. "Ready for whatever rolls your way, huh?" Caleb said, "Gun you took off the gangster's nightstand. Same time you took his woman?"

"And his money. And his Cadillac."

"Ever shoot it, check it out?"

"Hoping I don't have to."

"How about the woman?" Caleb grinned, saying, "You want I can show you, can help you get the hang before you go getting serious."

"We talking the gun or the woman?"

"Either one. You pick." Caleb reached into the cooler, getting two more beers, saying, "Did two tours and learned a thing about shooting guns."

Sitting on the bunched coat, Denny drank. "Two tours, huh? Flying in one of these?"

"Flew Hueys then, nothing like this."

"The choppers with the guns hanging out the side, flattening the grass, setting troops down, picking up stretchers. Cronkite showed it on the news," Denny said.

"Yeah, that was me, swarming the commie skies, raining hell and fire, picking up the wounded."

"Why they call them that, Hueys? Like it's funny."

"Huey's a damn fine warship. Bell UH-1 Iroquois, just ended up as Huey, way we like to shorten things." Caleb drinking his beer. "Sometimes called Frogs and Hogs, Guns and Slicks, depending what's aboard. Flew mostly with heavy fire teams, my bird called Gunslinger, with the shark jaws, white teeth and red blood painted across the nose. Had the mini-gun mounted at the door. No mistaking we meant business, flying in low, kissing the treetops and prepping a zone with that mini spinning and spitting four thousand rounds a minute. Gunner marking the LZ with that yellow smoke. Radioed coordinates for the Skyhawks and Phantoms, the warbirds coming on our tail with the sidewinders and heavy loads, lighting the zone like the Fourth of fuckin' July. No telling how many we killed. So the boys can take the ground. Kill the rest." He bunched his pant leg past his knee, showing an angry scar etched along his calf. "Trouble is those bastards don't know how to quit. Blasting everything from mortar rounds, SAMs, handguns, whatever they got. Took out our chin bubble same time I took one through here." Caleb pointing at the scar. "Medic called me lucky. Crew chief took one in the gut, had to pull out half his intestines. Man not as lucky, still walking with a hitch."

Denny was quiet, tipping his beer, saying he didn't want to think about that damned war.

Reaching past the styro, Caleb set a portable Ampex deck on top, pressing a button, a tape whirring its rewind. "Gonna fly this baby back to Mud Bay. Taking some time to myself, gonna find me a different kind of action — the warm and wet kind — and stay in bed two days straight." Caleb hit the play button and turned the volume knob. Smiling at thoughts about taking some time off.

Eric Burdon's voice filled the air, blessing the boys in high fidelity. Climbing across the passenger seat, Caleb got behind the controls, flipping gauges and getting set to take off. Singing along: *Sky pilot. How high can you fly?*

.

The Beaver lifted off the canal, flew over the freighter and winged for Mud Bay. Denny walking back down the pier, past the "Welcome to Alaska" sign. Sneakers slipping on the muck street, the sun warm on the road. Denny pulled off the cap and stuck it in a pocket. Watching the same kid with the hockey stick take a slap shot, pinging a tennis ball off the tin of a Coca-Cola sign. The kid yelling, "Scores!" His arms and stick going in the air.

Stepping across the puddle like a mote at Daisy's door, Denny went in, his eyes adjusting to the ill-lit joint, a musty tang greeting him. The plank floor creaked, spongy underfoot as he stepped to the counter. The rack of postcards, the handicrafts on display.

Coming from behind a beaded curtain, Daisy said, "Come for your change, huh?"

"Settle for a shot from that bottle you got in the bag." Denny glanced out the window, watching the kid shoot again.

"Ah, a hit-me-up." Grinning, Daisy went behind the counter, nothing more than a door set on piled crates, the kind fruit came in. Reaching the bottle, she poured a shot in a glass already on the counter, nodded for him to go ahead.

Tipping it back, not coughing this time, Denny was thinking he was starting to like that tasteless burn going down.

"Hit the spot, did it?" Daisy tipped the bottle again.

"Beat the hell right out of it," Denny said, watching her top the glass. "Gonna join me?"

"At my age, the trots'd dog me for days."

Denny asked if Mickey Rocket was around.

"Likely sleeping off last night. You try knocking?"

"Next thing on my list." Looking at the bottle in the bag, saying, "You sell it by the jug?"

She shook her head. "Don't want it on my conscience."

"One belt at a time, huh?" Denny smiled, thinking of the locals walking around armed, good idea not to sell them moonshine that could propel a rocket.

"Come to think of it, Mickey was out fussing with that eyesore he rents."

"The car's here?"

"What I said."

Denny reached in an empty pocket. "How much I owe you?"

"Same as before, you don't throw up, it's on the house. You know how it works."

Thanking her, he told her to keep his change, stepped past the puddle and went next door. Rent Me parked in the vacant yard, the four-eyed Corvair looking like it got a wash. Still had the keys in his pocket, Denny went and popped the hood, nothing but the jack handle in there. No diving gear. Opening the driver's door, he crouched and checked the ignition wires, cut and spliced and shoved up under the steering column. Pulled the Boppin' Beppe tape from the deck and dropped it in a pocket. Taking the metal stairs two at a time, Denny banged his fist on the door.

Slow to open it, Mickey snugged the sash of a bathrobe, looked like rodents lived in the pockets, his hair laid wet against his scalp. "Hey, man, what do you —"

Denny shoved him backwards, sticking the barrel of the Beretta under his chin, kicking the door shut behind him. Walked his man into the wall.

"What the fuck, dude?"

"What's the game, Mickey?"

Mickey held his hands wide. "Was coming to see you, get my keys, man." Tipping his head down, looking at the barrel. "Come on, man."

"We had a deal."

"What're you talking about? You parked her last night, right, figured you brought her back early. Figured something wasn't working right, why you hot-wired her. Like I said, was coming to see you about my keys."

"Paid you for the week, you remember that?" Denny put the Beretta away, reached for the keys, holding them up. "Why the hell'd I do that?"

"What am I gonna think?"

"How about the stuff in the trunk?"

"What stuff? Look, man, we can call the Doob, straighten this shit out."

"What's he gonna do?"

"For one, explain to you why I'd steal my own car, then park it in plain sight."

"Okay, maybe I jumped a bit." Denny backing off.

"A bit?" Mickey rubbed where the barrel had pressed into his neck. Denny went to the door and reached for the knob, looking back. "We still good till the end of the week, huh?"

"Gonna shoot me if I say no?"

"Said sorry."

"Yeah, fuck, we're golden. Just have it back end of the week, with the keys this time."

Denny went down the stairs.

"Oh ..." Mickey Rocket followed him to the door, clinching his bathrobe, coming down a few steps. "Was a guy come in Daisy's yesterday ..."

Denny stopped and looked back, motioned for him to close the robe.

"Was checking out the Yupiks, going through the post-cards like any tourist, you know, but asking questions."

"What kind of questions?"

"About you, mostly. Least, think it was you the way he was describing, and some chick with you. You got a chick with you?"

"What'd he look like, this guy?"

"Like nobody from around here. Kind of skinny, but tough, you know, a bit older maybe, and taller than you. Had a look about him."

"Kind a look?"

"Kind that gives you the creeps."

"What'd you tell him?"

"Said you didn't ring a bell, the way he was describing you. Told him tourists come and go, you know. Asked me if there was just the one hotel, then got in his T-Bird and drove off."

"That all you said?"

"To some guy not buying nothing, just asking questions, not tipping for information. Got what he paid for, you know what I'm saying?" Mickey said, still rubbing his neck.

Reaching in his pocket, Denny remembered his money was gone, saying, "Catch up with you next time, be a little something extra."

"Whatever, man." Mickey sighed, saying, "Didn't figure the dude for a friend, the look about him says he doesn't have many." Then stopped, remembering. "Had a gun under

his jacket, same as you. Just didn't go waving it in my face."
Mickey went back to his door, saying, "Maybe was him
jacked the car."

Clanging down the rest of the steps, Denny got in
Rent Me, stuck the key in the ignition and rolled down the
window. Whoever stole the car left the tape deck with the
eight-track in it. Popping in the tape and playing Boppin'
Beppe and dodging potholes along the main drag, Denny
slowed for the kid playing hockey. The kid's mother coming
to the stoop of one of the shacks lining the street, drying her
hands on an apron, nothing friendly in the way she watched
him drive past. Denny wondering if she leaned a twelve-
gauge by her door. He kept it to creeping speed, hanging
a left at the Wharf Road, steering around a crater, taking
Glacier past the stone border station.

Near the lookout a grizzly lumbered across the gravel,
big and brown, giving a lazy look at the Corvair, walking
like it had all day. Couldn't believe the size of the thing,
misjudging a safe distance, Denny rolled within a hundred
feet. Turning with a roar, the bear charged. Fumbling the
stick, Denny stabbed it into reverse, his elbow catching the
horn. The beast was faster, reared up and dropped its paws
onto the hood, its claws scraping down the sheet metal, the
springs sagging and bouncing as it got off. Unmatched by
this smogging heap of tin, and making its point, the bear
turned and crossed the lookout lot, disappearing into the
brush, on its way down to the river. The hood was dented
down, the windshield wiper on the driver's side stuck out
bent, the antennae was gone. Denny thinking of what Mose
said about yelling *Hah!* and knocking stones together.

Felt the sheet of sweat on him, driving the rest of the
way to Ripley, feeling the wobble at the front left tire, sure it

was out of align. Thinking how Mickey would take it, then thinking how much of what happened since last night he was going to tell Bobbi.

. . . thirty-two

Driving Ripley's main drag, Lee Trane was pissed about the muck and gravel thrown up at his fenders, couldn't believe the main drag being unpaved. This godforsaken place with its yellow hotel, an eatery called Klondike Kate's, a bingo hall and a schoolhouse, some shack selling Native art, and not much else to it. Pissed about chasing these fly-by-nights all the way to the Alaskan border. Thinking of ways Denny Barrenko was going to pay. Maybe drive back toward Vancouver with him trussed and gagged in his trunk, let him think about what was coming, then dump him in the Fraser and drown his ass. Lee thinking he could let Bobbi Ricci ride up front, give her a chance to talk him out of bringing her back, imagining what the Mad Dog would do to her. Lee coming around to feeling tired of Lonzo treating him like the hired help.

Parking in the slush by the curb, he looked at this place called The Ripley House, formerly The Brothel. He got out and walked to the door. The office out front of a courtyard, a flight of stairs in back leading to a few rooms up top.

The pick-up was a late-model Chev, a two-tone Cheyenne rolling down the street, stopping out front, parking the wrong way. The guy left the motor running, got out and walked in like he was mayor of the rednecks: a cowboy hat and a leisure suit with the boots outside the pants, going past the office and into the courtyard. Something about the guy had Lee stopping to light a smoke, watching him go up the stairs at the back. Watched him knock on a door. Getting no answer, the guy came back down and went in the office. Leaving a minute later, getting back in his truck, turning around in the street and driving off.

Finishing the smoke, Lee flicked the butt into the slush and stepped in the office, wiping his feet on the mat, a nod to the guy behind the desk. The nameplate saying he was Nils Skerrit, proprietor. Happy to serve.

"Was a brothel, huh?" Lee asked, putting on a smile, looking at a rack of tourist attraction pamphlets. Tour a national park, the hall of culture, go sled-dogging, see a fjord, fly over a glacier, cruise the Inside Passage, watch some whales. Another one: "See Skagway," Lee wondering what the fuck was in Skagway — skags? Everything up here about ice and snow.

"Yeah, back when the mines were going strong." Nils smiled, taking Lee for a tourist, drove up with his fancy car with the whitewalls, up here to see the sights. Reaching under the counter for his ledger, flipping it open. Saying, "Folks get a kick, you know, knowing what it once was. Of course, had it all stripped down and cleaned up, as you can see."

"Sleep in a bed one time used for mattress pounding," Lee said, grinning. "Tell your friends, say, 'Hey, guess what?'"

"Can if you want. Of course, the sheets get changed daily. All spic and span, I assure you." Nils turning to his ledger. "So, how many nights are you looking for?"

"Room at the top of the stairs, you got a woman in there?"

"Have to stop you there, sir. I thought I was clear." Nils frowned. "You want a woman, you need to bring your own."

Lee just looked at him, this redneck idiot. Taking the photo of Bobbi and Lonzo from inside his jacket, Lee spun it on the counter and let him have a look. "This woman."

"You with the law or something?"

Lee grinned, eased back the jacket enough to show the piece on his hip, saying, "Let's go with 'or something.'"

Then Nils getting a sly look, saying, "You sent by her husband?"

"Sure you want to know my business, friend?" Lee getting annoyed, showing it in his eyes.

"I just want no trouble here."

"Then tell me straight, and there won't be any."

"Understand, we have rules about confidential—"

Lee held up a hand, stopped him and he dug in his pants' pocket, laid a pair of twenties down, saying, "Best cure for rules." Tapped his finger on the snapshot. "Now, while we're still being friendly, how about it, Neil, this the woman?"

Taking his time, not correcting him on the name, Nils glanced at the shot, then the money. "Well, maybe I've seen her."

Lee pushed the bills forward. "She with a guy, sandy hair, about my size?"

"Was a guy like that, yeah, long hair." Nils made the bills disappear, running a finger down the register. "The Jeffreys. Yes, had a feeling about them. After a while, you get to know. Phony name, I bet."

Again, stopping him with the hand, Lee glanced at the nameplate, called him Neil again, then leaned on the counter, wanting to know their room number, then saying, "Other fellow was just in, cowboy hat and boots outside his pants, went knocking on Room 2, the very same room. How about him?"

Nils hesitated, getting a worried look, saying, "Don't know what it's about, but I want no part."

"Want me to jog your memory, Neil?" Lee reached in his pocket, could tell this guy was afraid of the cowboy in the leisure suit, took his hand out slow and set down another twenty. "Next time I got to reach in my pocket, won't be for money. You getting the picture?"

"Jack O'Dey, one of Mose Grillo's crew."

"Jack and Mose and a crew, huh? Saying it like they're people I ought to know?"

"Jack came in asking if I knew where they were, the same couple. Just letting you know he works for Mose. That's his bar across the street, deals in local art, at least by day. None of my business what they do at night." Nils pointing over at the bar.

"How do the Jeffreys fit in?"

"You'll have to ask them." Nils held up his palms, meaning that was all he knew, adding to it, "Did see Mr. Jeffreys going into Mose's place a couple nights back. Doubt he was looking at the art, more likely in the back room playing cards."

"This Jack fellow, he leave a message for them?"

"Yuh, said he was going to the burn site, be back in an hour or so. Said for them to hang around."

"This burn site . . ."

"A few miles out of town." Nils pointed east. "Can see it from the road. Guess it's about the mushroom business, another thing they're into."

"Mushrooms?"

"Mose sends his guys picking the wild ones, ships them to high-end eating places, New York and the like, the way

I understand it." Then Nils said, "Jack or them come back, you want me to say you called?"

"I wouldn't recommend it." Lee let his look do the talking, then he turned to the door.

Nils nodded like he understood. "So you won't be needing a room, then?"

"Maybe I would, except I was never here." Lee gave him a level look.

Nils nodded, understanding his meaning.

Lee Trane went out the door. Getting in the T-Bird, he drove east on the 37, the way the pick-up had gone, driving back out of town.

... *thirty-three*

"Not gonna believe this shit when I tell you." Denny looked at her on the bed, Bobbi finger combing, her hair a wreck. "But, right now we got a guy coming for us." Repeating what Mickey Rocket told him about the guy.

"Lonz?"

"Said the guy rode a T-Bird."

"Lee Trane." Bobbi was on her feet, a charge of fear going through her.

"Okay, we got to split out of here."

"And go where?"

Denny went to the window, looking out. "Figure it as we go."

"That's the thinking got us in this fucked-up place."

"This guy Lee Trane catches up —"

The rap on the door had her jumping into his arms. Taking the pistol from the holster, he motioned for her to get behind the Morgan chair, stepping to the side of the door. Bobbi thinking he was doing it the way he'd seen it done in movies. Funny he didn't look scared, looking over at her, motioning for her to get down, waiting till she crouched behind the armchair.

The rap came again, and Denny leaned flat on the wall, held the pistol with a cocked elbow, saying, "Yeah?"

"Open the door, you putz."

Denny relaxed. Edging it open, first a little, then all the way, he stuck the barrel in the man's gut.

Swatting it to the side, the old guy stamped his boots and stepped past him, looking around the room. "Want to tell me, what the fuck's going on?" The same guy she'd seen Denny with at Kate's — had to be Mose.

"Got questions myself." Denny still with the pistol cocked in his hand, looking out the open door, making sure Mose wasn't followed, closing and locking the door.

"That right, huh?" Mose practically laughing, giving him a dressing down by his look, saying he was unhappy hearing Denny had gone out to the lake, not clearing it with him first.

"I got to clear it with —"

Cutting Denny off, chopping his hand through the air. "I got to hear some guy in the life's come to town, my town, asking about you." Saying he'd sent Jack O'Dey over here to get the two of them, nearly an hour ago. And hadn't heard back from his man, so Mose drove over himself. Now seeing Bobbi rise from beside the chair, reaching the fringed coat from the chair, holding it across her bare legs.

He smiled at her, doing it in a way Denny didn't like. Saying to her, "Believe we nearly met." Smiling at her, nothing discreet about the way he was checking her out.

"Mose, like the guy in the Bible, yeah, I remember you." Bobbi stepped forward, saying her name, holding out her hand.

"Well, nice seeing you, Bobbi." His look saying he'd like to see more. Taking her in and shaking her hand.

"Sorry, guess I look a fright." Brushing fingers through her hair again, keeping the jacket in front of her, fringes tickling her thighs.

"Well, I don't scare easy." Eyes going down to her bare feet, Mose looking back at Denny. "You mind putting that away?" Waiting for Denny to tuck the Beretta away.

"So, where the hell's Jack?" Mose said. "Supposed to come get you."

Bobbi saying if anybody came by, she was down the hall, trying to get the taps to drip that off-color water, the goddamn pipes frozen. "What's a girl got to do to get herself cleaned up?"

"Just got back myself." Denny got in front of Mose, blocking the old man's hungry eyes, saying, "Was out at the lake scouting till some asshole jacked my ride, left me out there to die under your fuckin' northern lights. You know anything about that?"

"Sounds like those fuckers I told you about. No offense, Bobbi."

"Now I find out we got company."

"This company's what, your past catching up?"

"Not hanging around to find out."

Mose shifted and was back to looking at Bobbi. Bobbi standing like she didn't mind.

"You know, Mose, I'm done with you calling the shots." Denny stepping back in front of Bobbi.

"Some guy comes from the city, looking for another guy from the city, thinking you just do what you want . . ." Mose poked his finger at Denny. "You people got to learn it's my town."

"Man's name's Lee Trane," Bobbi said. "A pretty serious type of guy."

Mose turned to her. "And what makes you think I'm not?"

"Works for Tomasino Palmieri, guy everybody calls Lonzo," she said. "My ex, but a guy I . . . we . . ."

"We?" Mose looking from her to him and back. "Guy whose money you stole?"

"More like he owed it to me," she said, telling them both to turn around, then tossing the jacket on the bed. Standing in her bra and panties, getting dressed.

"Us," Denny said.

Mose saying to Denny, "You get her mixed up in this." Looking disappointed. "You rob a guy like that with no plan, and you end up losing his money at the bottom of the lake. Now, you got some hitter coming for you . . ."

"Yeah, and doing it in your town," Denny said.

"What's this guy look like?"

"Serious," Bobbi said, throwing in he drove a nice-looking T-Bird. "Be hard to miss."

"Well, Bobbi, know we just met, but let me tell you, I'm all about fun, normally speaking, but I got my serious side, too." He went to the door, telling them, "Now, get your stuff."

"Where to?" Denny said.

"Putting you two safe, then I'm gonna take care of Mr. T-Bird." Mose eased open the door, had a look out, before stepping past the door."

"Thinking we'll just split," Denny said.

"It sound like I'm asking?" The look was cold, Mose turning for the door. "Nobody drives his city car in my town, thinking he does what he wants. Make no mistake." Mose looked from him to her, stepped back over to the room phone on the dresser, picked it up, said to Nils at the desk, "Jack O'Dey come by?"

Bobbi could hear Nils saying he did go and knock on this door, came back down and left.

"He say where he went?" Mose frowned at the answer, then said, "Anybody come asking for these two, you say nothing, and you call my place right off, hear me?" Then Mose told him to patch him through to another number. Waiting for the click, he told Dalton Benning to get the Landrys and leave word for Gert, the guy he sent to the far side of Otter this morning, scouting morels along the burn area. Told them to get to his place, pronto, then he hung up. Looked to Denny and Bobbi and said to her, "You smart as you look, girl, then you follow right behind me." And he was out the door, taking the stairs.

Nothing to decide, Bobbi pulled on her bell-bottoms, tugged on the turtleneck and slung her bag over her shoulder and looked at Denny. "Don't get all red-blooded, huh?" Grabbing the fringed jacket, she followed Mose down the stairs. Leaving Denny to think it through, heard him coming down the stairs behind her as she asked if Mose had hot water at his place.

Mose saying he had everything at his place.

. . . *thirty-four*

Spotted it a few miles out, the two-tone Cheyenne pulled up on a dirt track on the north side, tire tracks showing in the muck ruts, on the edge of the burn area. A dead-looking place of charred trunks, the branches gone, the ground blackened with patches of snow. Wondering what the hell anybody would be doing out here, Lee guessed the cowboy was walking around looking for mushrooms.

Slowing past the pick-up, Lee swung the Bird around on the straightaway and parked fifty yards from it, this place with all the friendly of a graveyard. He got out, keeping a sharp eye, and walked along the burn, cutting up on the pick-up's tracks, stopping now and then to listen, trying for Native quiet as he stepped. Out of sight from the road, guessing what he heard now was the rush of a stream, or maybe it was the wind. Had his pistol in his hand.

Hearing a snap behind him, he started to turn his neck.

"Uh-uhn, wouldn't do it."

Lee held his hands wide.

"Who're you supposed to be?" Jack O'Dey said it easy, holding his pistol on this guy who followed him into the woods.

Lee turning a little more, smiling. "That door you knocked on, back in town ..."

Jack looked at this guy's outfit, city clothes and shoes. "Some kind of cop?"

"I look like that, huh?" Lee turned his head some more.

"You dress like city, talk like it, too."

"Looking for the couple in that room, same door you knocked on."

"Ah, how about this," Jack said. "I ask, and if I like what you say, then maybe you won't bleed out on the ground, mess up your nice outfit?"

Lee turned just enough to see the man now, checking the woods for anybody else.

"You got a name?" Jack said.

"Lee Trane."

"That real, or like one of them Hollywood ones, like Rock Hudson, the guy's real name's Leroy."

"Can see why he changed it. But mine's real, Lee Trane, like I said." Turning a little more, doing it slow, his pistol held wide.

"Kirk Douglas started as somebody else. And Carey Grant was Archibald. And Judy Garland was Gumm. You know the one, chick from *The Wizard of Oz*."

"One who sang 'Over the Rainbow.'"

"Yeah, that's it."

Lee edged halfway around to the guy with the cowboy hat, his pants tucked in his boots. The guy was aiming at his back, but looked distracted, glancing around like he was waiting for somebody else.

"Bunch of phonies, alright," Jack said. "But, you followed me out here, something more than Hollywood talk on your mind. Why you want those two?"

Lee smiled, saying, "Took something from the gent I work for. Sent me to get it back."

"You talking about the money at the bottom of the lake?" Jack grinned. "Thought that was a joke till now."

"Yeah, nothing funny about it."

"So, it's true, huh? There's money in the trunk."

"Not sure about the trunk, but half-mil got lifted from the wrong guy." Lee held the pistol loose, like he forgot it was there, his arm still extended.

"So, Lee Trane, you gonna toss it down, we can talk some more about the movies, or you want to play?"

Lee could make out the man moving his free hand to the brim of the cowboy hat, saying it like it didn't matter, his pistol pointed at his back.

"Just one thing, that true about you folks coming out here picking mushrooms?"

"It's about the nutrients in the ash, these burn areas gets them growing right. Can't believe what fancy restaurants'll pay."

"That right, huh? Thought they grew in cow shit, the way I understood it. The reason I don't eat them."

"That's your cremini and buttons, run-of-the-mill grocery store kind. Now, your morels, your exotics, they grow out here. Poke through the ground and grow wild, come in strong after a burn. You want to know more, you can go talk to Mose."

"The guy you work for. Yeah, alright, so where do I find this Mose?" Lee looked off, like he was distracted by something he saw.

"You don't need to go looking." Jack flicked his eyes to the side, just for a second. "You just keep asking the wrong questions, and the man's gonna —"

Lee spun and fired. All in one motion.

Jack staggered, felt he'd been punched, tried to keep to his feet, squeezing off a shot as Lee dove for the ground. Lee fired again and put a second one in his chest. Jack's legs went out and he sunk to his knees, couldn't lift the barrel now.

The bullet had grazed the meat of his arm, Lee feeling its sting, tore a swath through the fine merino wool. Taking a step, he toed the Walther away from Jack O'Dey's hand. Looked down at the man. The ringing loud in his ears. He knelt down, seeing the man was trying to speak.

"Mose Grillo. He'll be coming . . ." Jack forced out the words, barely audible. Looked like he was trying to keep his focus. Trying to stay in the world.

New growth showing around the blackened trunks. Lee looked to his left, fifty feet off the woods were green just past a creek, where the fire had been stopped. Looking at Jack O'Dey again, he reached down and tipped the cowboy hat over the man's face, not letting him see this one coming, ready to squeeze off the round, then stopping, thinking he heard something. Maybe it was a twig snapping. Staying low and moving to his right, he got behind a blackened trunk, listening and waiting. Something he was good at, like his time with the 23rd Infantry, moving on Heartbreak Ridge, holding that position till the Shermans rolled in. Lee leaving his rifle and crawling up the ridge with just his trench knife.

Staying in a crouch, not moving till he heard another snap, closer this time. Lee pinpointing its direction. When he stepped out, he had the pistol barrel pointing. Gert Kohn held the high-powered rifle across his body, seeing his buddy on the ground from a hundred feet away, then caught Lee's movement, too late swinging the rifle barrel when Lee fired, tapping Gert above the right temple. The man thrown backward. Lee stepped through a snowy patch, careful of his shoes, making sure with his second shot.

Walking back to the roadway, black ash and muck collecting on his shoes, Lee was reloading, getting the start of an idea, how to flush out Denny and Bobbi without Mose and a whole town of hicks getting in the way.

. . . thirty-five

Clay Jr. stuck the short length of two-by-four along the sliding door's track, clicked the latch and drew the curtains closed. The older Landry slid the bolt on his Remington with the scope, clanked the rifle on the kitchen table. Smelled of cleaning fluid and looked like it could bring down a moose.

Lifting the receiver from the wall phone, Mose made a call to Jack O'Dey's single-wide, not getting an answer and hanging up. Looking unhappy about it, saying, "The hell did he go?" No sign of Gert Kohn, either, the two of them supposed to be back by now.

"That for show or shooting?" The older Landry looked at Denny with his coat open, the Beretta in the holster. "Can't run a bluff every time, son."

"How about you don't worry about me, how'd that be?" Denny getting into the role.

Clay Jr. looked at Bobbi, leaned a Mossberg pump by the wall, telling her, "Just got to point it and pull this, darlin'. It kicks some, so hang on tight." Being smug about it.

"You want a kick, I can show you one, see for yourself if I can do it." Giving him a smile, pure sugar, liked watching the kid's ears go red.

The old man tugging his son by the sleeve, telling him, "Get outside."

Grinning, Dalton Benning strapped a six-shooter around his middle.

"Want to tell these boys the kind of company we got coming?" Mose said, looking at Denny. "And why we got it coming?"

Bobbi saying, "Like I told you, his name's Lee Trane, works for this guy I dated, Tomasino Palmieri."

"That's a name, huh?" the older Landry said.

"Goes by Lonzo. The man's a total bore, but not the kind you tell to his face." Giving the broad strokes, about Denny doing the driving, her doing the dating, both of them being used and getting fed up with it, deciding to even things up and strike out on their own.

"Uh-huh. You go with a guy like that, and don't like the way he treats you, so you hook up with his driver and take off with the man's money, steal his Cadillac, too." Dalton looked from her to Denny, laughing, "Don't know which one's got more balls ... Only trouble I see, you left a trail Ray Charles could follow, then ended up losing the money through the ice. May as well've sent this Tomato a postcard."

"And now we got to clean up your mess," Clay Jr. said, taking the Remington from the table, checking it over. Saying when they got the money from the lake, he wanted a piece.

"Fuckin' right." Dalton nodding.

"Nobody's asking ..." Denny started.

"My town," Mose said, pounding on the table. "Now, sit the fuck down." Looking at Denny, then Bobbi, waiting till they sat, saying, "Now, this guy, Tomato ... fill it in, the rest of it, who he is."

"Runs a dry cleaning business, vending machines on the side, a front for this family out of Montreal," Bobbi said.

"Family, like the mob?"

"Like that, yeah."

"Man should've stayed home," Mose said, looking at his guys.

"Won't be him coming," Denny said. "Like she said, the guy you ought to ask about's Lee Trane, one who does the wet work."

"Just one guy?"

"The man works alone."

The older Landry sucked air, saying, "Could just turn you over. Likely collect a reward."

"Except it's your town, right?" Bobbi said to Mose.

"Except for that." Mose looked from her to Dalton. "Nils said this guy drives a T-Bird. Baby blue with a fence for a grille, what he called it. You see it, you open up." Mose took his rifle and slung it on his shoulder, going to the sliding door and pushing the curtain aside, telling Denny and Bobbi to sit tight. Nodding to the kitchen, saying they'd find what they needed in the cupboards. Telling the older Landry to get the boys taking positions around the house, this Lee Trane sure to come calling. Meantime, he was going to find Jack and Gert, and join up with them later.

Landry saying it was under control.

The others filed out behind him. Dalton Benning turned, winking, saying to Bobbi, "I were you I'd lock it." Glancing to the front door.

... thirty-six

Mose put the rifle in back, next to the tank and diving gear he'd taken from Denny Barrenko's rental car, then left him by that boat launch to spend the night. Slinging the tarp overtop, grinning as he did it, thinking about the city boy out all night on his own, having to find his way back from the lake. Mose thinking he'd done him a favor — would have drowned before he got halfway down to the sunken Cortina. Fifty feet down in ice water was no rookie plunge.

And it didn't matter to Mose that he hadn't donned gear in a decade himself, he'd paddle the rowboat — same one Denny said he spent the night under. He'd make the dive in the thick wetsuit, knowing he had minutes before the hypothermia set in, the water robbing his body heat faster than the air. But for a cold, wet half-million, let his nuts shrivel.

Driving east, thirty over the limit, Mose reached for the thermos on the passenger floor, seeing Jack O'Dey's pick-up up on the dirt track near the burn area. Speeding past the T-Bird parked facing the other way on the shoulder. Not stopping, the charred trunks and naked earth going past. Guessing Jack had met Lonzo's man in the T-Bird. Maybe Gert, too. If he got past his boys, Lonzo's man would likely head to town and end up at Mose's place and get cut down by the rest of them. Landry good with a rifle and knowing where to bury the body deep in the woods. Make more fertilizer for the mushrooms.

Tipping the thermos, the coffee good and hot going down. The extra thermos on the rear floor was filled with hot water. This was his town, but he was picturing himself in a hammock, looking at palms swaying overhead, hot white sand under his feet, some rum drink in his hand. Leaving the cold, wet north behind, going to live his years where women were dark-skinned, nothing to hide in their bikinis, loving a white gent with money.

Headlights rounded a bend, coming toward him. Seeing it was a cop, he let up on the pedal, giving a wave to Henry Kendal's constable in the cruiser. Corporal Mikki Cook. Kind of a big-boned gal, not bad-looking, if you could get her out of that uniform long enough, get her thinking like a woman and drop the cop edge, trade the hundred-yard stare for bedroom eyes. Had crossed his mind, whether she had a thing going with the Doob. She waved, but didn't slow, wasn't interested in his speeding. Could be dealing with some roadkill report. Mose watched her in the rear-view, her cruiser disappearing past a rise. And he kept on, just ten more miles to Meridien. Freedom fifty feet down.

. . . *thirty-seven*

Stamping ash off his shoes, Lee Trane cursed and reloaded the pistol, his fingers stiff from the cold, goddamn this place. He tucked it away, walking back to his car, an idea taking shape. He'd tugged off the second dead man's coat, followed the footprints in the snow leading to the pick-up. Getting in it, he spun the tires and got it farther along the track, out of sight of the road. Twisting a coat sleeve, he shoved it down the gas tank's filler hole, got it soaked, stuck it back down. Took his lighter and lit it, watching the sleeve catch, then he walked to the road.

Opening the T-Bird's door, he was pissed, sure the sleeve had gone out. That's when he heard a car coming over the rise from the east. A cop car. Tucking the pistol behind his belt, he flapped the jacket over it. Goddamned shit for luck in the middle of nowhere.

•

Still wondering where Mose Grillo was off to in such a rush, racing his pick-up east, Corporal Mikki Cook leaned across the seat of her patrol car, rolled down the passenger window, the cap with the earflaps over her hair, the badge pinned on top, saying to the man, "Everything all right, mister?" Eyes looking at the fancy Ford parked to the side, nicest ride that wasn't a pick-up she'd ever seen. And the first time she'd ever seen whitewalls.

"You got me, Officer, caught me watering the horses." The man smiled, made it sheepish, like he was embarrassed.

Mikki nodded at him, saying, "You know a fellow, Jack O'Dey?"

"I supposed to?"

"Saw his truck sitting up on that track." She'd seen it on her way out to Meridien Lake, sure this was the same spot.

The man looked past his shoulder, saying he hadn't seen a soul since the crossroads.

Mikki catching the pistol shape at the back of the jacket.

"Like I said, I was just —"

"Watering the horses, right," Mikki said, her left hand staying on the wheel, her right moving to the three-on-the-tree. "Guess you're staying in Ripley, then?"

"Thinking of getting a room, that yellow place, used to be a brothel, right? Guess you know it."

"The Ripley House. I'm sure they can fix you up." Her hand firm on the shifter. "Guess you come for some early fishing, then?"

"More like sightseeing." A guy in city shoes, a jacket he might wear to dinner, with a gun tucked in back of it. Not a guy dressed for sightseeing.

Since being assigned here, Mikki knew Mose Grill and his guys were into all kinds of illegal activity. Possessing the kind of shit luck that got you sent to this way-out detachment, locals calling her boss the Doob, like he was dumb. Her foot stayed light on the gas pedal. "How about I get a look at your driver's license, Mister . . ."

"Verrick, Marty Verrick. Sure, I got it right here." Giving her a smile, she watched his right hand move to his back pocket.

Mikki forced a smile. No way she'd get the service piece unholstered in time, the one she'd only fired at the range.

Taking out his wallet, he flapped it open, showing the license. Holding it out, as if he meant for her to take it.

Glancing at it, she let him hold it, her left hand on the wheel, right hand on the stick, foot on the pedal. Surprised she wasn't scared, her eyes never leaving this guy's. "Okay, you can tuck it away, Mr. Verrick."

His gun hand held his wallet, and he kept the smile, tucking it in his pocket, his hand moving slow, stepping to his right as he did it. And he started to say, "Hey, you hear—" Then the *whoosh* coming from the woods behind him made him stagger, coming like an explosion.

Jamming the stick, Mikki stomped the pedal and dropped across the seat at the same time, the cruiser bolting forward.

•

Lee cleared his pistol and put a round through the door's RCMP crest, firing the clip, the rear window exploding. The cruiser jerked to a stop, and the cop twisted to get her service piece clear. He was running and diving onto the trunk, head first, punching and scrambling through the busted rear window and across the back seat, pushing himself forward.

She had the pistol in her right hand, grabbing the door handle with her left, trying to get out as Lee got a hand on her neck, the other grabbing her wrist, knocking away the pistol. Half over the seat, he overpowered her, the cop trying to punch up as he grabbed at her utility belt with his free hand, trying to get her cuffs. She twisted and tried to push him off.

Punching at her face, he felt her nose snap, her eyes rolling back as she went limp. Lee pushed her out of the driver's door, then got out and cuffed her hands behind her, getting her keys from the ignition and popping the trunk. She started to come around, and he clubbed her again, dragging her and shoving her in the trunk, shutting the lid. Woman sure had some fight in her.

Catching his breath, he pushed the cruiser to the shoulder. Could smell smoke and was crossing to his T-Bird when he heard something else over the crackling coming from the north woods. Double sets of headlights from a Trailways bus coming over the crest, bearing down and slowing at the sight of the patrol car with its back window smashed out, the T-Bird parked on the shoulder. Lee waving for it to stop, seeing bewildered tourist eyes looking out the side windows at a cruiser with glass all over the ground.

The driver in his blue jacket and cap worked the manual door lever, asking, "What's going on, mister?"

"Mountie went in there." Pointing at the woods, Lee said, "Sent me to radio for help, except the set's dead." He pointed to the smoke showing through the trees. A breeze was fanning the flames, creating crackling and a roaring sound, Lee feeling the heat.

"What happened to the window?"

"Got no time for that. This thing's spreading. Fast! Go get help. Please!"

"Right." The driver nodded, shutting the door, getting underway. Saying something to his passengers. A dozen faces, shocked, all looking out the window, passengers coming for the glaciers and northern lights, getting more than they bargained for, the driver throttling the Trailways and heading for Ripley, bound to alert the whole town.

When the bus was over the next hump, Lee was getting in his car, heard Mikki thumping inside her trunk. Knowing he should take care of it, but having trouble seeing himself shooting a woman, even one with a badge. The town would rush out here to fight the fire. They'd get her out of the trunk before the fire got to her. Meaning he had maybe an hour to find Bobbi Ricci and Denny the driver and get things done.

... thirty-eight

"Guess he's got enough guys." Bobbi went in the living room, Denny switching on the TV, turned the dial, the Galloping Gourmet getting worked up about broccoli with cheese. Mose and his crew out there on the lookout for Lee Trane.

Denny saying, "Armed like an assault team."

Bobbi saying, "He gets past them, think you could shoot Lee, or you expect me to do it?"

"He gets past those guys, I guess you're gonna find out."

One thing was sure, Lee Trane wouldn't come ringing the doorbell, stand and wait on the stoop. She watched Denny snug the drapes across the sliding door. Going to the front door, Denny checked the lock, went back and sat at the kitchen table.

Bobbi was going through the upper cupboards, checked the fridge, saying, "A lot you can learn from a man's kitchen."

"Already know more than I want."

"See here, take-out tubs from Kate's, looks like a week's worth, mean's the man's single and can't cook. Only fruit's Del Monte, and guess that's a carrot, like from last year." Taking it from the crisper and bending it, saying, "Not much good limp." Closing the door, she checked the freezer, a stack of Swansons and Hungry-Man. "See here, the man's big into macaroni and cheese." Going to the cupboard over the stove. "Chock Full o'Nuts." Tossing the carrot in the bin. "Gonna make a pot, huh?"

"Yeah, why not?" Looking at the TV from where he sat, the Beretta in the holster in easy reach. Graham Kerr working the studio audience, a glass of wine in his hand, the man with his long sideburns, asking the gray-hairs in the front row how many ounces in a cup. Then looking at the camera and going to commercial. Some cute kid singing about bologna. Joe Namath letting Farrah Fawcett suds up his face. Dodge trucks promising to go to any length. Graham Kerr coming back and keeping up the pace.

Sliding a cup in front of him, Bobbi took hers and went to the staircase, stopped at the bannister, saying, "Gonna see if he's got any hot water."

"You pick now to have a shower?" Denny turned and watched her take the stairs.

"I'm dying for one. Hotel shower's a cold dribble." The floorboards creaking underfoot, she went in the bathroom, getting undressed, running the water, calling back down the stairs, "You wanna save some water, there's room for two."

•

Some guy coming to kill them, and this girl wants to get wet and play pass the soap. Denny hearing the water running upstairs, a banner running along the bottom of the TV screen, saying stay tuned for *Beat the Clock* following the *Galloping Gourmet*. Graham Kerr whipping up something called *crème brûlée*, the gray-hairs watching him do it. Setting down the cup, taking the pistol and the dumb holster, Denny took the stairs two at a time, laid the pistol rig on the toilet tank. Her cup on the counter.

"What took you?" Bobbi drawing with a finger on the frosted glass.

Denny thinking she was drawing a heart, turned out to be a cock. Tugging off his shirt and climbing out of his pants, toes catching the elastic of his Jockeys, peeling them down, tossing his bunched clothes on top of the pistol, he slid back the glass door.

"Got more of that weed?" Putting a wet hand to his chest, stopped him from stepping in. Her hair matted flat, looking darker.

"I look like I'm holding?"

"Down in your coat. Come on, be fun."

"Not gonna need it." Taking her hand, he stepped in, feeling the heat of the spray.

"Promise?"

"Promise." Pulling her close, shutting the glass door, Denny took the bar of soap, rolling it in his hands.

... *thirty-nine*

Lee Trane had driven a half-mile, turning in the seat, seeing the heavy smoke rising above the treetops. Swinging in the bucket seat, he rolled on, trying not to think the woman cop could burn in the trunk, not something he planned on. Driving the Bird back to Ripley, he braked on the next rise another mile west, turning once more to the rising smoke. Yeah, this could work out, the fire giving him time.

...forty

A light chop on the water. Mose rolled up to a couple of birch on the edge of the path, too tight a space to squeeze his truck through. Grabbing the gear bag, extra thermos and tank, he left the truck and walked the path to the rowboat, its paint-can anchor smashed through its hull. Must have been Denny Barrenko, making sure nobody else got any ideas. Cursing him, Mose looked across the water. No other way; he'd have to swim out from shore and dive down. It wasn't just cold, it was hostile. The wind rippling the gray lake water.

He unzipped the gear bag, getting out of his jeans and pulling the dry suit over his long johns. Jerking up the suit felt like he was giving himself a wedgie. Snapping up the crotch strap, he shrugged out of his parka, adjusting the braces, pulling the brass zippers, tugging his own wool gloves over the Rocked in the Cradle ink, past the cuff seals. Pouring the thermos of hot water over his hood, he pulled it on, feeling the warmth. Checking his set-up, the gauge, the dumps, the attached light, pulling on the pack and tank, attaching the drysuit hose, eyeing the regulator, the weight, dropping the pry bar into the thigh pocket, strapping on the mask. Hadn't done it in a long while, but it was all coming back. Doing what Denny Barrenko had no idea about. Pouring the last of the hot water over the three-finger mitts, pulling them over the gloves. Grabbing his flag., floats and coiled lines, putting the flippers on at the shore, he waded knee-deep, feeling the cold, careful on the algae-covered rocks.

Mose looked down the shore. A green Dodge pick-up was backing down the ramp, a cap topper and a canoe sticking out the back, a couple hundred yards to the north. Goddamn Wim Dickens picking now to go for a stringer of ice-out trout. The old man getting out and untying the canoe, pulling it off the back and setting it on the ramp. Didn't see Mose, but if he paddled out, he'd likely spot the dive flag. Mose dropped it, leaving it behind.

Not thinking anymore about it, he counted to three and swam to where he figured the Cortina went down, and he dove down, adjusting for buoyancy. Five minutes tops before his tongue swelled and his head got cloudy. Hearing the air from the tank, everything getting darker as he dove.

There it was. Seemed deeper here than he thought it would be, but he'd make it. Shivering when he got down to the car, pulling the velcro side pocket, getting his hawk-bill and wedging it in the gap between the body and trunk, his toes and fingers getting numb. Pressing for leverage, he popped it with a thunk, air bubbles releasing. Shining the Ikelite inside, he grabbed the handles, clipping the line to the first case, taking his alternate air hose, filling the lift bag and letting it go. His breathing was quick and shallow; he clipped up the second case, filling the bag with air and letting that one go, sent it rising to the surface.

His head was clouding, thoughts of someplace tropical, his feet in sandals, one of those colored shirts with flamingos on it, eating passion fruit, wondering what it was like. Boat drinks with big-assed island girls that *no hablo ingles*, dark and shiny in Coppertone.

Pushing off the bumper, he forced his legs to pump, kicking his flippers. Looking up, following the floating bags to the surface, the buoys pulling him up — the light from above — but a strange droning got louder as he surfaced. Had to be the cold messing with his senses.

... *forty-one*

It was a diagram Caleb Hawkes had seen in *National Geographic* or someplace, detailing the parts of the brain using different colors, one lobe pink, the other purple, a pale blue cerebellum. Thinking right now his brain was a swirl of all those colors, the whole mess moving like a lava lamp.

By the time he stubbed out the roach, he put water on for coffee. Caleb stood in his briefs, spooned Taster's Choice in his cup, taking the whistling kettle from the burner. With the blinds closed, he wasn't sure what time of day it was. His splitting headache and that pasty mouth told him it was the morning after. Not sure who that was in the bed, long dark hair spilling across his extra pillow, likely a friend he made last night, asleep under his blankets. Hopefully of the female persuasion.

Switching on the Pioneer, he spun whatever LP was on the stacking turntable, setting the auto tone-arm down, hearing that scrape as the needle found the groove, Caleb thinking, Surprise me. Steppenwolf coming on, Side B with the organ and guitar riff overtop, John Kay doing the one about rain falling and feeling low.

He plunked himself on the sofa, his room overtop of the Driftwood, the bar downstairs. No charter today, meaning Caleb was free to sample some product. Had a key staring at him on the coffee table, some of it spilled on the glass top. A couple more tokes from now and he'd climb into his jeans, answer the craving for breakfast, thinking it was a flapjack kind of day, butter melting and syrup dripping. Maybe some berries or a banana if the Driftwood Room had anything like that. Spend the rest of the day filling the roach tray. Maybe whoever was in the bed would join him. Caleb searching for her name, trying to recall a face from last night's fog.

Grabbing his smokes, he looked around for his lighter when the phone rang. Lifting the needle off "A Girl I Knew." Taking a couple rings for him to get to it, saying hello, hearing the voice and wishing he hadn't picked up.

Early in the season for a wildfire, everything wet from the spring thaw, but smoke had been spotted a dozen miles west of Meridien. Captain Jim Wilem was calling in the emergency, saying the Dump Duck, the big Canso scooper, was getting fueled and set to fly from Mud Bay. Captain Jim saying he was needed.

Saying he was on his way, Caleb tried to will himself sober, filled the thermos with the hot coffee, found his jeans, taking a shirt from the laundry pile. Buttoning it up, he tried to think of the girl's name, wanted to write her a note and let her know he had to split. But he couldn't think of it as he stamped his feet into his shoes, hid the key of weed under the couch, grabbed the keys to his Jeep and went out the door, guessing she could just let herself out. What it meant to be on call, volunteering anytime an alarm sounded.

. . . forty-two

Was the first time he did it wet, middle of the day, the two of them under the shower's spray. Wanted to move them into bed, the king-size with the cannonballs on the headboard.

"You mean Mose's bed?" Bobbi making a face, snuggling against him, lifting and pressing a thigh against him. Hands circling around the back of his neck. Looking in his eyes, smiling.

"Might get soap in my eyes."

"You can shut 'em the whole time."

"Yeah, but, standing . . ."

"Never done it upright?"

"Not when there's a bed."

"How about some invention?"

"Mean like kinky?"

"That what it means to you?" Playing with him, her fingers getting a rise. "By invention, guess I'm an every-room-in-the-house girl. Every position, too."

"Talking like one-on-one Twister."

"More like *Kama Sutra*."

Smiling at this woman who went from wanting to shoot him, to spooning, to wanting to do it in every room. Amazing with her hand. Denny caving to what she was doing, having to hold it back.

"How about Lee Trane?"

"You thinking threesome?" Smiling at him, pressing at him, kept her hand working, feeling him pull away.

"Not a time for funny." Already seemed like more than the two of them. In this guy's house, with his army out there. Told her not to be a comedienne, Denny pulling her hand away, kissing the top of it. Then kissing her neck, moving his mouth down her body.

Urging him, Bobbi using her hand to guide him, breathing something about getting his Don Rickles in her Joan Rivers.

...forty-three

Lee Trane stopped the Bird out front of the Ripley House. Rent Me sitting out front, he walked by it and stuck his head in the office door. "They back?"

Nils shook his head, saying, "No sir, they were, but you missed them. Gone to fight the fire." Nils started to tell about the emergency, how he just got the call himself, everyone in town being mustered. "Means all of us got to —"

"Gimme the key." Lee held out his hand.

"I, uh . . . can't do that."

Going to the door, Lee took the sign from the small window next it, turned it from "Open" to "Back in fifteen minutes."

Then he dialed up the stare, putting it on Nils.

"I don't make the rules, top of which we got this emergency. Sorry, but . . ."

"Afraid and sorry. Hell, Neil, we're just getting started."

"See, in the hotel business, customer comfort and confidence, it's rule one, and I got to abide, then we got this —"

Grabbing the nameplate off the desk, Lee fisted it and bashed Nils in the face, waited while the man reeled and sputtered, clutching his face. Going from outrage to shock.

Getting his attention, Lee went on, "Survival, Neil. That's your rule number one. You can stick your comfort, and your saying sorry. You hear what I'm saying? You want, I can explain it some more, but, just so you know, my time's short, so we're gonna have to kick up the lesson." Lee looking like was going to hit him again, the nameplate in his fist.

Looking at the blood on his fingers, the phone within reach on the desk. Nils said, "Okay, look . . . guy called Mose Grillo came by, the three of them got in his truck and took off. Likely all volunteering, going to fight the fire."

That name again, Mose Grillo. "The key, Neil." Snapping his fingers. Lee giving him that look, one that said he had bigger problems than a fire.

Nils reached for the rack and handed it over. The desk phone ringing again.

Lee told him to go ahead and answer it, just be careful what he said, then he was out the side door. Taking the outside stairs to the room, he stood to the side and rapped on the door of 2. Could have shouldered it past the flimsy lock. Sticking in the key, he opened it, stood to the side, with the pistol in his hand. The room was empty, the bed unmade. Checking the bathroom down the outside corridor. Lee went back to the office, tossing the key on the counter, saying, "Point the way to this Grillo's place." Giving Nils a chance to think, was he more afraid of Lee or of Mose? Pointing to the darkened bar and gallery across the street. Mose nowhere in sight. Leaning across the counter, dialing up the look, Lee said, "Where's he live?"

"Don't know the address, but it's a log place, a big one on the west side just out of town, got trees all around. Think he's got a red birdhouse on a post out front." Nils pointed north, saying, "But he's got to be on his way, this bush fire's out of control, and Mose being captain of the volunteers.

Everybody in town having to go. You should be, too, help save the place." Nils wanting to go to the back room and get his coat, looking at Lee like he needed permission to do it.

Lee turned to the street, asking, "This shithole got no fire department?"

"Got the volunteers, meaning nearly all of us, plus the Scooper flying in."

"The fuck's a scooper?"

"Fire bomber. It's how we do it. Whole town on the ground, the scooper in the air."

"What's he drive, this Mose?"

"Uh-um, two-tone Ford, green and white one, a few years old."

"Pick-up?"

"Sure." Saying it like, what else.

Lee turned for the door, then stopped. "And Nils . . ."

"Uh-huh?"

"I wasn't here."

He waited for the man to bob his head like he understood, Lee went out the door, knocking down the "Back in fifteen minutes" sign, guessing Mose Grillo wouldn't be hard to find. The pair of mushroom pickers he left in the woods worked for him. Likely be others. The pump shotgun and bandolier of shells were tucked in the false panel of the Bird's trunk.

A brown Harvester with a tandem axel stopped across the street, and Nils was coming out, getting into his parka, locking the door without giving Lee a look, going and getting in back with a bunch of hicks all hunkered down in the bed, the truck lumbering off toward the fire.

Lee seeing the rising smoke to the east, thinking he could smell it, too, meaning the wind would push it this way. A good chance the whole town would burn down, just a bunch of hick volunteers and something called a scooper to stop the blaze. Lee thinking he was doing the place a favor, putting it out of its misery, looking at the wreck with "RENT ME" painted on its door. The thing looking like one of the beaters he'd seen at some wreck-'em race at the PNE back home.

Getting in the Bird, he put his thoughts on Bobbi Ricci, feeling close to catching up, taking care of Denny the driver, taking Bobbi on that long drive back to Vancouver, having to stop for the night, get a room in some other hick-town motel, use his Eddy Rush ID, maybe give Bobbi Ricci a couple of ways to go: get taken back to Lonzo, or maybe she could convince him not to. Driving through the dead town, slush slapping under his fenders, his whitewalls seeking purchase on the unplowed road. Lee driving through this dead place, everybody gone to fight the fire he started, just like he figured they would.

...forty-four

Henry "the Doob" Kendall was worried, unable to get Mikki Cook on the radio since he got word of the fire east of town. The streets empty, every man and woman gone to fight it, the way they did it in these northern towns. First sign of smoke, you considered yourself conscripted. Soon as kids turned sixteen, they showed up for basic training at the community hall. Non-compliance brought a hundred-buck fine. Second time meant going in front of the judge, the courthouse over in Smithers. Past that it was an automatic ten days, a guest of the county, didn't matter your sex or age.

Driving the main drag and then along the outskirts, Henry saw the men standing out front of Mose's place, a couple of pick-ups in the driveway. Guessing they were gathering to go fight the fire. Slowing the cruiser, he cranked down his window. Nobody smiling, the Landrys holding rifles. Casey Hopper and Dalton Benning looking at him. Not fire-fighting equipment, and no sign of Mose.

"Hey ya, Doob, what's shaking?" Casey Hopper made it sound friendly, the younger Landry grinning.

"Got a fire east of town." Henry waited, looking from man to man. Telling them about the call in, somebody spotting smoke. "You fellas planning to go and shoot the fire out?"

"Hadn't heard, but okay, we'll be along, Doob," Dalton Benning said, looking at him, but not making a move.

"Think the fire's waiting, Dalt?"

"Guess you heard me say we'll be along," Dalton said, stepping to the cruiser, the rest of them watching.

Grabbing his Stetson off the passenger seat, Henry started to open his door, putting his boot out.

Stepping in quick, Dalton Benning braced a knee against the cruiser's door, jamming it against Henry's leg.

Henry tried to pull his foot in, but couldn't, tried not to wince at the pain.

"Said we'll be along, huh, Doob. Now, how about you take my word on it now, okay?" Dalton eased back on the door, let Henry get his leg back in.

"Guess I see your point." Dropping his Stetson back on the seat, Henry put it in reverse and backed into the road, threw it in gear and jerked it forward. Getting out while it was still moving, the S&W in his hand, pointing it at Dalton, saying, "Let me make it plainer, so there's no mistake. Next one calls me Doob, I'm gonna take it personal, disrespect for the badge. And that man's gonna find himself cuffed and riding in back."

Dalton ran a hand along the stubble of his jaw, looking less sure in spite of the grin, but pressing it, saying, "Just how many cuffs you —"

Henry took a couple steps, raising the pistol and firing.

Dalton jumped, looked like he took a moment to know he wasn't shot. Turning and seeing the red birdhouse dropping off its post and lying broken on the ground. One of the pieces Mose paid to have carved overseas someplace and sent back here.

Henry stepped up, got in Dalton's face, saying, "Not gonna worry about you, Dalton, am I right?"

"Want us piling in back of your car, Henry?"

"Want you all driving out the 37, and I'm gonna trust you to do it." Henry casually swung the barrel past them, stepping over to his cruiser, reaching for the door handle.

"Guess you got on the uniform, gives you the last word," Clay Jr. said, keeping his distance.

"Any man wants, be happy to take off the uniform. And when I do, I'm gonna oblige the hell out of that man. But first thing, you're all going to put out a fire." Still holding the pistol, waiting till they piled in their trucks.

...forty-five

Yellow with orange across the wings, the big Canso's tail was marked the same way. The crew dubbed her the Dump Duck. Twin Pratt & Whitneys roaring above the pines. High-winged and big-flapped with an oversized tail, the Duck had the raw power to touch down on any body of water, needing a little over the length of a football field for the probes to scoop 8,000 pounds into its belly, doing it in twelve seconds at seventy knots. Lifting over the treetops with its belly full and flying over the smoke, dropping its load. Circling back and doing it again.

The training crew called themselves the duck pack, nervous guys sitting on the back benches. Caleb was in the second chair, still high from the weed, nodding to Captain Jim Wilem. Loving this, soaring over the miles of green looking like a carpet under them, the snow-spotted mountain and lake mirrored back. He was the No. 2, his main job this trip was to go over operations, this being the training crew's first real time out. Some of these guys still likely to get airsick. Back at training, Caleb had taken them through the basics: the splash-and-gos and wet landings, flying low and slow, going over the functions and operations, looking into the anxious faces, judging who'd make it and who wouldn't. These guys who started out not knowing the difference between a seaplane and a floatplane.

Shouting back a couple of last-minute instructions over the engines' drone, he got to his feet now, seeing the fear and excitement in their eyes, guessing a few hits of Thunderfuck could take care of that, but not something Captain Jim would approve of. Going down the row between them, clapping to time to get their attention, he started swinging his hips to a beat only he heard, throwing in some grunts and foot stomps. The crew looked at each other, smiling, knowing what was coming. Caleb doing this on the last practice run. Captain Jim gave him a thumb's-up, and Caleb was teaching the rookies how to crew, best way he knew, getting them to be easy with it, how to fight a fire from the air.

"I'm the fly, looking at the crumb in the river," Caleb sang out, not exactly Marvin Gaye, but putting some heart into it. "I'm going down, gonna get that crumb." Threw in some hand motions, the engines' drone sounding like back-up.

The guy closest was Jonsie. Unsteady getting to his feet, he clapped along and piped in, "I'm the fish looking at that fly. He comes down here, I'm gonna get that fly."

Caleb and Jonsie kept on clapping, moving like they were hearing the music. Caleb pointing to the next guy.

Manny came off the bench, grinning through the nerves, copying Caleb and Jonsie's moves. "I'm the grizzly, man, and that fly, fuck, he comes down for that crumb, and that fish comes up. Man, I'm nailing me that fish." Out of tune and no sense of rhythm, Manny clapped along, circled a dance move, getting into it.

Baker sat opposite and pulled himself up, holding onto a brace and called out, "I'm the man. And that fly goes down for the crumb, and the fish rises for the fly, and the grizzly gets the fish. Man, I'm shooting me that bear." Holding a pretend rifle, taking a one-eyed aim, putting his own dance moves to it. Clapping along.

Chuck was next to Baker, tucked his hair back and slapped his wet palms together and got up, high-fiving Baker, singing he was the mouse. Going through the same lines: the fly and fish and the bear and the man, then calling out, "And when that sucker's bagging the bear, I'm grabbing his sandwich."

The training crew stomped their boots on the metal floor, clapping their hands. No jitters now. Captain Jim was tapping the wheel, looking ahead at the gray mass filling the sky ahead.

Caleb did the part for an absent man, being the cat looking at the mouse, rhyming off the lines, saying he was getting that mouse.

Captain Jim took the mic and turned in his seat, singing and clapping, too, doing his bit, "That fly goes down and gets the crumb, fish gets the fly, and the bear swipes the fish, man shoots the bear. Mouse grabs the sandwich, and the cat lunges and misses the mouse, falls in the river." The captain looking back to the rookies, calling out, "And the moral of the story's . . ."

The crew shouting and stomping, all singing, "When the fly goes down, the pussy gets wet!"

Checking his altitude, the smoke boiling in the sky ahead, Captain Jim looked to Caleb, saying, "Here we go."

Young faces looking less scared, the scooper flying into that hell. Caleb taken back to Operation Rolling Thunder, a botched attempt to show U.S. muscle in the air. Scared shitless himself back then, but right now, he was feeling he could sign for another thirteen months. The chance of feeling alive, flying into Russian machine-gun rounds, missiles whooshing up from dense brush, arcing past them. Nothing on his mind, just feeling alive, keeping it steady, the Huey thundering and lighting up the jungle floor.

Rolling Thunder was long past and the peace talks had troops withdrawing. Here he was, left to flying supplies and weed and drunken hunters to remote spots. Crewing on the Dump Duck was like its own high. Except nobody was trying to shoot him down, and defying death had always made him feel alive, really alive.

Captain Jim dropped the Canso low over the water. Caleb got back in the second seat, switching the controls and scoops, catching a flash on the surface ahead, smiling to himself, thinking of Denny's car at the bottom of this very lake. The Canso skimmed Meridien's surface, felt like it was braking, the rushing sound of water forced into the tanks. Fifteen seconds and Captain Jim lifted off, Caleb retracting the scoops, the brute engines churning, lifting over the tree tops, an impossible angle for anything less than the Canso.

The crew in back were sitting now, stomping their boots, singing one by Jim Morrison about lighting a fire. Two hundred feet over the boat launch and they were kissing the treetops. Captain Jim swinging her in an arc and flying toward the hotspot.

Smelling the smoke and feeling the sting in his eyes, Caleb flipped the switch for the scoop doors, releasing the payload ahead of the advancing blaze. Tons of water hitting the mark. They circled, going for another scoop. The crew singing "Ring of Fire," doing Johnny Cash proud.

...forty-six

In a couple minutes, he'd be the richest man in the frozen north. And a man intent on going south.

That roaring sound was filling his head, growing louder as he surfaced, Mose thinking he came up too fast. Turbulence thrashed the surface, a rush and a giant shadow passing overhead. At first he thought it was a squall kicking up, then for a second he felt like he was passing over.

Breaking the surface, he was looking at the yellow lines snatched tight by the lift bags, water spraying off them, the Gucci cases whipped across the surface and up into the air. His mind moving slow, but putting it together. The bungee cords holding the Gucci cases together. The big orange plane snatching the yellow lines and lift bags, along with the cases, and roaring off — his fogged mind trying to make sense — the flying fucks were stealing his money. Trying to yell for them to stop, schlucking water. Started to swim after them, then survival instincts had him turning for the shore, Mose swimming, aware the Dump Duck was rising above the boat launch, the trail of lines, lift bags and cases. Seeing the distant smoke, being captain of the volunteers, he started to put it together, what it meant, his half a million bucks on the way to be dropped on a fucking wildfire.

. . . forty-seven

"Nothing wrong with the equipment." Bobbi using her hand, patting it like it was a good boy.

"Well, glad you got no complaint. Guess we're pretty good, you and me." Running his hand down her back, along her curves. "Who knows, maybe there's a next page for us." Denny looking down, liking what she was doing. Then tipping his head back under the spray, the hot water feeling good.

"If you mean like a forever thing . . . think that's a long a time."

"Well, we're good now, right?"

"Now, yeah. But, I'm not much for the house in the 'burbs." Bobbi worked her soaped hand, moved it gently, knew what she was doing, saying, "Or the kids-in-the-yard scene. Be like somebody's throwing ropes over me."

"Maybe you're overthinking it. Been going with guys like Lonzo too long." He reached and stopped her hand, got her looking up at him. Easing her back against the tiles, pressing against her, surprised the water was still hot, surprised he was up for round two, pushing himself in. Whispering, "Give it a chance, maybe see where it goes."

"I know where it goes."

"I interrupting something?" The voice had them jumping, both banging the wall.

Denny tugging open the sliding glass.

Lee Trane leaned against the doorframe, having fun with the moment, his pistol in his hand. Telling them to come on out, calling them lovebirds.

•

Bobbi stepped out after Denny, took the towel he pulled off the rack, the one he meant to wrap around himself. She held it in front of herself like maybe it stopped bullets.

"Let's go." Lee waved the pistol. Looking from him to her, both with their hair wet, skin dripping. "Downstairs, you're making coffee." Looking at him, then to her, "And you're making a call." Ushering with the pistol, he stepped into the hall and let them go ahead, Bobbi wanting to get into her bell-bottoms and turtleneck.

"You're fine how you are." Lee waving the pistol barrel, wanting them downstairs.

Denny walked ahead, naked, moving down the stairs. Lee followed behind Bobbi, saying even with her hair damp she looked good enough to eat. Following them into the kitchen, saying, "So, where's the money?"

"Bottom of the lake." Denny went and sat at the table, starting to shiver with the cold, the fringe jacket on the back of the chair.

"Could shoot you, leave you naked and dead, drag Bobbi out to the Bird and off we go." Lee saying, "So, how about we get to it, how you plan to get it back?"

"Can take you to it, right to the spot," Denny said.

Lee pushed Bobbi ahead so he could see her, then went to the wall phone. "Yeah, except you're already wet."

"Expecting me to dive for it."

"That what you were doing upstairs, practicing your dive moves?"

Denny reached back for the coat on the chair.

"Uh-uhn," Lee said. "Like you fine like you are." Then smiling at Bobbi. "You too, doll. This place got coffee or no?"

"I'm a woman, like I'd know that?"

"Look to me to be the instant type." Smiling at her trying to hide herself behind the towel.

Going to the cupboard, Bobbi reached a jar of Chock Full o' Nuts, saying, "This do?"

"It's coffee, right?"

Finding a kettle, she went to the sink and filled it, found a carton of milk in the fridge, opened it and sniffed its sour smell, found a sugar bowl in a cupboard, Bobbi asking how he liked it.

"Black and a sugar."

Lee saying they'd drive out to the lake, let Denny make the dive and bring up the money. He did it with a fuss, he'd tie the anchor rope to him and send him back down. He got it done, brought up the cases, Lee would make it quick.

"With no dive gear?"

Lee shrugged like it wouldn't matter.

"How about her?" Denny said.

"Got Lonzo waiting." Lee nodded to the wall phone, telling her, "Make the call."

Bobbi stepped over and took it off the hook. "Who am I calling?"

"Think you know. Dial zero, tell the girl who you want." Lee watching her from behind, saying she'd packed on a few pounds more than the last time he saw her, out by Lonzo's pool, but it all ended up in the right places.

"Makes me feel so good, you saying it." Bobbi rolled her eyes, picked up the receiver, the operator coming on, Bobbi saying she needed to call long distance, a matter of life and death. The operator asking which city, Bobbi getting switched over, giving the long-distance operator the number. Then waited while it rang.

Lee stepped in and took the phone from her, told her to fix his coffee, watching her spoon instant into a mug, adding sugar, pouring in the boiling water. Trying to keep the towel wrapped around her.

"Yeah, put Lonzo on," Lee said into the phone, then waiting.

"The fuck is it?" Lonzo's tinny voice heard through the earpiece, sounding like he just woke up.

"It's done."

"You got her, my Bobbi?" Lonzo back to calling her by name.

"Yeah, your Bobbi, standing right here, making me coffee."

"And the driver?"

"Denny, yeah, the whole happy family."

"And what belongs to me?"

"That comes next."

"Why the fuck haven't you —"

"Hold on." Lee held out the phone, saying to Bobbi, "Talk to this guy."

Bobbi started to bring his cup, Lee told her to set it back down.

Shrugging, Bobbi set the cup down, went and took the receiver, saying, "Hey, Lonz. You still sore at me, hon?"

"*Sei una stronza*, would've forgot who you are, except you got what belongs to me."

"Guess you don't mean my heart," Bobbi said.

"Know what I'm gonna do to your heart, do it with my teeth?"

"Take it easy. Jeez, the money's in a safe place, bottom of a lake." Bobbi held the receiver back to Lee.

Bringing his cup, taking the phone back in his other hand, he put it to his ear, watching the two of them.

Lonzo yelling, "How you gonna get it?"

"Turning the driver into a diver."

"Stop the bullshit, and fuckin' do it."

Looking at the dead phone in his hand, Lee hung it on the hook.

"Mind I get a smoke?" Bobbi said, looking at Denny, stepping to the table, her hand reaching for the jacket on the back of his chair.

"Stop." Lee told her. Reaching the pack in his shirt pocket, he tossed it on the table, saying, "Know that shit'll kill you, huh?"

"I like it on the edge." She flipped open the pack, Lee tossing a book of matches on the table. Denny lighting it for her, coughing from the smoke.

Lee laughed, watching Denny's face go red, coughing some more. Saying to him. "How the hell you gonna make the dive?"

"Not much good if I catch pneumonia first. What say you let me get something on?"

Lee waved the pistol, said he was bored of looking at him anyway, making him go first up the stairs, Bobbi behind him, Lee following, the pistol in his hand. At the top of the stairs, Lee ushered Bobbi to the side in the hall. Lee told Denny to go first, watching him reach his clothes from the toilet tank.

Denny reached for his underpants. "Got to watch me, huh?"

Lee just shook his head at him.

Bobbi dropping her towel. Put her hands up, saying, "Oopsie."

That got Lee turning.

And Denny had the Beretta, Lee late seeing it.

And Denny shot him, Lee stumbling backward, getting off a wild shot, trying to aim on Denny. His words cut off as he tumbled backwards down the stairs, the pistol going off again, firing into the ceiling.

Lying at the bottom of the stairs, he tried to speak, watched the two of them coming down the stairs, felt the blood bubbling from his throat, past his lips as he started to choke. Bobbi and Denny looking down at him, watching him go.

•

The ringing still in Denny's ears as he got dressed.

Bobbi, back in her bell-bottoms and sweater, stepped past Lee Trane, his blood matting his shirt and jacket, pooling on the carpet. Picking the receiver from the wall phone, she dialed the operator again, asking for the same number, then she waited. After the click, she said, "Hey ya, Aldo, long time no see. How you doing?"

Quiet for a moment, then Aldo said he was doing fine. Bobbi told him she was good, too, asking him to get the old man, waiting till Lonzo came on.

"What the fuck now?"

"Your boy got his chock full of nuts."

"You crazy bitch, what're you saying?"

"Saying we shot him — well, Denny did."

"You fucking with me ... Put Lee on, right fucking now." Called her something in Italian, then yelling, "Now!"

"I do, just gonna get dead air, sweetie." Bobbi loving this, saying, "He shot him with your little ol' Beretta, one I took from your drawer."

"You and him, huh, the driver?" Like he didn't believe it.

Stepping past the body, she pulled the phone cord tight, the coiled line straightening. Taking Lee's cup from the counter, sipping, thinking it wasn't bad for instant, even lukewarm. "Yeah, the two of us are going someplace nice, where they got some sun and palm trees. Gonna spend your money, every cent."

"The dead don't spend."

"You want it back, baby, then why not come and get it? Maybe you can beat us to it. It's sitting right on the bottom of the lake."

"I'm on my way, coming to bite your heart out. Gonna let that fuck watch." Calling for Aldo to go start the car.

"Yeah, okay, good, you got a pencil, hon? Gonna give you directions."

"You think it's a joke?" Lonzo cursing in Italian.

"Look, Lonz baby, I got stuff to do, a real mess to clean up here." Handing the phone to Denny.

Lonzo going on, Bobbi still able to hear, "The day you took my money, I stashed two more cases. Think you hurt me, you can't hurt me, *lupa*. I got money like that Getty and broads like Hefner."

"And don't forget the cock socks, baby. Some of those skanky girls —" she called.

Denny said into the phone, "Calling Nat Adderley jungle music. You got no class, Lonzo. You ask me, you got what you deserve."

"And you got balls for a draft dodger, talking on the phone. Not gonna have 'em long. Gonna catch up and cut them off, hand them to you."

"Let me guess, with your teeth? You know what, I'm starting to see what Bobbi's been saying, about you being a bore." Denny hung up.

Bobbi smiled and drank some more of Lee's coffee, offering him the cup, Denny taking it from her, having a sip, looking thoughtful and saying, "The man just gave me an idea."

"Like where to run?"

"Said he stashed two more cases, right? How much you wanna bet they're in the same spot?"

"Under the shoes?" She looked at him, her eyes sparkling, the smile spreading across her face. "You got to be crazy, even to think it."

"The man's on his way up here as we speak. Heard him tell Aldo to go get the car, right? So, I say we head back down, his place in the Properties, and help ourselves."

She was shaking her head. "Denny Barrenko, you're something else." Stepping to him and kissing him on the mouth. He was finally thinking south.

When they finished, he reached down and fished around in Lee's pocket, found his wallet and the keys to the T-Bird. Took the bills from the wallet and tossed the leather aside, then took her hand, leading her out of there.

"How about him?"

"You want, can leave Mose a note, say sorry about the mess. My guess, the man's been compensated, that is if he makes the dive. Can pay his girl comes once a week to clean it up at the end."

Denny guessing Mose drove out to the lake while he sent his boys to go hunting for Lee Trane. Had a feeling it was him who stole Rent Me, with the diving gear in the trunk. Denny putting it together when he spent the night under the rowboat, the reason he bashed a hole in its hull, knowing it would slow Mose down. Make him work for it.

Driving out of Ripley in the T-Bird now, the town looking more deserted than usual, smelling of smoke. Looking over at her, Denny said, "It's all falling in place, huh?" Going to the front door, holding it for her.

"We drive to Vancouver while Lonzo drives north. And let me guess, you're gonna tell me we're going to trade cars, steal some egg-beater that doesn't stand out."

"Not this time." Denny going to the Thunderbird.

"We going in this?"

"I've got an idea." Shoving the stick into gear, Denny took the road to Killik, drove past the lookout, then past the border crossing and along the canal. Parking at the foot of the pier, Denny shut the engine and got out, told her just to trust him, taking her hand and walking to the Beaver tied at the end. His ears had stopped ringing from the pistol shot. Opening the door of the plane, he reached into the cooler, helping himself to a bottle of Labatt's, looking for a church key.

"What are we doing?"

"Waiting on our pilot." Denny knew Caleb Hawkes was crewing on the Scooper, one he called the Dump Duck, out there fighting the blaze.

"Told you I don't do planes."

"With Lonzo coming north and us going south. Yeah, this time we're flying."

"And this pothead guy Caleb, he's gonna fly us, huh?"

"Doesn't know it yet, and may need you turning up the charm, but yeah, he's going to fly us." Denny betting Caleb was ready for a new adventure.

"And if he says no?"

"Who says no to a three-way?"

She raised her brows.

"A three-way split."

The sound of the engines got them looking north along the canal that never freezes, the big Canso flying in low, right down the middle, past another freighter being loaded, Denny not sure what flags this one was flying. Opening the beer, he handed it to her and reached for another. As the Canso flew closer to the water he saw something flapping underneath. Not sure at first, then he made out a yellow line, and what was left of one of the Gucci twins caught on the end of it. Bobbi put a hand to her hair and kept it from blowing around, sipping the beer, watching the Dump Duck touching down, the open case skipping in its wake.

Acknowledgments

Many thanks to my publisher, Jack David, for his continued support, and to the entire ECW team who excel at everything they do. As always, it is a pleasure to work with them. For their contributions, thank you to Michel Vrana for the perfectly sinister cover design, Kathryn Hayward for her exacting copyediting and Jen Knoch for her proofreading talents. Also, to Emily Schultz who has edited each of my novels, I am grateful for her brilliance.

Thank you to my family, Andie and Xander, for their generous hearts and for tolerating my sometimes insufferable wit.

And of course, thank you to those who read my stories.